TIMELESS LOVERS

Turning to stare toward Grace in the darkness, Fox asked, "How is it that you don't find the idea of me . . . of me being here, in this time, unacceptable?"

"I don't know for certain." Grace rolled to her side. "Wait, I do. As I see it, there are three possibilities. Ye are mad, which I don't believe to be true. The second is that ye're lying to me."

"I'm not."

"I did not think so. Which leaves the third likelihood."

"That I traveled through time."

"Aye. 'Tis not unheard of, ye know. The ancients speak of it."

It had grown darker, and by this time Fox couldn't even make out Grace's shape. But as they'd talked he'd been unable to escape the subtle scent of heather that clung to her like a gossamer veil. Every sound she'd made, every breath, honed his senses to her. When he brushed warm skin, it was as if his resolve to fight his need for her dissolved. "I can't stop thinking of you. Wanting you." The pulse beneath his fingertips quickened. "Tell me you feel the same."

"Do not ask me that."

"Why? Nay, do not turn away. Answer me. Please."

"Ye are known to me. Here." Grace's hand covered his, dragging it down till his palm covered her heart. . . .

Books by Christine Dorsey

TRAITOR'S EMBRACE
WILD VIRGINIA NIGHTS
BOLD REBEL LOVE
THE CAPTAIN'S CAPTIVE
KANSAS KISS
SEA FIRES
SEA OF DESIRE
SEA OF TEMPTATION
MY SAVAGE HEART
MY SEASWEPT HEART
MY HEAVENLY HEART
SPLENDOR
THE RENEGADE AND THE ROSE
THE REBEL AND THE LILY
THE ROGUE AND THE HEATHER

Published by Zebra Books

THE ROGUE AND THE HEATHER

Christine Dorsey

Zebra Books
Kensington Publishing Corp.

http://www.zebrabooks.com

ZEBRA BOOKS are published by

Kensington Publishing Corp.
850 Third Avenue
New York, NY 10022

First Printing: April, 1998
10 9 8 7 6 5 4 3 2 1

Printed in the United States of America

To my family. I love you all. And as always for Chip.
And to John Scognamiglio, a true gentleman.

Chapter One

"Did you have the dream again?"

Lord Foxworth Morgan watched his breath fog the
wavery window glass, then let the red velvet drape fall,
obscuring the early-morning mist swirling about the courtyard. Without turning, he shrugged broad naked shoulders. "I couldn't sleep 'tis all."

"Isn't that what I'm here for?"

The words, so thickly laced with seduction, earned a
smile from Fox. He glanced about, taking in the delight-
fully debauched form of Katherine Salinger draped sensuously across the oversize bed. "Are you certain you won't
come to Ashford Hall with me? It will be damn lonely
without you."

"And leave all this?" Kate asked with a sweep of her
pleasingly plump arm, which encompassed the bedroom,
richly appointed with carved mahogany and gilt. "You

know I adore you, Fox. But I think we might rub each other the wrong way were we to spend too much time together.''

''Speak for yourself, Kate,'' Fox responded gallantly, but he didn't pursue the subject. He had a notion she was right, and really wasn't certain why he'd suggested she accompany him in the first place. Except he meant what he said. It would be intolerably lonely at Ashford Hall.

But he didn't think Katherine Salinger was the answer. Even as Fox made his way back to the bed they shared, twinges of regret slowed his step. He shouldn't have come here last night. Shouldn't have drunk as much as he had. Shouldn't have gamed away . . . he wasn't certain how much he'd lost at the tables downstairs. He was full of regrets.

But mostly he regretted ever telling Kate about the dream.

He wanted to believe she wheedled it out of him, but the truth was less palatable. It had been nearly a fortnight ago. He'd been drinking heavily, loose-lipped from brandy, feeling oddly melancholy about his brother Dalton's death, and chilled from the thoughts that haunted his sleep. Kate had offered a kind word, a soft, velvety breast on which to rest his head, and he'd spilled the all of it.

Embarrassing to think on it now.

Embarrassing, too, that she could read him so easily. Despite the years he'd known her, the nights he snuggled into her bed.

Of course, it was the dream that awakened him nearly two hours ago.

In the grainy light Fox could see Kate's eyes narrow as she drew him into her warmth. He hadn't realized how cold he was till he felt the contrast between her luscious flesh and his own.

What did he expect standing in front of a cold window

reliving a battle best forgotten? But the problem was he could not forget Culloden. Awake or asleep, the visions, the screams, the smell of death, held him in a grip he seemed unable to break.

"I think it best I call my man and return home."

"Oh, but Fox, it's early yet, and from the feel of things you don't really wish to go off just yet." The blue eyes twinkled as she leaned over him farther, allowing her magical hands to roam down across his body.

The sexual assault didn't stop until his fingers circled her wrist. "You could arouse a corpse, Kate, but I do need to return to St. James's Square. And contrary to the way things might seem, you did an excellent job of wringing me dry last night."

"I would say it was a mutual endeavor."

A chuckle rumbled through his chest as Fox swung his legs over the side of the bed. He took a deep breath and rubbed both palms down across gritty eyes and the dark stubble of beard shadowing his jaw.

"When are you leaving for Ashford Hall?"

He'd planned to start the trip this morning. Had told his staff as much. But the idea of heading south toward Devon held little appeal . . . and he didn't think it only because of the regimental drums pounding in his brain. With a shake of his head that stirred the beat and brushed dark wavy hair across his collarbone, Fox acknowledged his indecision.

"Did you ever think that spending some time in the country might be a good thing, Fox?"

Twisting about, he gave Kate a look that a more demure maid would have found frightening. Kate Salinger simply plumped a pillow behind her head and returned his stare. "We both know you haven't been . . . yourself since Culloden."

"And who, might I ask, have I been?"

"Your sarcasm is lost upon me, Fox, so you may as well save it for someone more easily wounded by the sharp edge of your tongue."

"I'm not interested in wounding anyone, thank you."

"Aren't you?"

Despite the rat-a-tat-tat, Fox pushed to his feet. This is why he shouldn't have come tonight. He knew Kate loved to mother. Her girls. Her clients. Especially the ones she personally liked. Especially him.

"You did your best that day, Fox," Kate said as she pushed up to her knees. "Nothing that happened was your fault. You must accept that."

Damnation, he didn't wish to speak of this now. Not with the dream, the reality of it, so fresh in his mind. He must have been insane to tell Kate of this. "What I have accepted, Kate, is that my best, as you put it, simply wasn't good enough." Fox decided against ringing for his man and jammed a long leg into blue silk breeches.

"No one blames you for anything, Fox."

Fox paused, clawing at the fabric, which suddenly seemed twisted. Growling when Kate suggested she help him. "I can pull on my pants myself, damn it. And figure out that I did nothing contrary to orders that day. Nothing to be ashamed of," he finished before managing the second leg.

"Exactly, Fox. So you should go to the country. Rest. Enjoy being lord of the manor so to speak. Forget that silly battle."

"It was only a dream for God's sake, Kate." Fox yanked on his shirt, then followed that with an embroidered waistcoat and jacket. "You make too much of it," he said with a forced smile. "But you do have the right of it about one thing. I think I will be off to Devon today. It's about time the new Lord Morgan visits his county seat."

* * *

He hadn't fooled her. Fox stared down at the amber liquid swirling in his glass and acknowledged the truth. Kate could see through him too easily. Which was reason enough to thank whatever gods looked after fools that she hadn't agreed to his hasty invitation to accompany him to Ashford Hall.

Fox sank onto a settee in the library of his St. James's Square town house. He wished his sister Zoe was there. She could wash away this gloomy fog that had settled over him. But she was off in the Americas breeding with the ease of a broodmare with that damn Scot she had married. The two had made him an uncle thrice over, and that was only what he knew of. But damn she seemed happy. Her posts were always full of chatty tidbits about her sons, who appeared to be as robust and wild as her husband.

Fox let his head fall back against the cushions, accepting his own role in his sister's marriage. Hoping he'd done the right thing.

He'd tried to make up for that early-spring day three years ago, when the mist and the sleet had painted the moors of Culloden slick and cold. When his soldiers had slaughtered so many. He could still hear the screams of the wounded. Smell the gun smoke. Feel the icy fingers of water inch down his collar.

It was there he met Keegan MacLeod, the Scot destined to wed his sister. And Padraic Rafferty, the Rebel, Fox thought with a snort. Odd how their lives had twisted together, melded, then snapped apart.

Fox slammed the rest of the brandy against the back of his throat, relishing the sting, then pushed to his feet. He'd already sent the coach with his belongings south, toward Devon. He was to follow. He didn't have time to sit reminiscing about such foolishness. In the courtyard behind the house a horse awaited.

Taking one last look about the book-lined room, Fox stalked from the house. His mount was strong and frisky, anxious to be on his way. Fox rode from St. James's Square, following narrow, crowded roads toward London Bridge. Perhaps Kate was right. Leaving the city and all its vices behind might be just the thing. But as Fox approached the Thames he reined in his mount, allowing the wave of humanity to flow about him.

As if he were naught but iron filings, he felt the pull. Leather straining, Fox shifted in the saddle. His dark eyes narrowed, looking north toward the hubbub of London, but seeing farther, much farther.

It took him near a fortnight to reach Drummoissie Moor. A hard ride over muddy roads, sleeping in the hovels the Scots called inns. And for what? To gaze again over the desolate countryside of Culloden? To wonder what in the hell had come over him? No one knew where he was. Damnation, the staff must think him dead. As soon as he'd had his fill of staring at the nothingness, he'd find some semblance of civilization and send a messenger to Ashford Hall. Then he'd follow and forget this foolishness.

Could it be he was losing his mind? The thought was unsettling. Yet how else could he explain this madcap ride north to visit a sight that held only unpleasant memories for him? Did he think seeing the moors again would have some healing effect? If so, he'd been wrong.

No feelings of absolution washed over him. He came to no terms with what happened. He was simply there. On that bleak expanse of barren moor, noting how quickly nature reclaimed her own. No one would know, looking about, what had happened three years ago.

Fox paused and rubbed his whiskered chin. Was it only three years? It seemed like a lifetime since that fateful day. But yes, he'd been thirty-two, and he was now, today, thirty-five. What a grand way to spend one's birthday.

Alone.

Standing in the chilly drizzle, listening to echoes of thunder roll in from the bay. Hearing instead the incessant pounding of artillery, the screams of the wounded, the beating of his own heart.

Mad. He was mad. And seemingly unable to do anything about it. Even when the skies opened, pelting the heather and bracken with a hard-biting rain. Not even when the thunder rumbled or the lightning seared the cloud-darkened sky.

Soaked to the skin, Fox lifted his arms. He turned his face toward the heavens, wishing to be washed clean of his transgressions. To be born again.

When the tingle ran through his body, prickling the hair on his nape, Fox didn't flinch. He somehow knew what was coming as the lightning shot, white-hot toward him. His last thought was of the date, April 16. The day of the battle of Culloden. The day of his birth.

Odd it should also be the day of his death.

Chapter Two

"Ye've got to be the most stubborn, hardheaded woman in all of Scotland, Grace MacCammon."

"Because I've no desire to wed ye?" Grace tilted her head, glancing up toward the man who tromped through the matted bracken beside her. "Now that sounds a wee bit conceited, even for ye."

"Don't ridicule me, Grace, and don't make light of my proposal. 'Tis made in all seriousness."

Grace's smile faded. "I know it is, Alex, and I appreciate the thought, I really do, but—"

"Dugald's been dead for nearly four years, Grace. I loved him too, like a brother, I did, but we've got to come to grips with his death, and move on."

Shading her eyes against the morning sun with the curve of her hand, Grace halted her headlong stride across the moor, then turned to face him. "Is that what ye think I'm doing? Holding on so tight to Dugald's memory that I feel my life is over?"

"Isn't it?"

"Nay," Grace said instinctively, then, after a moment's thought, "Nay." Dugald's death grieved her to be sure. And the circumstances still bewildered her. She'd always thought him a good man with strong beliefs and a willingness to stand by them. She hoped she was right.

"Memories are short, Grace. Most have forgotten what happened."

Grace's smile was sad. "Do ye really think that?"

"It doesn't matter." Alex reached for her hands. "As my wife, no one would dare show ye any disrespect."

"I once thought Dugald ... myself ... above public shame. Now I know no one is exempt."

"So that's it then? Ye'll allow a small group of ignorant riffraff to dictate yer happiness? I thought ye stronger than that, Grace."

"It wasn't a small group, if ye recall. 'Twas most of Scotland." Her green eyes softened as she looked at her friend. "With a few notable exceptions."

"Ye know I never believed what they said about Dugald."

"Or me, Alex. Do not forget it was Dugald they thought capable of theft. But me they thought willing to drive him to it."

"How could they think such of ye?" Alex kicked at a clump of dried bracken. "I would see all the pompous lot of them kneel before ye in apology or face the point of my sword."

"Alex." Grace placed her hand on his sleeve. "I don't want ye involved in this."

"But I am, Grace." His hand covered hers. "Let me make it as it should be for ye. No one will hurt ye. I swear to ye."

"I know this may be difficult for ye to believe, Alex. But it really isn't fear that keeps me from Edinburgh."

"What is it then? Why do ye hole yerself up at Glenraven,

I'm wanting to know." Mist swirled as he kicked again at the seepy ground. "There's nothing here for ye but solitude and wasteland. Come with me to Edinburgh. We can be married there and live among people, not damn rooks." His arm swept with a jerky motion toward the birds cawing overhead.

"I'm hardly alone. Have ye forgotten Maude?"

"Wish that I could. Nay, Grace, I did not mean that in truth. Bring her with ye. She's welcome, to be sure."

Grace doubted the sincerity of that, but didn't push the issue. Studying Alex, the set of his chin, the straight-backed stance, he seemed to ooze disbelief that she would not find his plan a worthy one. Marrying him. Leaving Glenraven. Despite everything, Grace could hardly fault him his confidence. A handsome man, to be sure, Alex had copper curls that caught the sun and eyes as blue as the sky. His strength knew few equals in the Highlands. He was clever and passionate, kind and true. A friend.

And Glenraven? Why had she exiled herself at her ancestral home when Dugald died? There were none left to greet her. It was not even the home of her youth. Though there were those who blamed her for Dugald's possible shortcomings, Grace believed in her heart she was guiltless. Sighing, she lifted her eyes, scanning the wide expanse of brooding landscape.

"Grace, have ye heard a word I said? Do ye plan to give me an answer?"

"Alex." Grace looked up at him and considered saying yes to his proposal. Perhaps she should leave this place, go with him. Marry him. She really didn't fear public censure for herself. But just as she opened her mouth to say the words, her horse snorted and gently nudged her shoulder. When Grace did speak, it was a gentle reprimand that she uttered. Absently she let her fingers drift across the horse's silky nose.

"That's it?" Alex stomped off, his boots seeming to disappear in the low-lying fog as he trod across the uneven ground. "Ye give me no answer, yet ye speak kindly to a horse."

"Alex," Grace said, then lifted the dampened hem of her riding habit and tramped after him when he didn't stop. "Don't be this way. Ye know how much I value yer friendship."

When he whirled about his eyes were dark as the sky at eventide. "That's all I am to ye then? A friend?"

He spoke the word with such disgust, Grace wished she could fully explain to him how much his friendship had always meant to her. But he appeared in no mood.

What did one say to a spurned suitor? Grace wished she knew. Wished she'd had some forewarning of his proposal. But she'd never suspected a thing. Certainly not when he arrived a sennight ago. Very few visitors found their way across the moor to Glenraven, and though that suited her temperament at the moment, it was always wonderful to see Alex.

He was traveling from his clan's stronghold in the Highlands, making his way to the capital to take his seat in Parliament. On the morrow he was to leave for Inverness, and the packet waiting to carry him south to the Firth of Forth and Edinburgh. He was understandably anxious about the upcoming session and had spent most of his visit talking of little but politics and the damnable English, as he called them.

If she'd had any idea their ride along the moor would lead to such a misunderstanding, Grace might have stayed abed, pleading headache or chill. But she'd readily accepted his invitation. And now must deal with his proposal.

"Alex," she said. "Ye've always been my friend. Even before Dugald."

"Were that I never brought him to ye. Were that I never met him myself."

"Ye don't mean that, Alex." Grace's voice was little more than a whisper, yet his response shattered the eerie stillness.

"Don't I?" Alex's hand shot back through his curls. " 'Twas I who introduced ye to him. 'Twas I who helped convince yer da that Dugald would make ye a fine husband." With his pointer finger, Alex stabbed at his chest as he made each point. Then his anger seemed to melt as the mist. "Have ye any idea how much I envied him ye? Ye sitting in the drawing room, quietly smiling a welcome. Ye entering a room on his arm. Ye sharing his bed."

"Alex, please."

"Please what? Gracie." He reached out, touching her cheek. "Ye think I never thought of that? Of ye kissing him, and opening yerself for him."

"Ye should not talk so." Grace turned away, unable to meet the fierceness of his expression.

Again ten fingers ruffled his hair. "Ye're right, Grace. I owe ye an apology."

"I'm not asking for one, Alex."

"But ye'll get one all the same." Alex blew air through his teeth. "And ye know I did not mean what I said about Dugald."

"I know." Grace's heart went out to him. They were together, she and Alex, when they found him. It was a Wednesday, clear and bright like today. Rumors ran wildly about the capital, and had for months. The New Caledonia colony at Darien was lost, the colonists dead.

A pall hung over the walled city, and on every tongue the question was the same. "What happened?"

The idea had been such a good one. Everyone had invested, expecting fabulous returns. Now many were penniless, and most wished a scapegoat.

One had been easy to find. Dugald MacCammon was one of the directors of the Scotland Company. He'd convinced many to invest. They'd lost fortunes. And he appeared to have gained one. Talk was of little else.

Dugald knew it. Grace knew it. As did Alex. He'd arrived at their house one afternoon urging them to accompany him. The earl of Maymont, Hugh Archey, was giving a dinner, and all the members of Parliament and officials would be there. Hiding away, as they were, simply fueled speculation that the rumors were true, he said. It was time for them to declare their innocence.

Grace agreed, as did Dugald. But he couldn't leave yet, her husband had insisted. They must go, and he would join them directly.

She and Alex had pleaded, but Dugald wouldn't be swayed. He had something to do, he said. All during the dinner, as one person after another turned away from her, Grace silently cursed her husband. He should be here with her, proclaiming his honesty. Explaining his newfound wealth to the multitudes . . . to her. But he never came. And so she and Alex returned to her house.

And found him.

Grace brushed fingertips across her brow, trying to dislodge the memories filling her head, but they wouldn't leave. She could see it as clearly now as when it happened. Dugald slumped over his desk. The blood spattered wall. Then there were the smells, evil scents that hung in the air, making it difficult to breathe. Gunpowder and death. She'd screamed when she saw him, the sound growing more shrill when she noticed what he held in his hand. The sound echoed in her head now, making her swallow down nausea and look away.

"I couldn't have borne . . . borne any of it without ye, Alex. Ye must know that."

"We helped each other, Grace."

Grace nodded. Alex had been a rock, taking charge of Dugald's body. The house. Of her. And she'd allowed it. Until the day she left everything behind and took her household to Glenraven.

Alex had argued with her over her decision. "Foolish," he'd called her and worse. There had been a few times over the years when she'd agreed with him. When the solitude seemed to close in upon her. But those moments never lasted long. She'd done the right thing to come here . . . to Glenraven, to the moor.

Chapter Three

Alex stepped closer and Grace allowed him to grasp her shoulders and draw her near. His kiss began innocently enough. Soft and gentle. Slow and sedate. Giving her plenty of time to back away. To leave him again.

But she didn't. Grace stood still, her mind rebelling against what was happening, but her emotions and her body were weak. It had been so long since she'd been kissed. Longer still since she'd been kissed with passion. And every cell in her body knew there would be passion from Alex.

He didn't disappoint her. As soon as it was obvious she would not object, his arms wrapped about her, pulling her into a warm cocoon that buffeted against the winds whipping across the moor. His mouth was firm, demanding, masterful enough so that Grace could appreciate the practice he'd had. He played with her bottom lip, nipping, then soothing with his tongue, sending goose flesh rippling over Grace's body.

She remembered this feeling and liked it. Her toes wanted to curl, and her knees sagged. When Grace lifted her arms, wrapping them about his neck, she could feel Alex's smile agains her lips.

How wonderful it would be to cuddle into him. To let desire sweep over her and feel cherished again. She'd loved that sensation more than anything, and she'd missed it terribly when it was gone.

And it was gone long before Dugald's death.

Despite her desires, Grace knew no good would come from this. Leaning back, she managed to separate her lips from his. "Alex?"

"Hmmm?" He was now moving down the side of her neck. The scrape of his whiskers sent chills through her body.

"Please stop. Please."

"What's the matter, Gracie? Are ye fearful I'll have my way with ye, and then rescind my offer? That will never happen. I'll wed ye no matter what. If I bed ye before or after, it will be the same." Alex emphasized his pledge by spreading his hand over the curve of her breast.

"No, please." Grace twisted away, then glanced over her shoulder. His expression was as bewildered as she expected. Why shouldn't it be? Up until that moment she'd participated wholeheartedly.

"What is it, Gracie? Am I rushing ye? I'll wait. I swear I will. Just come with me. I desire ye so. Tell me we'll be wed soon."

"Alex." Grace's voice faltered. "I cannot wed ye. Now or ever. Please understand, it's just—"

"Ye were kissing me, Grace. Kissing me and liking it."

"I'll not deny that."

" 'Tis a good thing, I'm thinking." Agitation colored his voice.

"I said I won't deny it!" Grace found herself more

annoyed than she liked. Alex wasn't the only object of her ire. How could she have let him kiss her like that? All that she'd said to this point about wanting to remain friends and not wishing to marry seemed as so much drivel after her response to him.

"What are ye trying to do to me, Grace?"

"Nothing." Grace whirled about to face him. "I did not ask ye to bring me here. Or propose to me. Or kiss me, for that matter."

When he only stared at her, Grace looked away. "I should have not allowed the kiss. It was my mistake."

"It did not feel like a mistake at the time, Gracie."

"But it was. I may not have acted as I should have, but it's not something I wish to happen again."

"I never thought ye were a tease, Grace."

"I'm not."

"Well, it's hard to tell that from where I'm standing. And I'm not just referring to the kiss, though Lord knows that is enough."

"There's nothing else." Grace felt her horse push at her shoulder.

"Think that if ye choose."

"Don't talk such rubbish."

"Rubbish is it? Is it rubbish when ye stayed with me till well past midnight last night? Or when ye touch my arm whenever ye say my name? Or when ye smile at me as ye do? Or when ye fell asleep, yer head against my shoulder?"

She'd done those things and more. Grace couldn't even deny anything he said to herself. But she'd been so glad to see him, so surprised when he arrived. And they'd always been so comfortable with each other. Even before Dugald died. Even before she met Dugald. There had always been Alex. Her friend.

"I never meant for ye to think . . ." What? That she loved him? "Alex, please understand." He was walking away from her now, his step, everything about his carriage radiating anger. When he reached his horse, Alex grabbed up the reins and leapt astride.

"Alex, won't ye even talk to me?" Grace ran toward him, but he paid her no mind. With a twist of leather he turned his mount's head toward Glenraven.

"Dugald always called ye his ice princess," Alex yelled down to her as he dug his heels in the horse's flanks. "Now I know why."

"I am not an ice princess, nor a tease," Grace yelled at his retreating form.

"I'm not," she repeated, then, feeling tears burn behind her eyes, yelled across the vast, sweeping moor, "I'm not!"

Grace took a deep breath, and, in one fluid motion, scooped up a clod of dirt. She squeezed and it molded in her hand, dark and moist, smelling of peat, of Scotland. With little enthusiasm she tossed it toward a mound of mist-swirled bracken. It landed with a plop short of her aim.

With a snort she clawed through the winter grass, prodding another handful of dirt from the ground. Feeling somehow driven to hit the target, she threw again, enjoying the challenge, the energy, the freedom. Spurts of temper were not part of Grace's character. Even as a child she was the calm one. The quiet one. Dugald had commented upon her composure the first time they met. Refined and serene, he'd called her—to her face. Obviously behind her back he was calling her less worthy names. Ice princess, indeed.

Recalling Alex's words made her aim truer and fueled her arm with power. At least she wasn't a thief, or a coward. She threw another clump, a mixture of dirt and root. And what of Alex just leaving her here on the windswept moor? Certainly she could mount and ride for home. She often rode the moor alone. It wasn't far to Glenraven, and she'd leave in just a moment. But for now pummeling the rise held too much appeal. She scooped and threw, scooped and threw, rocks, dirt, it mattered not. Nor did she mind that at times she missed, for more often than not, she didn't.

How could something so simple feel so good? Grace stared down at her dirt-encrusted hands. With all the time she spent wandering the moor, why had she never tried this before?

With each toss she moved closer, threw harder. Grace's breathing rasped in her ears, and her face grew damp from exertion. One more clump of dirt and she'd wipe her hands and ride off toward home. Just one more.

"Ouch! Damnation woman, 'twas not I who called you an ice princess."

Startled by the sound of another human, Grace turned to flee. But her skirts seemed alive, wrapping themselves about her legs like wet tentacles. Her arms windmilled; her knees crumpled. She landed hard, smacking her hip on the ground. Despite the pain Grace fought for footing, yanking at the heavy wool, looking furtively about her for some sign of who'd spoken.

It wasn't till the mound of bracken moved that she had a clue. Fear made her even clumsier. Her eyes widened and her mouth seemed full of dust. With all her strength Grace sidled away, putting as much space as possible between herself and the mound.

From the mist-shrouded lump a man emerged. At least she thought it was a man. He sat, slumped forward, head hanging low, black hair shielding his face. He didn't move, a signal that gave Grace a bit of courage. She stopped scooting backward.

"Who are ye?" Grace finally gathered the nerve to ask, though she thought perhaps it should have been "What are ye?"

He didn't answer, only slowly lifted his head. The tangle of hair separated, showing a slim triangle of dirt-smeared skin, a straight nose, a glimmer of eye. Enough to tell her it was a man and not some goblin or monster emerging from the moor's depths.

"I know ye can speak. Ye did it before. So why won't ye answer me? Who might ye be? What are ye doing here on the moor?"

A grime-covered hand lifted and tentatively touched his hair, spreading it more. "I," he said, clearing his throat when the sound grew ragged, "I don't remember."

Grace pushed to her knees and studied him more thoroughly. He wore a jacket and waistcoat, though that, too, was blackened almost beyond recognition. "Ye don't recall who ye are, or what ye're doing here?"

"Neither, I think." His head dropped, only to jerk up. "No. Wait. The battle."

"The battle?"

"Aye. You'd best leave. This is no place for a woman." He looked about himself so intently, that Grace found herself doing the same. "They . . . we are killing everyone." He shook his head, a strand of hair catching on his eyelashes. "Bodies everywhere."

Chills raced down her spine. Despite what her eyes told her, Grace found herself almost believing his words.

She opened her mouth to speak, then thought better of it. What did one say to this. Did he see bodies where there were none? But no, he didn't. His next words proved that.

He sat straighter. "What happened to them? The Scots? The soldiers? Where did they go?"

"I don't know." He was making her more nervous by the moment, and she'd been quite frightened from the beginning. Inching her mist-heavy skirts away from her boots, Grace tried again to stand. But the grasses beneath her were slippery, and this time she landed unceremoniously on her bottom. Her movement gained his attention. His expression solemn, he shook his head.

"They were here. I saw them. Certainly you heard the artillery."

Grace swallowed hard. Why hadn't she simply mounted and ridden after Alex? "They aren't here now," she said, deciding that stating the obvious was her best tack.

He seemed to accept this, at least on the surface. "So I see." Awkwardly he tried pushing to his feet. The motion sent Grace scurrying backward again. He noticed and lifted a darkened hand. "I won't hurt you."

Assuring words, but it was more the fact that he appeared too weak to rise that stopped Grace's furtive flight. She studied him again. "Ye're wet, soaked actually. Where ye in the bay?"

"The bay?" He lifted his arm, staring intently at his sodden sleeve. "I don't think so." He glanced toward her again. " 'Twas the rain that made me wet."

"Rain?"

"Yes, I remember now. The storm came from nowhere. Hard, lashing sheets of rain. And thunder that rumbled across the moor. And lightning." The excitement that built with each word disappeared, and his eyes closed.

"What is it? Are ye feeling ill?" Grace wanted to reach toward him, but prudence kept her at a distance. After all, though her emotions were captured by his plight, little he said made sense.

Soldiers, dead Scots, even a storm that never was. Not unless he'd lain on the moor for over a sennight.

Tucking a lock of red hair behind her ear, Grace offered a bit of truth. "There's been no storm."

"That's absurd. It was raining this morn. You obviously weren't awake in time to see it."

"Was that during the battle?" Grace wasn't certain why

she encouraged him in this farce. Perhaps only to point out that if he remembered a battle that never was, surely he could be mistaken about the weather.

"Yes, of course, it was raining. Didn't I just say as much. There was a storm. I watched it blow in from the bay. Thunder. Lightning—"

Despite her resolve to keep her distance Grace pushed to her knees and reached toward him. He'd suddenly grabbed his head with both hands as if he would squash it like a melon.

"It was sleeting. Driving, icy rain." He looked up at her now, with an expression of bewilderment that tore at Grace's heart. "How could it be doing both?"

"And neither."

"What?"

"There's been no storm, no ice either for days. I haven't a clue how ye managed to get yerself so wet. But I'm thinking ye might be a bit feverish. Who could blame ye, lying out here on this moor."

"Feverish? Yes, that must be it." He let his fingers slide down the side of his face. "If you'll bring my horse, I'll find my regiment. Perhaps the surgeon can give me a powder." He tried to rise again. "And you might take heed to my words and find some safe haven before the troops return. What is it?"

"There is no horse but my own."

He didn't even question her. He simply sank to the ground.

"I suppose we could—"

Grace stopped talking when the clip-clop of hooves echoed across the treeless flats. It didn't help her state of mind when her first thought involved returning troops. But she knew there were no troops, and shading her eyes she noted it was Alex galloping toward her. She'd forgotten all about his angry departure. But the stranger on the moor hadn't. He glanced up as well, his mouth thinning. "Your suitor, I suppose."

"He isn't my suitor," Grace said. "Just a friend."

"What kind of friend leaves a woman defenseless out here?"

"I wasn't defenseless," Grace insisted, adding, partly because his words rang too true, "I could ask what kind of man listens to a private conversation?" Despite the annoyance in her tone, Grace thought she noticed a glimmer of the strange man's white teeth before he spoke.

"It was beyond my control. I simply awoke."

"And kept yer presence a secret."

"You could have been anyone. Besides, it didn't seem the thing to disturb such a touching and, I might add, romantic, interlude. Now what kind of man would do that?"

Grace was saved answering when she heard Alex yelling her name. He'd obviously spotted the stranger, and taking him for a blackguard, which Grace had to admit, he could very well be, feared for her. Alex raced now across the moor, his mount's hooves kicking large divots.

"For God's sake, Grace, get away from him! I shall cut yer liver out if ye touch her."

"Your suitor appears a bit possessive."

"Would ye stop calling him that. He did not know what he was saying." Grace tried again to rise, this time gaining her footing. "Isn't it obvious he thinks ye untrustworthy?" Grace shook her mud-encrusted skirt, then started hiking toward Alex.

Nearly three rods from her he leapt from his horse, then yanked a broadsword from his saddle.

"Alex, wait." Grace reached for his arm, missing, as he raced past, heading for the stranger. "For God's sake, Alex." Grace lifted her skirts and took off after him. But he didn't stop till he loomed over the man, his broadsword lifted high above his head, poised to split the stranger's head open.

Only then did he deign to glance toward Grace. "Are ye all right? Did he do anything to ye?"

"Nay." Grace saw Alex's jaw tighten and hurried on. "I mean aye, I'm fine." When he stared pointedly at her muddy gown, Grace hastily added. "I fell. He shocked me, is all. Look at him, Alex. He's too weak to hurt a fly."

Alex did as she asked, but Grace had to admit the stranger appeared less innocuous than she would have liked. He still sat on the ground, but his back was straight and his expression, especially the look in his intense, dark eyes, gave no hint of capitulation. Nor did his words.

"If I had done harm to the lady, you'd have only yourself to blame."

Grace saw annoyance stiffen Alex's shoulders. His hands tightened on the sword's basket hilt.

"Alex!" Grace pushed between the two men, placing herself as a shield for the stranger. "He's feverish. Speaking nonsense. We really should see that he gets some care."

"Or we could simply leave him here," Alex growled, obviously angered by Grace's interference. He seemed to stare through her toward the man she protected. But Grace stood her ground, waiting for Alex to think about what she'd said. When his gaze dipped, meeting hers, she let her breath out.

"Who is he?" Though his tone held the same ring of belligerence, Grace knew he'd thought better of his actions.

"I don't know. He doesn't know. He can't remember at the moment." Grace decided to skip the details that made the stranger sound mad. No need to mention dead Scots or icy rain.

"He sounds English."

"He may be. We have no way of knowing now, do we?"

Alex's eyes narrowed. "What's he doing here?"

"You needn't talk as if I can't hear. If you wish to know something concerning me, simply ask."

Aye, so ye can tell a story so strange that those hearing it would call ye mad, Grace thought as she quickly answered for him. "He's isn't sure. Lost, I imagine. But as I said before, he's feverish. Nearly out of his mind with it."

Alex lowered the sword. "Aye, well, as long as he didn't hurt ye any, I suppose we can take him someplace. I'll get my horse."

"And mine, too, please."

When Grace turned back to the stranger, he was leaning forward. "I need no protecting from you."

"Is that so?" Grace brushed at the dirt on her hands. "If ye believe that, ye're madder than even I thought. Alex could have cleaved ye with just one stroke."

"Not before I blew a hole in his gut." The stranger's nod was nearly imperceivable, a slight movement, but it drew Grace's gaze to his hand. Almost hidden in the bracken, visible now that she looked closely, was a pistol. The sun gleamed off the barrel, showing its tilt aimed at her heart.

Grace drew in her breath, and her eyes lifted to meet his. So the stranger was not as feverish, or vulnerable as she thought. "Are ye going to kill me, then?"

The silence that followed her question seemed unending. Grace could hear Alex gathering the horses, sliding his broadsword into its leather scabbard. She considered screaming, but realized it would do no good. The stranger could pull the trigger, and she would be dead before Alex could do more than drop the reins.

The stranger shifted, and Grace searched her mind for a prayer. But he didn't squeeze the trigger. Instead with practiced ease, he twisted the weapon till the butt reached toward her.

Grace's heart pounded, and her knees felt like porridge. He was handing the pistol to her, and she felt almost too weak to take it. With a grunt he shoved it into her hand. "You keep this for the time being. I don't think I trust myself with it at the moment." His fingers, blackened by soot, closed around hers, shaping them to the hand-warmed ivory. The contact was brief, the look he gave her unreadable, but in that moment Grace knew what she had to do.

With Grace's words of encouragement and Alex's strong arm, they managed to get the stranger onto her horse. Used to Grace, the mare shifted beneath the extra weight, but she waited patiently for her mistress to mount behind Alex.

Once on the horse, the stranger appeared less awkward. But now that she could see him clearly, Grace was even more perplexed. His clothing appeared charred. What could have happened to him?

Alex insisted upon leading her horse, and that arrangement gave Grace a clear view of the Englishman as they trotted along the road. He ignored her, keeping his eyes straight ahead while Grace tried to imagine where he'd been and what battle he saw in his mind. The more questions she came upon, the more certain she was that she needed the answers.

When they reached a fork in the horse path, Alex pulled on the reins. "If memory serves, MacGreevey's bothy is right behind that rise. We'll leave him there with a guinea or two, and they'll take care of him."

"Nay." Alex had already nudged his horse when she spoke. Grace waited for Alex stop the horse.

"What?" He shifted in the saddle, twisting his head to look at her. "What's wrong with MacGreevey, then?"

"Nothing." Grace dampened her lips. "It's just . . . well . . . I think we should take him to Glenraven."

Alex's expression was incredulous. "Have ye lost yer mind, Gracie?"

Grace decided to ignore that question, for truthfully she wasn't sure. "It is for the best. Maude can care for him there."

"He's English, Grace. A Sassenach, for God's sake."

"He's a human being who is in need of help."

"Aye, but not yer help. Nay, Grace, I won't allow it. There's no sense looking at me that way. I will not permit a stranger to move into Glenraven."

"Alex."

"The decision is made, Grace. We're taking him to Mac-Greevey's."

"We're not. At least I'm not." Grace felt Alex's back stiffen, knew she hurt him with her refusal to follow his dictates, but there was no help for that. "I found him, and I'm taking him to Glenraven. Now I'd appreciate yer help, but will understand if ye feel as if ye can't. I can share his mount."

"My God, Grace, do ye know what ye're saying? Look at him. Look, damn ye. Forget that he's English. He could be anyone. He could be a thief, or a murderer."

"He's no murderer. Of that I'm sure." The weight of the stranger's pistol pressed against her thigh.

"Grace."

"My mind is made up, Alex. I could not live with myself if I didn't do what I could for him."

Alex jerked his mount's head back toward the path to Glenraven and sent him to gallop with a sharp heel to his flanks.

Grace tightened her hold, but her gaze would not leave the stranger who rode beside her. And she could not stop wondering why she cared so much about what happened to him.

Chapter Four

Slowly, Grace turned the key, wincing when the metallic tumble reverberated through the night quiet. Glancing about the wide, dimly lit hallway, Grace almost expected Alex to leap from the shadows and demand to know what she was doing. With a shake of her head Grace inched open the heavy door. Inside, thick, needlework hangings shrouded the room in darkness. Lifting the flickering candle, Grace sent its feeble light into the gloom.

On quiet slippered feet Grace glided over the stone floor toward the massive bed in the corner. The threadbare curtains draping from the high tester were drawn back, allowing an unblocked view. He lay there, the coverlet pulled to his chin. For a moment Grace simply stared, watching the rhythmic motion of his chest as he breathed.

The stranger appeared sound enough. Of course Maude had told her as much. But lying abed, unable to sleep, Grace had wished to see for herself. She would have come before she retired, saving herself this nocturnal sojourn through the castle, if not for Alex. Poor Alex had considered it his duty to spend the afternoon and evening admonishing her for her foolishness. How could she bring a stranger, an English stranger at that, into her home? Especially now. He had pleaded and scolded, urged reason, and lamented his need to leave on the morrow. All to no avail.

Shifting the candle, Grace noted that someone, possibly Maude, had cleaned the soot from his face. Dark whiskers still tinged his jaw and chin bluish in the thin light. His hair, too, had been brushed, though it lay now, black as midnight, in disarray on the pillow cover. He looked more human than when she found him on the moor, but no less feral.

Perhaps she was a fool to bring him into her home. A man with no name. A man whose mind conjured pictures of battles unfought. Finding him did not make her responsible. Yet for some reason that was exactly how she felt.

With a sigh Grace turned to leave. She gasped when a large hand locked about her wrist. The candlestick wobbled, and only through effort did she keep it from tumbling to the floor.

"What are ye doing? Let me go."

"Tell me where I am first." Though he kept his voice low, his tone was insistent.

"Ye're at Glenraven." Grace searched the shadows for his face. "Do ye not remember coming here?"

"The moor?" He hesitated. "Yes. You're the woman with the jealous suitor. From the battlefield."

His fingers loosened their hold, and Grace slipped her arm free, then lifted the candle to see him better. "There was no battlefield," she said softly, ignoring his comment concerning Alex. "How are ye feeling?"

He took a deep breath. "As if I've been poleaxed."

"Maude thinks perhaps ye were struck by lightning."

"Lightning?"

"Aye, ye did mention a storm when I found ye, though it must be days ye lay out on the moor afterward."

"Yes, I remember the storm. And the lightning."

"That must be it then. Maude said she's seen people before with singed hair and soot-covered skin. Though usually she's looking at a corpse when she does."

That brought a smile to his face—a smile that Grace returned.

"So I'm lucky to be alive, am I?"

"According to Maude, aye."

"Is Maude that old witch who had me soaked and scrubbed till I thought my skin would peel from my body?"

"That would be she. Though I doubt she'd take to being described as an old witch."

"She's hardly young," he stated dryly.

Grace tried unsuccessfully to suppress a chuckle. "Maude is my sister-in-law. A fine woman and one versed in the art of healing, which I might add ye can be thankful for."

"And should I be thankful that she held my nose till I drank the foulest-tasting liquid this side of hell?"

"Ah," Grace said with a nod, for she'd had her share of Maude's medicines and thought his description accurate. "One of her tonics, I imagine."

"Not a witch's brew, then?"

"Nay," Grace said with a laugh. " 'Tis to make ye sleep and give ye strength. So are ye? Feeling stronger, I mean?"

"I suppose. Especially if the alternative is more medicine." He twisted, raising to an elbow as if to prove his words, then moved, shifting back against the deeply carved headboard.

"Let me help ye." Grace set the candle on the bedside commode. He wore a nightshirt of fine linen. Grace decided it must be one of Alex's and vaguely wondered how

Maude convinced her friend to lend it. The very idea of the two of them arguing over the matter made her smile as Grace reached for the stranger. Her fingers slid across his shoulder. A second later they quickly jerked away.

Grace stepped back, feeling foolish. She'd reacted as if his flesh were searing hot. As if she'd never touched a man before. As if she were naught but a young maiden.

Hoping he hadn't noticed, for he was still pushing himself back, Grace moved to assist him again. But at the last moment, when she would have touched him, it was the pillow she fluffed against the headboard.

The movement sputtered the candle, splashing feathery rays of light across him. He was sitting now, the covers pooled about his waist. The nightshirt, untied at the neck gaped open, showing a V of bare chest. Grace averted her eyes, but not before noticing the wedge of skin, burnished in the candlelight, peppered with dark, curling hair.

Pulling the shawl that covered her night rail more tightly about her shoulders, Grace tried to halt the fanciful thoughts racing through her mind. She was a widow, after all, and hardly a young one, having reached the age of eight and twenty. Far too old for such foolishness. True, she had come to a man's room in the middle of the night, but her reason for coming was innocent. A rescuer checking on her ill patient. Grace did her best to focus on that as she reached for the candle, but the very air about her seemed alive and sensual.

Her fingers still tingled where she'd touched him. His scent tickled her nostrils, and when he spoke the sound of her name on his lips all but vibrated through her body.

She took a backward step, then another. "I must go."

His eyes narrowed. "Have I offended you in some way?"

"Nay." Grace tried to keep her voice steady. "It is simply . . . I should let ye rest."

"I've slept most of the day."

"True, but I haven't."

"You aren't believing your suitor's words, are you?"

With an effort Grace stopped her retreat. How did he know of Alex's sermons? "He really didn't say all that much."

"Then you didn't receive the same lecture as I."

Grace stepped closer. "Alex came to yer room?"

"And told me exactly how much he trusted me, which I may add was not at all."

"He had no right to—"

"He's concerned about you. And I can't say I blame him."

"It seems strange ye would take his side in this."

Fox shrugged. "True, we aren't exactly close. But that has naught to do with what he told me."

"And what did he tell ye?" Grace replaced the candlestick and folded her arms.

"That someone tried to kill you in your sleep."

"Will he never let that rest?" Grace said, shaking her head. "I should not have mentioned anything to Alex."

"It hardly seems the kind of information one should keep to oneself."

"It was a dream." Grace settled into the chair beside the bed. "A silly nightmare, that seemed real at the time, but . . ."

"Fades with the light of day?"

"Aye. Exactly."

He stared at her a moment, silent. Then leaning his head back, he said, "I seem to be having my share of those lately."

"The battle?"

When his head turned, his eyes held hers. "There was a battle. I was there."

What could she say to that? He was a man who knew not who he was. Yet, the intensity of his expression held her, as if she had no will of her own. He believed what he said, almost enough to make her believe. Grace found herself wishing she could. But even in the otherworldly feel of this encounter, reality could not be denied.

"I dreamed I awoke from a deep sleep," she began. "Someone stood beside my bed. Draped from head to toe in flowing black. It was dark, near impossible to see." Grace swallowed as the memory flowed, filling every rational crevice of her mind. "I almost convinced myself I was imagining everything till I saw the knife. Fear sliced through me. The silver-tipped knife cleaved the air, swooping toward me."

"Go on."

Grace laughed self-consciously. "I screamed, or thought I did, and my nightmare disappeared."

"Are you certain that's all it was?"

"Now, aye. Admittedly at first I was unsure. Unfortunately, Alex called on me the next morning, and I was still quite upset."

" 'Tis an upsetting dream."

"True." Grace took a deep breath. "But I had just lost my husband, and couldn't sleep without one of Maude's brews. It was no more than that. I can accept it now."

His gaze again caught hers. "There was a battle."

"Of course."

"Do you think I can't hear the patronizing undertones to your words?"

"I do not know what ye wish me to say."

He smiled, his teeth flashing white in the mellow light. "Nothing. 'Tis I who is being difficult. And after all you've done for me."

"I did little." Grace felt her cheeks warm and hoped he couldn't notice. "If ye recall, it was Maude who saw to yer well-being."

"I'm not likely to forget that," he said with a laugh.

"She can be a bit . . ."

"Strange?"

"I was going to say overwhelming. But she is devoted to our family."

"What would she say if she knew you were here with me now?"

All the imagery she'd tried to squelch, with only limited success, came rushing to the forefront of Grace's mind. The semidarkness. The hour. How alone they were. Together.

As if she watched through a crystal-clear window, Grace could almost see herself slipping the night rail from her shoulders, letting it slide sensuously to the floor. Feeling the silky-smooth sheet beneath her back. The heat of his hard body. A shudder trembled through her as Grace twisted away. She could not allow him to read her thoughts.

"Maude does not control me. Glenraven is mine, and I do as I please."

"I've offended you."

"Nay." Red curls fluttered as she shook her head. Swallowing, Grace forced herself to look back at him. Forced herself to face him. "I do not offend as easily as that."

Grace smiled to prove her words, and because the image had faded. He was a man. Nothing more. She was allowing her fancy too free a rein.

Perhaps Alex was right. Maybe she did need more people about her. Fewer lonely days on the moor. A husband. Or lover.

Grace swallowed again. "Alex thinks of himself as my protector," she said, surprising the stranger and herself.

"Do you need protecting?"

"I did, at first." Against her better judgment, Grace let her eyes meet his. "When my husband died. I was very young when I married, and then he was gone. My parents were dead. Most of my family as well. There was only

Maude, who, though I'm fond of, is not one to give comfort.''

"So you turned to Alex."

"We turned to each other. He was my husband Dugald's best friend. We were friends." Grace laughed self-consciously. "I can't imagine why I'm telling ye this. A stranger."

"Maybe because I am a stranger. Even to myself."

"Perhaps." Grace fought to look away, to keep the next thought to herself. "Alex will be leaving on the morn. One night's protection is all I need."

"Are you certain of that?"

The gleam in his dark eyes made her skin prickle and her heart race. What was she doing? Grace searched her mind for some explanation for her behavior. But she could find none and did not answer his query.

After a silence that seemed charged to Grace, he turned his head to stare straight ahead. "I will leave tomorrow, too."

"Leave? But—" Disappointment flooded through her. "But where will ye go? Ye don't even know who ye are."

His eyes closed, and the skin on his face seemed to grow taut. She wanted to touch him. Desperately.

"It will come back to ye. All of it. In time." Her tone lightened. "Perhaps Maude can do something. In the meanwhile ye must rest." *And stay here,* she wanted to add.

"I am rested." He forced air from his mouth. "I'll surely lose what's left of my mind if I sleep any longer. I cannot simply stay abed."

"Ye are, of course, free to go." Grace tightened her hold on the shawl, almost expecting him to leap from the bed and rush out the door. Instead he sighed, and the anger seemed to sift from his body.

"Please accept my apology. I don't seem to be myself at the moment. At least I don't think I am." His laugh held no mirth. His hair whispered across the linen as he turned his head to face her again. "I think perhaps I do need more rest."

As dismissals went, this one was at least couched in politeness. But Grace felt no less compelled to leave. When she'd closed the door behind her, she took a deep breath, leaning her shoulder against the stone wall. Every part of her body felt drained. It was all she could do to push away from the wall and make her way up the curved stone staircase to her own room.

When sleep did come it languished amid dreams of erotic torment.

"Are we boring ye that much then, Grace?"

"What? Oh, nay." Grace stifled another yawn, hiding her mouth as best she could behind the pewter mug. "I just seem a bit tired this morn, is all."

" 'Tis hard to imagine anyone slept last night, what with an English stranger among us." Alex leaned back in his chair, a sour expression darkening his handsome face.

"Alex, please." Grace had decided this morning that, for the sake of peace, she'd not argue with Alex before he left. But he'd spoken of nothing else since she'd joined him and Maude in the dining room.

"Please what?" Alex jabbed his spoon her way. "Forget that ye seem to be going mad? How do ye think I feel, Gracie, forced to leave this morn, knowing ye're harboring a dangerous man under yer roof?"

"He's not dangerous."

"Oh, ye know that for a fact, do ye? Have ye heard nothing I've said to ye since I arrived? The Sassenach are doing their best to ruin us. And ye're helping them."

Grace felt her temper unraveling. "For goodness sake, Alex, it is not as if I'm supporting the English army."

"No? What if this man is a spy? Ye scoff, but it could be so. 'Tis hardly good to trust yer own brother anymore."

Grace let her gaze stray toward Maude, but as usual the older woman was most intent upon clearing her plate of food. She scooped porridge into her mouth with a flattened hunk of bread, seemingly unaware of the discussion flowing about her.

" 'Tis clan chief against clan chief now, and the English are doing their damnedest to flame the controversy. Money is flowing north into Scottish pockets, sending reason flying."

"Ye're not accusing our Englishman of that, now are ye? Did he have so much as a pence on him, Maude?"

Maude's bony fingers stopped spreading clotted cream on a scone. She shook her head. "I had his clothes burned, but I looked through them before I did."

"There, ye see." Grace stared at Alex over the rim of her cup.

"I see nothing." His voice gentled. "Grace, ye know how I feel about ye."

Grace glanced nervously toward Maude. She didn't wish to discuss Alex's feelings or his marriage proposal in front of Maude. But Grace's concern appeared unfounded. Maude showed no sign of having heard anything. Relieved, Grace turned her attention back to Alex, who was rambling on about knowing what was best for her.

"Ye should pay Lord MacDonald heed, Grace."

Surprised her sister-in-law had spoken, Grace paused, her spoon midway between her plate and lip. When she looked toward Maude, the older woman continued.

"The Traveler is not for ye."

Spoken low, with little inflection, the words seemed to haunt the great hall. Which was ridiculous. Perhaps her thoughts wandered to areas best left unexplored, but Grace had done nothing wrong. Lowering the spoon, she looked

Maude straight in the eye. "I don't know what ye're talking about. I have only taken in a poor stranger who is hurt and confused. Ye did no less yerself."

The older woman pushed back her chair and stood. Most of Maude's face was hidden in the shadows of the plaid draped about her head. But Grace could swear Maude looked at her with pity. "Ye will see, my pretty. Ye will see."

When she was gone, Grace simply stared after her, not moving until Alex cleared his throat. "What is she talking about?"

"I . . . I haven't any idea."

He shook his head. "I don't know how ye can stand living here with only that old woman for company. And I'm not trying to convince ye to come with me. At least that's not my purpose in saying it."

"She misses her brother."

"Aye, and we all do, but—"

"Don't concern yerself, Alex. She will forget this as soon as she goes out on the moor to collect her herbs."

"She can be frightening."

The laughter that followed his statement seemed to cut the tension. Grace took a swig of milk and smiled toward Alex.

"I've been thinking about what ye said yesterday on the moor." When his face brightened, Grace wished she'd waited to talk to him. But it was too late now. "When Parliament recesses will ye be coming back this way? Back to Glenraven?"

"I can. I will, if ye wish me to."

Grace took another swig of milk. Her mouth seemed too dry to form words. "I do."

"Oh, Grace." Alex reached across the table toward her. "Ye don't know how happy I am to hear ye say that. But must we wait? Come with me now. I'll see that nothing harms ye in Edinburgh."

"I know ye would, Alex. But not now. When ye return, we'll talk on the matter more."

"Then I have incentive to see my work done quickly." He stood, moved around the table, and knelt beside her chair. "Ye will not be sorry, Grace."

She was sorry already. Or frightened. Grace couldn't tell which. But this was what she wanted. What she needed. Wasn't it? Last night as she lay in bed pondering what her life had become, the idea of marrying Alex held some appeal. They were friends. She found him attractive and attentive. He made her laugh. He loved her. The notion of being held, of being loved, had seemed so tempting, concealed as she was by darkness.

Yet now, in the light of day, everything seemed so settled. She'd only wished to let Alex know her mind was open to the possibility of wedding him. She should have known he would consider the subject settled.

"And ye'll turn the Englishman out? Nay, now Grace, listen to my words." He grabbed her hand and held tight. "If we've an understanding between us, ye must see that I cannot allow him to stay here."

Alex stared at her till Grace felt she could take it no more. She pulled her hand free and stood, pushing away from the table.

"Ye found someone on the moor, lost and bewildered. It's only natural the romantic side of yer nature wished to take him in. But for the love of God, Gracie, he's a raving lunatic."

"He is not."

"Gracie, he doesn't even know who he is."

"That's not entirely true."

The sound of the stranger's voice drew Grace as if she had no free will. She turned toward the opening where he stood. His eyes met hers briefly before he bowed toward her. He ignored Alex.

"I apologize for entering unannounced," he said, his tone sounding not the least contrite. "However, I thought you should know that my memory has returned."

"That's a relief," Alex said, returning to his seat.

"Aye. That's wonderful." Or at least it should be. But Grace couldn't help thinking, *Now he will leave.*

"Well, don't keep us in suspense. Who are ye?"

"Yes, do tell us. But first sit and break yer fast." "Please," Grace added, when he appeared reluctant.

With another bow he took a seat. As did Grace. He looked much better this morning. Taller than she'd thought. And more handsome, even wearing an ill-fitting jacket, more suitable for a servant. She tried not to stare.

"Tell us what sparked yer memory."

"I simply awoke this morning knowing."

"Very convenient."

What was wrong with Alex now? He wanted the Englishman gone. And he would be. Grace tried to compensate for his rudeness. "Perhaps rest is what ye needed after all."

"It would appear so."

"Well, this must be a comfort for ye."

"Yes, but I must send a message forthwith to let people know I'm safe."

"Of course. Certainly. Why everyone must be concerned. Yer family. Yer wife." Grace could think of nobody else to add. The word, "wife" seemed to hang in the air.

"There is no wife. Or family either. But I was expected at my estate in Devon over three weeks ago."

"No wife." Grace felt her cheeks heat and lowered her eyes.

If Alex noticed, he seemed too busy finding fault with

the stranger to comment. "Devon seems some distance from Inverness. Did ye lose yer way perhaps?"

It was a taunt, one the Englishman met head-on. His dark eyes narrowed, his voice hardened. "Nay." When he looked toward Grace his expression softened. "Do you suppose one of your servants could take a message for me to Ashford Hall?"

"Certainly," Grace answered, but her reply was all but drowned out by Alex.

"Ashford Hall, ye say? That's yer estate?"

"Aye. I'm Lord Foxworth Morgan, Earl of Clayborne."

"Earl of Clayborne? How interesting." Alex leaned forward. "So tell us Lord Morgan, why *did ye* come to Scotland?"

"I had my reasons."

"Reasons ye can't share with the people who saved yer life?"

"Alex." Grace was beginning to feel as if she should banish him from Glenraven. "I'm certain Lord Morgan's purpose is his own."

"Not when it affects Scotland, it's not."

"I assure you, my coming here has naught to do with anyone but myself."

"Which is all the explanation any of us need, I'm sure." Grace thought that might be the end of it, or at least she hoped it was. But Alex stood so violently his chair tilted back.

"I'll take my leave now, Grace."

"But Alex, ye haven't finished—" Grace took a deep breath and thought better of arguing with him. "As ye please."

"I'll await my horse near the stables," Alex said. He strode from the room, leaving Grace staring after him.

After he was gone the silence seemed overpowering.

Grace tried to think of something to say, but it was the Englishman who spoke first.

"Perhaps I was insensitive. Of course animosity continues. It hasn't been that many years. And the Disarming Acts were not passed with healing in mind, I'm afraid. Was your friend a follower of the Prince?"

"The Prince?"

"Don't concern yourself, madam. I am not here to ferret out traitors. Nor will I mention his plaid or manner of dress to anyone. My own wounds run too deep."

"I'm afraid, Lord Morgan, I have no idea what ye're talking about."

"I shouldn't have mentioned it. Do accept my apology. In your place I would answer no differently. I was simply trying to reassure you after all you've done for me."

"Then I suppose I am . . . reassured, that is." Grace still had no clue as to what he was talking about.

"If ye wish to send a message after ye've eaten, I will summon someone."

"That is very kind, but I believe I might make as good a time myself. That is if I may prevail upon you for the loan of a horse. Mine seems to have disappeared in the storm along with my belongings."

"Certainly. And I believe ye will need some supplies and perhaps a change of clothing." Grace did her best to speak calmly, while inside she felt anything but. He had come into her life one day, and was leaving the next. Which was how it should be. She knew that. Then why was she feeling so saddened, as if she was missing something very important? All so utterly foolish and ridiculous.

No more than an hour later, Grace sat in the great hall. She'd moved her embroidery frame next to the window, but spent her time staring out toward the moors. When Alex rushed through the doors, she jumped to her feet.

"My word, look at ye." He usually paid his appearance

much heed. But now his hair was tangled about his head, and his face shone with sweat. He smelled strongly of horse. "What are ye doing here? I thought ye left."

"Only to ride to Argyle House and back. I've no time to apologize for my appearance, Grace. Where is he?"

"Who? Alex, sit down before ye fall down."

"I'm fine." He paced to the window. "He hasn't left yet, has he?"

"Are ye talking about Lord Morgan? For if ye are, the answer is nay. But I can tell ye, Alex, I want no more of whatever ye were doing this morn. Not in my home." Grace straightened at the noise Alex made. "I mean it."

"Lord help us, we must be courteous to Lord Morgan . . . except, that man is not who he claims to be."

"What are ye saying, ye heard him, same as I."

"I heard him lying to ye. To both of us."

"Alex," Grace sighed. "I know ye don't like him, and I suppose, well, he is English, and I found him just after we fought—"

"That's what ye think, Grace? That I'd dislike a man, nay, call him a lair, because of that? Do ye think me so shallow then?"

"No." Grace rose and moved to where Alex stood, his bent arm draped over the mantel. Below a peat fire burned, slowly warming the room. "I didn't mean it to sound like that. It's just—"

"Lord Morgan is one of Scotland's most vocal enemies in the English Parliament. He was chief among advisors who pressured Queen Anne into refusing to sign the Act of Security."

"But . . ." Grace was at a loss. "He doesn't seem that kind of man."

"He also fought against the Darien Project with all the power at his command. And he has considerable power."

"What would he be doing here then?"

"An excellent question. But I have one for ye. How old a man would ye say the Englishman is?"

"I don't know. I hadn't thought on it."

"Well, think on it now."

"Thirty, perhaps. Nay, five and thirty," Grace corrected when she remembered the tiny lines radiating from the corners of his eyes. "What difference does it make?"

"Because, Grace, the real Lord Morgan is near fifty."

Chapter Five

"Lord Foxworth Morgan, Earl of Clayborne. Lord Foxworth Morgan, Earl of Clayborne." Fox said his name aloud, listening carefully to the inflection, trying to memorize the way his tongue moved, the set of his lips. He wished never to forget it again. Never.

Now that his memory was with him, he could admit, to himself anyway, how frightened he'd been. How weird it was to look at his hand, check his reflection in the mirror, and not know who it belonged to. He'd known it was his. But who was he? "Foxworth Morgan, Earl of Clayborne," he repeated. "And I'm going to Ashford Hall. My home."

He was tempted to take up residence in London again. To surround himself with the familiar. He hadn't lived at Ashford Hall since he was a boy, and his memories were not the best. At St. James's Square, everyone knew him. The cook, the butler, the chambermaids, his acquaintances at the clubs, Kate. They all called him by name. "Lord

Morgan. Fox." How pleasant it would be to respond to a smiling face, addressing him by name. His name.

With a shake of his head, Fox crossed the stone floor and peered into the wavy-looking glass. The face he'd known for thirty-five years stared back at him. He couldn't help smiling.

The pounding on the door sobered his expression. Fox lifted the outdated jacket from the chair back and slipped his arms into the sleeves, jerking around when the door flew open. He wasn't surprised to see the rejected suitor.

"Why in the hell did ye not answer when I knocked?"

Fox's stare was hard. "I'm not in the habit of responding to such."

"Aye, because ye're the exalted earl of Clayborne."

Before Fox could answer, Grace swept into the room. She'd obviously been hurrying. Her cheeks were flushed, her eyes bright, and the fontange perched atop her curling red hair, askew.

"Oh, ye're still here." She leveled a look at Alex and continued. "I thought perhaps ye'd already gone to the stables."

"I planned to leave momentarily. But not before thanking you again." Fox bowed toward her, grateful he hadn't done what he'd considered last night. He had no doubts he could have seduced her. In the wee hours, she'd been as vulnerable as he, as aware as he. But Grace MacCammon deserved more than a quick romp between the sheets. And he didn't need any more regrets.

She smiled at him, her green eyes shining, and Fox had a moment of indecision. He could leave tomorrow, or next week perhaps. The suitor's voice slammed into the sensual illusion.

"Ye're not going anywhere without explaining yerself."

"Explaining myself?" Fox noted the slight expansion of the other man's chest. Not a good sign. Whatever the problem, he didn't wish to continue this confrontation. Not in front of Grace. Fox kept his voice level. "I thought I already had."

"Yer lie ye mean?"

"Alex, I'm sure there's a logical explanation."

Fox shifted, the uneasy feeling becoming stronger. "What is it you're implying, MacDonald?"

"I'm not implying anything, I'm stating a fact. The earl of Clayborne is near fifty years old. And ye who is claiming to be him cannot be a day over five and thirty."

"Several days over actually."

"Aye, but hardly fifty."

"No." Fox turned to gather the saddlebags that had been packed for him. Yes, it was definitely better he leave now. "However, I am the earl of Clayborne. My brother died recently."

"And ye inherited, I suppose."

"I did. Now if you'll excuse me."

"So, if ye're the heir, ye must be twenty and two, and a rakehell of a hellion."

"A hellion I may be. But I'm clearly not twenty-two."

"Which makes ye neither Thomas Morgan, nor his son James."

"Nay, it makes me Foxworth Morgan, which I told you." Fox shook his head. How backward were these Scots? He'd noticed the clothing and their complete lack of knowledge about political affairs, but this was too much. "Thomas Morgan was my grandfather, James, the rakehell, my father."

"I told ye there was an explanation, Alex." Grace linked her arm with his. "Ye see, his father is . . ." Fox watched as puzzlement spread across her face, clouding the meadow green eyes. "But yer father cannot be two and twenty?"

"Hardly. My father is dead."

"I see."

"Ye see what?" Alex extricated his arm. "Grace, will ye listen to what he's saying? 'Tis a lie. Every word of it. I spoke not an hour ago to Lord Argyle, just to make certain I was correct. The real earl of Clayborne is in Edinburgh. He's there as a representative of the Queen. This is not Lord Morgan."

She was clearly confused, looking from one man to the other. Fox wished he could say something to ease her mind, but he'd only be repeating himself, and dragging on this encounter. Besides, much more listening to that damned MacDonald, and he'd start to doubt his own memory.

No, he knew who he was. He could remember everything. Clearly. His sister, Zoe. Her Scottish renegade of a husband. The battle, Culloden, where they'd first met. The Irishman, Padraic Rafferty—

Padraic Rafferty. Fox swallowed, then slowly turned his head to stare at the suitor. Alexander MacDonald was his name. His face was red with barely controlled anger. Other than that, there was nothing distasteful about his appearance, if you didn't count the unfashionably long hair, and billowy coat. Fox was certain he'd never seen him before yesterday. Yet . . . Yet, there was something oddly familiar. Something . . .

Any idea Fox had of grasping what it was about the man vanished when Alex drew the sword hanging at his side.

"Alex! What are ye doing? Put that away this instant."

"That will be enough from ye, Grace. This be man's business, and I'm telling ye this liar needs to be gone from here before I run him through."

"Ye won't." Grace stepped between the two men. "I'll have none of that at Glenraven. Lord Morgan is my guest."

Fox wanted to kiss her. Had a sudden memory, nay, thought, of what she'd feel like in his arms. How she'd smell. The smooth texture of her skin. He could swear her taste tickled his tongue.

But he could not know. And he could not continue to cause her problems. Staying was impossible, as much as he might desire it at this moment.

Stepping around Grace, Fox faced the suitor, and the tip of his sword. His eyes were narrowed, his stare icy. "I am leaving."

They stood thus for what seemed hours to Fox, but what he knew was merely seconds. Probing, each one daring the other to move. It was Alex who blinked, lowering the sword so it no longer pricked Fox's woolen waistcoat.

Fox heard a sigh of relief, thought at first it was his own, then glanced around to see Grace, hand pressed to her heart. Without another word he exited the room.

"Ye're angry with me."

"I don't wish to discuss it, Alex. Not now."

"When? I'm leaving within the hour." He strode to the window, jerked aside the draperies covering the leaded window, then turned to stare at Grace. She sat in the parlor before her embroidery frame, and though her needle occasionally slipped through the stretched fabric, her mind wouldn't focus.

"Damnation, Grace, I should have been in Inverness hours ago."

"Then why don't ye leave?" The words came out more brittle than she liked. With a sigh, Grace added. "Alex, I know ye think I blame ye for what happened with . . . with the Englishman. But truthfully, I don't. I'm simply . . ." She shook her head and jabbed the needle through the fabric. "It was unsettling, and I don't wish to discuss it further."

"Ye know he wasn't who he claimed."

If she didn't know, it wasn't through lack of information on Alex's part. Grace nodded her head.

"And it was a lucky thing we found him out when we did. Lord knows what information he might have extracted."

"Aye, Alex. He was a spy to be sure."

"Ye mock me, Grace, but I can think of no other explanation for him showing up here the way he did."

To tempt me? Grace pushed that thought from her mind. "Ye misunderstand me, Alex. I'm agreeing with ye. But must we speak of it further?"

He crossed the room to kneel at her side. His smile radiated warmth as he reached for her hand. "Not if ye do not wish."

"Alex." Why had she stopped him from berating the Englishman? Surely listening to that was preferable to another proposal.

"Don't worry. I'm not going to begin a lament about how I can't live without ye. Or how I'll miss ye while I'm away. Though I truly shall." He paused a moment, perhaps waiting for her to respond in kind. When the silence lingered, he hurried on. "I really should be off."

And so Grace was left alone again. Which is what she wanted, or so she told herself as the days passed. Maude was keeping to herself. An irksome habit, but one Grace doubted the old woman would ever change. When Dugald was alive, he had managed to curb his sister's reclusive habits to a point. But with him gone, Maude made little pretense of enjoying company. She'd seemed especially annoyed by the Englishman.

The Englishman. Despite what Alex told her, Grace thought of him as Lord Foxworth Morgan. And she thought of him often.

" 'Tis bordering on obsession," she mumbled as she speared the fabric in her hands, completing a petal of a perfect pink rose. Leaning back, peering at the embroidery critically, Grace sighed. How many flowers had she created with silk and thread? She had a talent for it, or so she'd been told. And a compulsion to create. But as with the Englishman, her needlework left her feeling unfulfilled.

Though beautifully crafted, her rose seemed lifeless. Grace glanced about the room. Hanging from the walls were some of the other embroideries she'd stitched over the years. They were all aesthetically pleasing, but . . .

Rising, Grace stepped around her frame. Slowly she walked about the room. Cocking her head, she studied the heralding angels over the mantel, then the MacCammon coat of arms above the desk. One wall was nearly covered by a battle scene featuring Robert the Bruce. A grouping of smaller pieces, depicting flowers and fruits of the different seasons, decorated the west wall. The piece she'd just started was to complete the series. Summer roses.

But she had no taste for it. After a moment of contemplation an epiphany struck. Her embroideries, pleasing to the eye as they were, lacked emotion. Intricate, colorful, correct in line and space, her angels, her battle scene, her fruit, her flowers, every stitch she ever made, simply lay on its fabric backdrop.

Moments later Grace found herself sitting behind the embroidery frame, extracting the stitches that made her rose. When she began stitching again, she had no plan. She wasn't stitching Robert the Bruce because Dugald asked her to, or the family crest because she thought she should. She simply allowed her fingers to roam at will.

A servant shuffled in, bringing tea, which Grace barely touched, and lighting candles, which she barely needed. How many hours passed before she surfaced, Grace couldn't tell. But darkness had shrouded her view of the moor through the east windows.

It didn't matter. The moor, its bleak, windswept longing, lived on the stretched silk before her. Not finished certainly, but complete enough for her to feel the bracken underfoot, to catch the scent of heather. To sense the yearning.

Grace slept little that night, or the next. She didn't work on her embroidery all the time. There were hours she simply stared out the window, memorizing the slant of light on the vast moor as the sun slid across the sky. But mostly she stitched. Her back began to ache, and still she stitched.

By evening of the third day, the fingers on her right hand hurt too much to bend through the handle of her teacup and her eyes throbbed. She retired early, not surprised when Maude knocked on her sitting-room door a short time later.

"This will help ye sleep."

"How did ye know I needed it?" Grace opened her door further, a silent invitation for her sister-in-law to enter, but the old woman remained in the hallway. The candle she held threw strange shadows across her plaid-shrouded face. She ignored Grace's question, choosing instead to mention the embroidery.

"Where do ye plan to hang it? 'Tis not a very pretty piece of work."

"I hadn't thought." Grace accepted the bowl Maude held out to her. "My bedroom perhaps. Don't ye think it might look nice on that wall?"

The old woman simply shrugged. Without another word she walked away.

Grace drank the foul-tasting potion, then lay on her bed. She looked about the room, imagining the needlework hanging in different places, wondering why Maude thought it not pretty. But though she tried to stay awake, within minutes a heavy sleep settled over her, the deep, dreamless sleep of the drugged.

Grace wasn't certain what woke her. It was dark when

she lifted the draperies to look out the window. Still, she splashed water on her face to wash away the cobwebs filling her mind, and dressed without calling her maid. Flexing her fingers, Grace slipped from the room, thinking she'd work again on her embroidery.

But it was to the stables she went. By the light of a lantern, Grace saddled her horse, then mounted and rode out just as the eastern horizon pinkened. Her undressed hair flowed behind her, and the cool morning air filled her lungs. Beneath her, her mount galloped, covering large expanses of mist-shrouded turf with her stride. After days in the castle, Grace felt alive.

She knew it was the moors that called her, and with an open heart she answered. Desolate, even in the early-morning light, the land stretched bare and barren as far as she could see. Nothing but quiet and solitude.

Until she saw him.

Grace didn't question who it was, any more than she'd questioned her need to come here. He stood, staring out over the wild moor the wind catching his dark hair, a lonely sentinel.

As she galloped toward him, she knew he heard her, but he didn't turn when she approached. Grace slid from the saddle and let the leather reins slip through her fingers. She was beside him before he glanced around.

Their eyes met briefly before he looked away. Lifting his arm, he pointed toward the northeast.

"We came at them from behind yon rise. We were overwhelming that day. Under command of the king's brother." Fox's mouth tightened. "He was a cruel bastard. I'd thought that before, but after that day, little doubt remained." He snorted. "Except in England, of course. William was hailed a returning hero. Honored at this ball and that. Who didn't wish to entertain the duke of Cumberland?"

Fox took a deep breath. "I had my share of invitations as well, let me assure you. Everyone thought my wound was the reason I declined." He shook his head. "I was afraid to go out in public. Afraid of what I might say or do if someone praised my heroism. So I tried to persuade Zoe, my sister, to go with me to Ashford Hall. She pleaded poor health, and I couldn't stand the thought of going by myself, so I went to an inn south of Lanchester instead." The wind whipped his cynical laugh toward the bay. "The innkeeper thought I was mad. And maybe I was." His gaze snared hers. "Just a little."

"But I digress. It was the battle I described." His head tilted as if once more he could hear the blast of artillery, the mournful cries of the dying.

Grace listened as well, but it was only the wind she heard sweeping across the plain.

"We came across the moor, bayonets fixed, murder in our eyes. Revenge is what we were seeking, you see. The Prince and his hapless followers had come dangerously close to London. Panic had closed shops, and my God, you mustn't mess with commerce. 'Tis not the British way.

"So we drove over them, killing as we went. They didn't stand a chance, your foolish kinsmen, not against the king's army and those Scots who didn't follow the Prince.

"I tried." When he looked down at her there were tears sparkling his thick, dark lashes. "God knows I tried to do what I could to stop the massacre. But there was bloodlust in the air, and the orders from on high were to kill any survivors. To slaughter them."

His eyes closed, and Grace placed her hand on his where it hung limp by his side. He allowed the contact at first, but soon pulled away.

"No, don't touch me. I know you don't know what I'm talking about. I cannot find a living soul who does." He took a deep breath. "It is as if the battle, the entire episode, never happened."

"Ye're right." Grace stepped closer as she spoke. "I have no idea of what ye speak. There's not been a battle on this moor. Not that I've heard. But that does not stop me from sensing how ye feel. In here." She grabbed his hand up, pressing it to the front of her bodice, over her heart. "I know yer pain, as if it were my own."

He stared at her, searching. "After I left Glenraven I decided to ride for Fort George. I'd been stationed there after I returned to service. It was a few years ago, but I figured some of my fellow officers would still be there. Someone who would advance me some coin, a suit of clothes, perhaps. I don't know, anything that didn't make me feel so out-of-date." His brows lowered.

"The road south wasn't there. I mean it was, but only a horse path. I didn't know anyone at the fort. And they'd never heard of me." His voice calmed. "Then I rode back to Inverness."

Grace didn't ask what happened there. The expression on his face showed clearly, the experience still had him confused.

"I considered returning to Glenraven."

"Ye should have."

He shook his head. "I rode south, intending to leave Scotland behind me."

"Did ye?"

"Nay." Fox let his hand slide from her grip. "It was in one of the border towns where I stopped to sup that I heard the constable talking."

"What was he saying?" Grace realized she'd been holding her breath and let it out. Something was happening. She could feel it. The energy was everywhere.

"He spoke of things in England. Of the Queen."

"Aye, what of her?"

"I don't recall." Fox shook his head.

"Then I don't understand. If ye can't even remember—"

"The Queen, Grace. He spoke of her as if she were still alive."

"But she is."

His eyes widened. "Queen Anne is who I'm talking about. Anne Stuart."

"And I'm speaking of the same."

He whirled about as a raven flew overhead. "This cannot be, you see. England and Scotland, Great Britain, are ruled by King George II. It's been years." Fox searched his mind for bits of history he'd learned. "Since 1714 when she died. None of her children survived her and so the crown passed to the Elector of Hanover. His son—"

"Stop!" Grace sank to her knees, her hands pressed flat against her ears. "Don't say anything more. I can't bear this."

"You can't bear it." Fox dropped down to face her. His hands covered hers, pulling them from her head. When he spoke again, his nose, nearly touched hers. "This is happening to me. This strangeness. 'Tis I who your suitor says does not exist. 'Tis I who cannot find roads where they should be." His fingers tightened. "They should be there. Why aren't they?"

"I don't know." Tears streamed down Grace's cheeks, but it was not from any physical pain he caused. "I swear I don't."

His eyes met hers then slowly he lifted a hand, using the pad of his thumb to wipe away the tears. His voice gentled. "Don't cry, Gracie. 'Tis I who's going mad, not you."

"Ye're not."

"Well, I'd relish another explanation, then." When she didn't respond, only continued to look at him, her eyes shimmering, Fox shook his head. "Would you like to know the irony of it all?" He wiped away another tear sparkling down her cheek. "For once in my life, I wish I were perfectly sane."

His hand slid to bracket her face, fingers molding about her head, lost in the fiery red curls. He leaned forward and their breath mingled. When his lips finally grazed hers, Grace felt the touch to the tips of her toes. She melted toward him, knee to knee, torso to torso.

It was as if she'd been far, far away and had just found her way home.

Even as the feeling swept over her, Grace knew how foolish it was. She was not the lost one. Oh, but she could be. So easily. Her arms wrapped about his waist, and she held him as if this time she would not let him go.

But, of course, she had no choice.

He pulled back, then let his forehead rest against hers. "I shouldn't have done that. Please forgive me."

Grace giggled, then started to laugh. She simply couldn't stop herself. His beg of pardon would have been much more effective if they were not pressed together, breast to chest. Apparently he saw the humor as well, because soon, his deep laughter joined hers. But they didn't separate.

"Come back to Glenraven with me."

"What, you want a madman as a guest?"

"Ye're not mad. There must be some explanation. We'll find it."

"What of the jealous suitor?"

"Alex?" Grace hadn't given him a thought. "He's gone to Edinburgh."

"Grace . . ."

"Where else will ye go? Ye can't continue riding all over the countryside."

"I not thinking clearly, inviting a man, who you must realize desires you mightily, to stay with you."

"I'm not inviting ye to share my bed, Lord Morgan," Grace said. "Only my home. Besides, we'll be chaperoned. Ye haven't forgotten about Maude, have ye?"

"Nay," Fox said with a chuckle. "Nor could I."

It was full light, the day holding a tiny hint of spring, when they came upon Glenraven. The decision for him to come had been more lack of alternative, than actual agreement. But he was there, riding with Grace along the trail leading to Glenraven.

For the first time Fox took note of the castle. There were towers that appeared to date back centuries, seemingly held together by newer additions. But all was in disrepair. Several of the towers were crumbling. Yet the whole held a stark beauty perched as it was, on the edge of Drummoissie Moor. Fox wondered that he hadn't noticed it when he was in Scotland before. Battles and war could do that, he supposed, close a man's eyes to the beauty about him.

His gaze turned to Grace. He'd been in Scotland, this area, many times over the years. Strange their paths never crossed. She was younger than he, true, but not by that many years. She would have been married when he was here last, but that had never stopped him before, certainly not in noticing a woman of her spirit and inner glow.

All he could do was shake his head. So much did not make sense to him.

No one was about when they entered the hall, which was fine with Fox. Time alone to think, was what he needed. Grace was right. There must be a logical explanation for his confusion—one he would find more appealing than the idea of going mad. Though there was always that to fall back upon.

Grace seemed willing to give him the time he needed, for which Fox was grateful. She curtsied, waving him off toward the room he'd used before. "Ye may break yer fast whenever ye choose. I believe I shall have mine sent to my room.''

"Thank you, Grace."

She paused on the stairs, her hand, small and pale against the stones. The smile she gave him tugged at Fox's heart as few things ever had. It seemed to evoke a memory, nay, a feeling, so faint he could barely wrap his mind about it. So fleeting it was gone before he could grasp its meaning. But he could swear the scent of heather lingered.

He looked around quickly, expecting to see bunches of purple flowers filling vases, but there were none.

He was thinking like a fanciful maiden, when what was needed was logic. Forcefully pushing aside the sensual spell, Fox remembered something he'd wanted to ask since he first saw her this morning. He'd sent a message to Ashford Hall the day he left Glenraven. The seventeenth. Since then he'd been wandering about the countryside and had lost track of time.

She was near the top of the curved stairs when he crossed the hall and called out. "Grace, one more thing if you please. Could you tell me the date of today?"

"Aye, 'tis the twentieth day of April, in the year of our Lord, seventeen hundred and five."

Fox watched till she disappeared around the corner. So it had been less than a sennight since he sent word to Ashford Hall. He should be— His thinking on the matter slammed shut as if an iron gate dropped. What had she said? Seventeen hundred and five? No, he must have misunderstood. 'Twas seventeen forty-eight. Forty-three years later. Aye. forty-three years later! What—

The scream, her scream, sent even that thought flying as he raced up the stairs.

Chapter Six

Fox raced into the room just as Grace whirled around. He took one look at her stricken face, another at the bed, and grabbed her by the shoulders.

"Are you all right? My God, were you hit?" He brushed red ringlets back from her face.

"Nay . . . I mean yes, I'm fine." But as hard as she tried, Grace couldn't seem to stop shaking. "It was silly of me to call out." In an attempt to curb her trembling, Grace wrapped her arms about her middle. "It's just . . ."

The rest of her words were muffled against his coat as Fox pulled her toward him. He held her there, rubbing her back, the loose tendrils of curly red hair, till her quivering stopped and her breathing slowed.

Hesitantly, reluctantly, Grace pulled away. When she could see his face, she attempted a smile. " 'Tis foolish, I'm feeling. It's just when I walked in and saw—"

"And thought about what would have happened if you'd been in that bed . . ."

"Aye. It did give me a fright." Grace laughed self-consciously. "I should have had it taken down long ago."

With a final pat to her arm, Fox left her by the door, and moved toward the center of the room. Slowly, he walked around what was left of the bed. A huge, iron chandelier lay twisted and bent amid the rubble of splintered tester, shredded fabric, and goose feathers.

" 'Twas never used, at least not since I came here. I simply liked the look of it, so primitive, as if some ancient Druids sang chants and wrought it over flames burning into the night sky." Her hand lifted. Her fingers grazed one cheek, before she balled them and let her hand drop back to her side. "That sounds so fanciful. Quite unlike me, really. But there'd been something about the piece that seemed to call to me. To my soul." Shaking her head, she added, "As if something made of iron could do such as that could. But—"

"Grace."

"Aye." She looked up, grateful he'd stopped her babble. Grace had no idea what had gotten into her to talk on so. Perhaps agitation over what might have been if she hadn't dragged herself from slumber this morning before dawn.

"I don't think this was an accident."

"Of course it was." Moving close to what used to be her bed, Grace pointed toward the ceiling. "It hung there for years, perhaps hundreds of years. Glenraven was originally built in the twelfth century. I wouldn't wonder if the luminary isn't as old. Rest and decay are bound to take their toll."

"So is a knife."

"A knife? I don't understand ye."

Stepping over the rubble, Fox dragged the heavy iron chain with him. " 'Tis true what you say about rust, but that's not what sent this thing falling. See for yourself." He held the end of the chain up for her inspection.

"I see nothing but a broken link."

"Look closer." Dirt and rust drifted from the clanking chain as Fox held it higher. "Here. Feel it right there."

" 'Tis smooth." Grace met his gaze. "But how?" She lifted her eyes to stare at the single link still remaining overhead. "And why would someone do such a thing?"

"I don't know the why," Fox grunted as he pulled and pushed the tallest piece of furniture in the room, a carved chest, toward the center. Hands planted on the polished surface, he vaulted himself up.

Near as primitive as the chandelier, the tower room was octagonal in shape. Windows, narrow affairs that looked out over the moor, had replaced arrow slits, but little else seemed modernized since the castle was used as a stronghold. The stone walls sported no paneling or paper and were softened only by sets of needlework hangings. The ceiling lacked plaster. Dividing the chamber in eighths were rough-hewn beams, timbers actually, which began maybe ten feet from the floor and ran toward the ceiling center.

Fox grabbed hold of one of the beams and, pulling himself up, began inching over and up toward the one remaining chain link.

"Do be careful." Grace tilted her head to watch. "If ye should fall—" What? He more than likely would kill himself.

"Is there another way up to the ceiling?" Fox grunted his words. "A room over top this one perhaps."

"Not that I know of. Oh, what happened?" Grace rushed to stand under him, only to be motioned away. His right hand had slipped and he momentarily hung upside down, caught only by his crossed legs.

"Damn splinters." Fox muttered through clenched teeth as he swung himself up till he could catch on again with his hands. The timbers disappeared into the mortared stone just shy of the center. Fox positioned himself as close as he could to the beam's end, then reached toward the link. Straining and stretching he could just reach it. But he wouldn't have been able to use his hands to saw through the metal.

"Well, it could have been done this way, though I doubt it."

"What of a ladder?"

" 'Tis possible I suppose. Though moving the bed might have been a problem."

"But why would someone do such a thing?" Grace shook her head. "It must have been an accident."

"I don't think so."

"But—"

"Hand me something long. There, that piece of bedpost. That's it. Can you lift it? Good. Now hand it up to me. Wait, I'll work my way down a bit."

"I don't understand what ye're doing," Grace said, after she managed to hold the staff of wood high enough for him to reach.

Instead of answering, he used the pointed wood to knock at the different stones forming a circle around the lone link. Tap tap tap. Fox jabbed and prodded, cursing under his breath. Each stone seemed firmly embedded. Until he hit one directly across from him. Powdered mortar sifted down through the ray of sunlight streaming through the window.

With renewed energy he shoved at the rock, moving it enough to see a dark band of separation between the mortar and the rock. One more push and the stone disappeared, leaving a hole large enough for a good-sized fist to fit through, not half a foot from the broken chain.

Fox looked down toward Grace. She stared back at him wide-eyed. "How did ye know that was there?"

"I didn't. But a chain doesn't just cut itself." Fox

dropped the piece of wood. It clattered to the stone floor. "Do you have any idea how to get to that space above your ceiling?"

"Nay. I didn't even know 'twas there. But I do recall once hearing that Glenraven was full of secret passageways and such. They were used as escape routes."

"Well, it seems as if this one was put to a different use." Hand over hand, Fox moved along the beam till he could hang down and drop to the floor. He brushed his hands together, audibly catching his breath when Grace came around beside him, taking one of his hands in hers.

"But who would do something like that? I mean go to such elaborate means to have the chandelier drop. Is this the hand with the splinter?" Clear green eyes glanced up at him.

"Yes. Ouch."

" I see it." Grace bent over his flattened palm. She used her short, rounded fingernails in a tweezer like fashion. "Does that hurt?"

"Nay." He could only see the top of her head, but he couldn't help smiling at it. She was using such care to remove a tiny sliver of wood. A sliver he'd have ignored. Something about her ministering to him this way soothed his heart. Made him feel soft inside.

With a bit of throat clearing, Fox pulled his hand away. "It really is fine now."

"All right. I think I got it anyway."

"Good." Fox took a deep breath and leaned back to stare at the ceiling. "To answer your question, I'd say someone wants you. . . . They wish your death to appear accidental."

She couldn't help it. Her knees nearly buckled, and a chill like the winter wind off the moor swept through her. "My death?" she said, trying her best to appear calm as the goose flesh prickled her arms. "That can not be."

When he said nothing, only shifted his head, leveling his dark eyes on her, Grace took a breath meant to calm her racing heart. "But who would wish me dead?"

"You'd know that better than I."

"Know what?" Maude, a plaid draped over her head, and around her shoulders crept into the room. She made no sound as she surveyed the crushed bed and twisted metal.

"Maude!" Grace hoped no one had noticed her jump when the older woman spoke. " 'Tis glad I am ye're here. Lord Morgan wishes to know about the secret passages. Do ye have knowledge of them?"

"So that ones back, is he? I didn't think he'd be gone long."

The silence that followed sent uncomfortable prickles down Fox's spine. She looked at him with eyes as old as time. Eyes that appeared to see beyond the here and now.

"He's trying to discover how someone could have cut through a link of the chain holding the chandelier."

"Probably just broke from age. Told ye not to use this room when we come here."

"Do you know about the secret passageways or not? His tone wasn't exactly amiable, and Fox felt the censure in Grace's stare, even though he didn't deign to look her way.

"There are passages all over the castle. They have been used through the ages by Scots. 'Tis said King Charles hid in one before fleeing the country. I'm not certain I should tell a Sassenach like ye."

"Maude."

Fox held up his hand to silence Grace, then brows lowered, stared hard at the old woman. "Do you know of one over this room or not?"

Instead of responding, she shuffled across the room.

Lifting a bony hand from beneath her plaid she ran her palm across the stones under one of the hangings. Within minutes she was shoving at one of the wooden beams dividing the room. The beam creaked and squealed as it slid across the stones. In its place gaped a narrow aperture, dark and forbidding.

Twisting her head slowly, Maude pursed near-colorless lips. "There is yer passageway, Traveler."

He'd never been fond of tight spaces—it was one of the reasons he'd put off boarding a vessel bound for the Carolinas to visit his sister. But there seemed no help for it. Fox hesitated, then moved toward the opening. He could just about squeeze through into the cobweb-laced mystery beyond. As he turned sideways, his gaze met Grace's worried one, then the challenge in Maude's black eyes. With a silent oath he pushed into the void, and was immediately consumed by smothering dark.

"A candle," he called back between coughs, as the dank air permeated his lungs. He thrust his hand back into the room. While he waited Fox tried to acclimate himself to the musty oblivion. He could see nothing, yet he knew how close the sides were. The walls seemed to press in upon his shoulders.

The weight forced against his palm was familiar, but certainly not a candle.

"Ye may need this," he heard Grace say as his fingers closed over the pistol butt. Fox transferred it to his other hand, then took the lighted candle.

Perhaps it was better not knowing what was in the tunnel. All Fox could see was drippy stone walls and cobwebs. He inched forward, using the hand holding the gun to push aside the labyrinth of gossamer threads crisscrossing his path. And as he walked deeper into the darkness, pretended not to hear the squeaky chatter of rodents.

*   *   *

Grace jerked around when she heard the clatter of boot-steps in the hall. The Englishman stood in the open doorway, the pistol in one hand, candle in the other. His dark hair and clothes were matted with a grey film. She took a step toward him, then decided to keep her distance. "Did ye find anything?"

"Bats," came his succinct reply.

Grace smiled, despite herself. "Besides that, I mean."

Fox lowered the candle, then took a few swats at his jacket, finally shrugging at the impossibility of cleaning himself. "I didn't find the tunnel leading above your room, but I do know someone has been using these secret passageways."

"How can ye tell that, Traveler?"

Fox glanced toward Maude. "Cobwebs, or lack thereof. From a certain point in that maze till I stumbled out into the hall, I actually didn't encounter any of this foul substance." This time he brushed fingers through his unfettered hair.

Grace watched him pocket the pistol, then turn toward her. "Can you think of anyone who would wish to harm you?" he asked. Before she could answer, Maude spoke up again.

"If I were asked, I'd say 'twas ye."

"He had nothing to do with this. Lord Clayborne was with me when the chandelier fell."

"Well, 'tis obvious ye weren't together in this bed."

Grace sucked in her breath, surprised at her sister-in-law's implication. "We were on the moor, riding."

Maude's shoulders seemed to lift her body beneath the wraps of plaid. "Ye cannot fight what will happen, any more than I. It just is a good thing my brother is dead, is what I'm thinking."

"How can ye say such a thing?"

Maude pulled her plaid tighter about herself, then trudged toward the door. "Better dead than knowing what his wife is about."

Grace stared after her, not wishing to turn and face the Englishman. When she finally did, her words stumbled over each other. "Please accept my apology. I know she can be difficult, but . . ." But what? "But this is more than is bearable. I shall have a long talk with her about . . ." Grace let the unfinished sentence drift into nothingness.

"I was right the first time." Fox waited for Grace to raise her brows in question before continuing. "She is a witch."

"Nay." Grace looked away, but not before a giggle escaped. "She is different, that is all." Grace should have let it rest there. Grace knew it. But the next words were out of her mouth before she could stop them. "She knows I would do nothing to disgrace Dugald's memory."

"But you're thinking about it."

Grace let her gaze meet his, then looked away, certain they were both thinking the same thing, wishing it wasn't the truth he was speaking.

"How long has your husband been dead?"

She didn't look at him . . . couldn't. "Nearly five years."

"That seems long enough not to concern yourself with what he might think of your actions."

"I doubt Maude would agree with ye."

"I'm not talking to Maude."

"My husband was a good man," Grace said, knowing her statement had no relevance to what the Englishman said. "He was a scholar and a merchant. That might seem a strange combination, but he read and learned. And what he believed was that commerce and trade were the heart and life of any country. He wanted that for Scotland." She glanced up at him. "Ye've heard of Darien?"

"Scotland's attempt to establish a colony in the New World?"

"Aye. Dugald was one of the Scotland Company's directors. He worked so hard on making it a reality. He wanted badly for it to succeed."

"And in the end lost everything?"

"Very nearly." Grace turned away, before he could see the tears shimmering her eyes. "I really should clean this mess."

Fox ignored the subtle shake of her head when he drew near. "Is that why you live here in this crumbling castle? Because he left you with nothing?"

"Nay. I've other places to go." She twisted her head, looking up at him through burnished lashes. Grace searched for a word to describe why she came to Glenraven. Why she stayed. It was not love of the old castle, or devotion. It was more as if she couldn't bear to leave it . . . or the moor. "This is where I choose to make my home," she finally answered.

Now that the initial shock of the attack on Grace was lifting, Fox remembered what he'd been thinking when he heard her scream. It was just as unsettling now as then. Just as unbelievable.

He left her side to move around the crushed bed. "Tell me again where your friend Alexander MacDonald went."

"Ye don't think he could have had anything to do with this." Grace gestured toward the mess. "For I can tell ye right now, he would not do such a thing."

Fox raised his hand, palm out. "I never considered him."

"Good. For he wouldn't."

"Are you in love with him?" Fox had no idea what made him ask that, except her defense of him seemed so absolute. The fact that her denial was as well, cheered Fox inexplicably.

"I do not love Alex. Not in the way I assume ye mean."

"I shouldn't have asked."

"No, it's all right. I simply feel he wouldn't—"

"Hurt you?" Fox finished for her. "I happen to think you're right. But that still doesn't answer my question."

"About his whereabouts? He's headed for Edinburgh. He's a Lord of the Session in Parliament." She shook her head. "He's so fearful an act of union will be passed uniting Scotland with England. He's as passionate in his patriotism as Dugald was."

Fox peered out the window as she spoke. Now he tore his stare from the moor and turned to face her.

"It passes."

Grace's brows lifted. "What passes?"

"The Act of Union."

"Well, it may, certainly, but—"

"You don't understand me. I'm telling you it does. Parliament passes it in—" He waved a hand trying to pull up bits of history he'd learned from his tutor. He never did have a good head for dates. "Seventeen-oh-seven, I believe. The Scottish Parliament, basically dissolves itself. Scotland has representatives in the English Parliament, of course, but it's a pittance."

Grace's head cocked to one side. "But how could ye know that?"

Fox brushed her question aside. "Tell me the date again, if you will."

"The date?"

"Yes."

"Ye asked me earlier. I don't understand."

"Just tell me."

"Nineteenth . . . nay, the twentieth of April, seventeen hundred and five."

His stomach seemed to sink. With effort he kept talking. "I'm going to assume you're telling me the truth."

"The truth? I've no reason to lie to ye. Why do ye look at me so strangely?"

"Because when I left London a little over a fortnight ago, it was March fourteenth, seventeen hundred and forty-eight."

"Forty-eight? But that's impossible."

"So it would seem." Fox paused, then shook his head. Was he a fool, to say such a thing? Or mad? Without another word, he left the room.

He found Maude hunched over a low table in a ramshackle outbuilding. By the yeasty smells oozing from the rotting wood, Fox guessed at one time it was a bakehouse. But she didn't appear to be kneading bread. Laid out on the warped plank serving as a tabletop were bunches of dried weeds. As he watched, she pinched a few leaves from one spray and sprinkled them into the hollowed-out rock she used as a bowl. Putting her weight behind the pestle, she ground and ground, singing a tuneless ditty as she did.

Fox made no sound as he stood in the doorway, but he wasn't surprised when she slowly turned her head. Her face nestled in shadows, but he could tell she stared at him, though she said nothing.

"What did you mean earlier, when you said neither of us could stop what will happen?"

"What do ye think I meant, Traveler?" She turned her head, concentrating again on her grinding.

Fox stepped over the stone doorsill and moved into the shadowy interior. "Do you always answer a question with a question?"

"Do ye?"

Crossing his arms, Fox allowed a grin to play with the corners of his mouth. "Why do you call me Traveler?"

She tore off a scraggly section of root, tossing it into her mix. "That what ye are, isn't it?"

Fox leaned against the unlit fireplace. "Are you going to tell me anything?"

She gave one last twisting crunch to her mixture and angled the pestle in the bowl. "What is it ye wish to know?"

"You said something was going to happen that we couldn't stop. What is it?"

She snorted. " 'Tis already happening. Ye can't see it?"

"What?"

She peered at him a long moment, searching from behind the shadowy plaid hood. "Yer knowing won't change anything."

"But that doesn't keep me from wanting to know, damn it." Fox took a step toward her, not liking the thoughts rushing through his head. He'd never knowingly harmed a woman, but by God he felt like grabbing this one and giving her a good shake.

She knew it, too. Fox could see the laughter in her eyes as if she was daring him to do it. Instead, Fox let his clenched hands fall to his side.

"I would like you to explain to me what you meant . . . please."

"Ah, ye've had a change of heart, Traveler. But yer true heart will not change. Yer love will stay yer love for always."

"What kind of strangeness are you saying now?"

"Explaining it to ye, Traveler. That's what ye wanted, isn't it? To have yer reason for being here deciphered for ye?"

"I don't know what you're talking about."

"Don't ye now?"

Chills ran down Fox's spine. "What's happening to me?"

"Nothing that doesn't happen to most. Ye've just traveled a might farther to find it, is all."

"Find what? Your words make no more sense than the recipe for one of your brews. A little of this, a pinch of that. You say no one can stop what will happen. Now you say I'm searching." Fox shook his head. "I can find no logic to your ramblings."

"There is more to life than logic, Traveler. I think perhaps ye are beginning to understand that."

He understood nothing. Nothing.

The damn witch. Fox leaned against the crumbling garden wall, berating Maude, life in general, and his situation in particular. Why couldn't she just talk like anyone else? All he wanted was a simple explanation. "Ha," Fox said aloud. There was nothing simple about it, and he knew it.

"I thought I might find ye here."

Fox jerked his head around, unable to stop the pleasure washing over him as he watched Grace pick her way through the overgrown garden. When she was beside him, he let his gaze drift again to the landscape he'd been watching.

"Moors have always fascinated me."

"Some find them desolate," Grace said as she, too, looked out over the windswept expanse.

"But you don't."

It was a statement rather than question. As if he knew . . . had known from the beginning. Grace wondered again about the feelings this stranger evoked in her. She'd never seen him before finding him, ragged and bewildered on the moor. But it was as if she'd known him forever. "Nay, I don't," she finally said.

They stood in companionable silence, watching the setting sun paint shadows across the moor. When Grace finally spoke her voice was soft as the coming night. "I . . . What ye said this morning about the date—"

"I don't blame you for doubting me."

"Did I say I doubt ye?"

Fox's laugh was mirthless. "You're saying you believe

that ludicrous tale about being forty-some years earlier than it was last month?'' When she said nothing, Fox looked her way. Their gazes met. "I think I may be going mad. Seriously mad.''

She still only stared at him, and the next words erupted from him. "For God's sake, first I can't remember who I am. Then I do, but find myself somehow swept back in time. If that's not madness, I don't know what is.'' He shut his eyes, then rubbed both palms over his face.

When he looked at her again his expression showed bewilderment. "But, then how can I recall everything so clearly? Names. Dates, well, maybe not the dates so well, but events. Ask me anything about what has happened in the last forty-odd years. Yes, ask me something.''

"I . . . what shall I ask?''

"Anything.'' Fox had a difficult time controlling himself. "Ask about the king.''

"Back on the moor ye said Queen Anne had died.''

"Yes, in, let me see, 1713, no, '14, aye, 1714. I was two at the time. Don't recall a thing. Except, of course what Mr. Bartholomew, he was my tutor, my brother's and mine, told me. The throne passed to a German, George Louis, Elector of Hanover.''

"Why?''

Fox shrugged. "Religion played a part. And power. But he was king, George I.''

"Was?''

"He died as well. His son, George II, is king now.''

Grace took a moment to assimilate all he'd said. Not that she believed him, necessarily. They were playing a parlor game, were they not? He was imagining a world for her, a world of the future. That's what was happening. Wasn't it? "The battle ye spoke of.''

"Culloden.''

"Aye, Culloden. Tell me about that.''

"It was dreadful. Hundreds of Scots were killed, most in battle, but afterward orders were given to slaughter the survivors."

"By the king's brother."

Fox looked down and smiled at her. "You have a good memory. Yes, Lord Cumberland. Even those who escaped were hunted down. It was a dark time for Scotland."

"Tell me why."

"Why the battle?"

"Aye." Grace watched him now, openly assessing how he said each word. Waiting for something to show he was making this up to tease her.

"When Anne died, so did the direct Stuart line. At least as far as their legitimate claim to the throne." Fox realized he was giving a one-sided view, the English view, and started again. "The Hanovers were in power, but there were those, especially in Scotland, who favored the Catholic Stuart line. The Stuarts lived in exile in Italy, but James's grandson, Prince Charles, decided to test the waters, so to speak, in Scotland. There'd been a Jacobite Revolution in 1715, but that was quickly squelched."

"By the English?"

"Yes. This time, however, the Scots had the young Pretender to rally about. He raised his standard in Eriskay and the Highland clans swarmed about."

"He raised an army."

"Aye."

"I don't imagine this pleased the king, George II, was it?"

"Not in the least. Especially when the Jacobites had success. They won victories at Prestonpans and Falkirk, actually advanced into England, making it very close to London before turning back. With the English army close on their heels."

"And ye were in that army."

"I was. I was a major. There were skirmishes, but the main battle, the one that changed the course of Scottish history, happened out there." Fox swept his hand to include the moor stretched before them.

Grace followed his gaze and almost thought she could see what he did, the ghosts of her kinsmen. They were there haunting the moor, their spirits restless.

But how could that be? To believe that was to believe he had traveled back from another time.

Yet, if it were true . . .

If there was going to be a battle, if her people were to suffer, was there not something someone could do? "What exactly did the Jacobites want?"

"Besides a Stuart king?" Fox shook his head. "I don't know. I mentioned earlier the Act of Union. Many Scots considered it unfair. Most didn't have any say in the matter."

"What if they did? What if the Highlanders' opinions were asked? Do ye think that would make a difference?"

"I don't know. Possibly not. I doubt much can be done to change history."

"Yet ye're trying to convince me ye've traveled through time."

"Am I?" Is that what he thought? That he'd traveled through time? Fox leaned against the rock wall. Time travel was impossible. Yet, was there another explanation? He could think of none. Even the madness theory was losing some of its appeal. He didn't feel mad. He had no desire to rant and rave. And other than the situation he found himself in, he felt perfectly fine. With a shake of his head, Fox pushed away from the wall. "Grace, I don't know what I'm trying to say, except I remember it all so clearly. It can't be 1705. Hell, I wasn't even born till 1713. Eight years from now."

"What else happens?"

"I beg your pardon?" Fox looked down at her, surprised to find her face alight with inquiry.

"We seem settled into this fantasy. I'm just wondering what else changes in the world over the next forty-some years. Surely some good happens."

"I suppose so." Fox shouldered himself away from the wall. "Let me see. What good happened during my lifetime?" His lips pressed together in thought. "Ah, roads have improved. In Scotland as well as England."

"That's certainly a good thing."

"Yes." Fox didn't mention that the roads in Scotland were built by an English general to make travel in the Highlands easier for armies, namely the English army.

He bent his mind to think of something frivolous and fun that had happened. Jack Broughton winning the boxing championship from James Figg? No. Cricket coming into vogue? Not that either. "I have it." Fox folded his arms in satisfaction. "The quadrille."

When she looked at him quizzically, he continued. "It's a dance, French I believe, but becoming quite popular in London."

"The quadrail."

"Rille, quadrille. It's fairly simple really. Let me show you."

"Here?"

"Why not here?"

"We've no music for one thing."

"Don't we?" Fox reached for her hand, smiling when she gave hers willingly. He'd done this before. The idea came to Fox from nowhere, and it wouldn't dissipate. No amount of rational thought dimmed his perception. He'd reached for her hand, and she'd given it. He recognized the weight, the slide of soft skin, the scent of her, and the way her fingers curved ever so slightly about his. But he couldn't remember when it was.

And then he stopped trying. It was enough that she was with him now, laughing softly as he led her toward their turf-covered ballroom.

"We would stand in a square, which of course, we can't do with only two of us. But we must pretend there is another couple."

"Aye." Pretending seemed to be what she and Foxworth Morgan did best.

"We must begin with the Grand Round. Here. We must set, and rigadoon. Point your right toe to the right, and back quickly. Yes, that's it. Now do the same with the left. Good. Now bend your knees, give a little hop, and there we are. Now we all take hands."

"The imaginary people and ourselves."

"You are catching on. Yes, and now we chasser, slide step, eight counts to the left, then back to the right. Very good."

"What do we do now?" Grace asked with a giggle.

"Any number of things. We can Grand Chain." Fox demonstrated their positions, and told her they would again rigadoon. "Or we could Weave Rings." He passed by her shoulder, looking down at her as he did. "Perhaps we should give it a try."

In the dusk, they faced each other as Fox began to hum, in the slightly off-key, tuneless way he had. But Grace didn't seem to notice as she took his hand. They pointed their toes. They laughed when Grace hopped when she should have bent her knees. They held hands, staring into each other's eyes as they began the Grand Chain.

He'd always found the Weave Rings seductive, but never so much as now. It was as if invisible silken threads kept them bound even when the steps forced them to separate. They were always drawn back.

They repeated the changes four times, and with each step they grew closer, and his tuneless song, slower. When they faced one another, barely room for a breeze to wend its way between, Fox stopped humming. His hands lifted to bracket her face. Hers snaked about his waist.

"The other couple would be scandalized by our behavior," Fox whispered in her ear, as he bent to nuzzle her neck.

"We imagined them," Grace sighed. "We can imagine them gone."

Fox lifted his hand only long enough to click his fingers. "They are no more." Then, with barely controlled passion, he pressed his lips to hers.

Chapter Seven

What in the hell did he think he was doing?

Fox lay on top the coverlet, his legs crossed at the ankles, his hands stacked beneath his head. Staring. Watching a delicate-legged spider weave a web in the corner of the tester. Seeing, but not really seeing.

The hour was late. Long past the time he usually rose. If he were still in the military, his men would wonder at his indolent behavior. But, of course, he was no longer in the service of King George. There was no King George.

Fox squeezed his eyes shut and swallowed hard. Not a damn thing made any sense to him, and all he could do was lie abed and study the industrious arachnid.

Forcing himself to focus, Fox began sorting through the facts, or what passed as facts. His name, his age, his reason for coming to Scotland, they all were clear to him. He'd even pinpointed the moment everything changed. It was storming, thunder exploding, and lightning streaking the sky with fire. He remembered lifting his arms, taunting the gods. Feeling their wrath.

It was the moment of awakening that thrust his life into turmoil.

Each night since then, as he laid his head upon the pillow, he'd considered the possibility that when he awoke he'd be in London, or Ashford Hall, or at least in the correct decade.

But it was obvious a simple matter of opening his eyes wasn't going to change anything. The time had come for him to take some action. Some action other than. . . . Fox unpiled his hands and scrubbed them down across his face.

What was he thinking dancing with Grace MacCammon in the moonlight? Kissing her? If everything else that happened to him wasn't enough to prove his madness, that was.

He'd wanted her, wanted her so badly that even now the urge to find her and finish what they'd begun last night nearly overwhelmed him. And Grace would have him too. Arrogant as it seemed, Fox knew her attempts to stop him were halfhearted. One more kiss. That was all it would have taken.

But some long forgotten shred of decency buried deep in his soul had surged forward, forcing him to pull away. To accede to her wishes. At least to the ones she dared to speak.

Fox groaned. He had to leave this place. Today. Before he found himself longing to stay. In her castle by the moor. In her time. Fox grimaced as he pushed to his feet. *In her time.* He almost had himself believing he'd traveled from one era to another.

Fox found her in the large drafty hall she used as a parlor. A peat fire burning in the fireplace battled the chill. She'd moved her embroidery frame close to the east windows to catch the morning light, he thought. The streaming sun did magical things to her hair, setting it ablaze. Forcing that thought aside, Fox strode across the stone floor, clearing his throat as he did.

She pivoted on her chair, and now the sun seemed to turn her hair into a flaming nimbus, surrounding a face as sweet and perfect as any he'd ever seen.

He cleared his throat again and forced himself to look down at her needlework. Perhaps he was wrong about moving herself to the window for the light. For it was the moor, the view from the window, that she'd sketched across her canvas with needle and thread. Fox averted his eyes before he became sucked into the landscape.

He would tell her now. Tell her he was leaving. But before he could she took a deep breath.

"How can it be changed?"

Fox raised a brow in question.

"The . . . the fantasy ye told me last night. If one were to believe it true, believe it actually to be the future, or the past." She paused, lifting two fingers to her forehead. "I'm trying to reconcile this in my mind. To be careful with my words, though I truthfully do not know why."

"I certainly will not think ill of anything you might say."

"I would imagine not." Grace rose, then sank back into her chair. "What ye said last night has not strayed far from my thoughts."

"The battle?"

"Aye and its aftermath. And all the rebellions and curses borne by my people before the defeat." She touched the needlepoint moor reverently. "Culloden," she whispered. "How can we stop it from happening?"

His eyes met hers. Fox realized he should be pleased to have her, anyone, believe his tale of years lost. But he wasn't. He didn't want anyone to believe him. The entire idea of coming back from the future was preposterous. Couldn't she understand that?

Oh, she called it a fantasy, but it wasn't. Not to her. Fox could see the truth in the depths of her crystalline eyes. She believed everything he said. Perhaps her mind needed to adjust to the concept, but her heart, her spirit, accepted and believed. A flame-haired temptress given a glimpse into the future's crystal ball. And she did not like what she saw. Damnation, he needed to escape.

"Lord Morgan?"

"Yes?" Fox blinked. "What did you ask?"

"There must be a way to change what happens. Can ye tell me what it is?"

Change history? Or the future? Fox turned toward the fire. His hands folded behind him, he stared into its bluish blaze. The very idea seemed as foreign as traveling through time. He doubted either possible. He questioned whether either should be done.

Not that the idea of averting Culloden didn't have appeal. He had only to close his eyes to experience again the death and destruction. But it happened. Nothing could change that.

He glanced over his shoulder. "There's naught can be done."

"I can't accept that." She turned away, back toward her work, as if to continue looking at him would prove him right.

"There were . . . are events, a series of them, that lead to Culloden. I can't recall, or perhaps never knew, all of them. Possibly most of them are already in place."

"What are they? Tell me what ye do remember."

"Grace." His eyes pleaded with her to stop this nonsense, but then remembered that he'd started the talk of the future. He'd tried to prove to her that this wasn't the right time and place. He could indulge. With an expulsion of breath he turned and walked back toward her, settling himself in a chair. If he were going to force his memory, he might as well be comfortable.

"Let me see. The most obvious reason for Culloden was Charles Stuart's assertion that his grandfather was the rightful king, and the army he raised to back his claim."

"Aye, ye mentioned as much. But that happens years from now. What of this moment? Ye came to this moment. There must be a reason."

Fox shook his head. "You accept too readily." When she only stared at him, Fox forced his mind back to the history lessons he could recall. The process was as grueling now as it had been when his tutor had expected him to learn them in the first place.

"There was controversy over the ascension to the crown after Anne. Not many in Scotland approved of the Hanoverian Elector, George I. Of course, there were many in England who felt the same, though he was Protestant. But I believe you Scots wished a separate sovereign. Of course, that was before the union. What is it?"

"The union." Her eyes lit up. "Could that be it? Ye said last night it comes to pass, and I know Alex and many others oppose it."

"I imagine it isn't too popular in Scotland. But it does happen."

"When?"

"It went . . . goes into effect in 1707, to the best of my recollection."

"Why did Scotland approve it? Ye mentioned she gets very little from it."

"I don't know."

Grace glanced around. "There must be a reason. Were there battles, threats of war?"

Fox shook his head. "Nay, not that I recall. This all happened before I was born, you understand," Fox said, before realizing how foolish that sounded. Fox pushed out of the chair. "Memory fails me. If I'd have known this . . ." His hands lifted in a shrug, "this thing would happen, perhaps I'd have listened more carefully when my tutor spoke of things Scottish. Though in truth, I doubt he'd have given me any anti-English facts.

"I see."

"Grace." Fox sat back on the edge of his chair, and reached for her hand. "There's nothing to be done."

"How can ye say that after telling me of the battle and the aftermath. Of the hangings and punishments. I could tell it moved ye."

"Moved me aye, Grace. But reality is reality."

"Strange words coming from ye."

Leaning back in the chair, Fox closed his eyes. She had the right of it there. He was the last person on earth to be speaking of reality. He who could no longer tell what was real and what was not.

When she began speaking, Fox watched her through lowered lids. "Things might be different if the Darien Project had succeeded."

"Perhaps another try."

She was shaking her head before he finished speaking. "There's no more money. So many of us gave all we could. Loans were promised, then withdrawn because of English pressure. 'Tis even rumored a British man-of-war attacked one of the reinforcement vessels heading for the colony. Then there were the Spanish. There's nothing left."

Her demeanor, usually so bright, radiated defeat. Fox wished there was something he could say to cheer her. But even her own attempts to find a solution were met by his skepticism.

"Perhaps there is something we can do so that the Prince, James's son, is successful. Or James. Did ye not say he came to Scotland on several attempts to regain the throne?"

Fox shook his head. "They were short-lived, sad affairs, doomed to failure. Besides, England would never sit back idly and watch the Stuarts regain the throne. Any attempt would bring more bloodshed and suffering."

"We wouldn't want that."

"No. I'm afraid, Grace, there's nothing to be done."

"Nay, I'll not accept that. At the very least the lords and barons, all the members of Parliament, must know the import of what they're doing."

"How do you propose to let them know?"

Her expression brightened. "We'll tell them."

"About me?" Fox asked with a guffaw.

"If we must."

"And you expect anyone to believe this . . . this nonsense?"

"*I* believe *it.*"

"And it's enough to make me wonder at your sanity." Fox realized he shouldn't have said it, the moment the words left his mouth. Her lips thinned, and she returned to her embroidery, stabbing the stretched fabric with her needle. Fox forced air through his teeth. "I cannot imagine you convincing anyone an Englishman has come from the future to save Scotland."

"Well, I must try." She glanced toward him. "And how can ye be so calm, knowing what ye do? I mean, the lives of hundreds are at stake, and ye keep giving me reasons why we can't, or shouldn't, do this or that. Have ye no compassion? No fire in yer belly?" With that she jabbed the needle into the fabric and stood. "Why do ye think ye were sent back here?"

"I don't know, though I doubt it was to argue with you. If indeed I was 'sent back here' as you call it."

Her countenance softened. ''Of course ye are confused and—''

''I'm leaving. Today.''

''Leaving?'' She sank back into her chair. ''But where will ye go?''

''Home. To England. London. Or Ashford Hall, I haven't decided yet. But I know I can't stay here.''

''I see.'' Grace folded her hands. ''Well, as it happens, I'm leaving too. For Edinburgh.''

''Grace.''

''Perhaps ye're convinced nothing can be done, and we should just allow events to take their natural course, but I'm not. I can't be. Not now. Not knowing what I do.''

''For God's sake, Grace.'' What if he was wrong? What if he was mad? Then she would be off preaching the tales of a madman.

''I'm convinced everything happens for a purpose. And I know there's a reason for yer coming here at this time.''

All Fox could do was stare at her. She appeared so certain, of herself, of him. And he was neither. How could she be so sure his life meant something whichever time he inhabited? For as long as he could remember, he'd been wandering about, not knowing what he should do with himself. He'd joined the army, but though he'd risen in the ranks quickly enough, he'd never felt as if he belonged there. But then civilian life seemed unsuitable as well. How many times had he resigned his commission only to buy it back again? Even his trip to Scotland had been the act of a desperate man. He'd left his town house, heading for Devon, yet found himself in Scotland instead, standing on a battlefield that wasn't a battlefield at all. At least not yet.

No, nothing was certain to him, and it never would be. Right now all he knew was that his head felt as if it might explode if he continued to dwell upon this. He took a breath. "I'm going to England."

"So ye said." She wove her needle through the outer edge of her embroidery and loosened the frame. "And I'm going to Edinburgh."

She stood, then walked, her head high, toward the door. She was a stubborn woman, Fox could say that for her. One that would no doubt get herself into trouble.

"I'll accompany you there." When she looked over her shoulder, Fox shrugged. " 'Tis on my way."

She simply nodded, but he'd wished for a smile."

Damnation, he'd forgotten about the sister-in-law.

He'd postponed his departure a day to give Grace time to prepare for her trip. Actually, he'd resolved himself to waiting a sennight, and was pleasantly surprised when she'd sent word that same evening that she was prepared to leave. And that Maude would accompany them.

Fox had resigned himself to traveling with less speed because of Grace. Now he decided it might take months for them to reach the Scottish capital.

He shook his head and continued to stuff clothing into the saddlebags he'd been lent. He had two suits of clothing, and four shirts. One shirt was of the fine linen, from Lord MacDonald, he assumed. The others, plus the suits, were more apt to have been borrowed from one of the servants given their coarseness of weave and workmanship. Though to be honest, Fox had noted that the servants in Grace's household appeared well cared for. There were also more of them than he would have thought she would keep, given the disrepair of the castle.

Fox shook his head. He couldn't concern himself with such things as servants who didn't do their jobs.

He brushed his hair, pulling it back in a simple queue.

For what he hoped would be a long day on horseback, Fox donned a jacket of grey wool decorated with silver buttons—one that reminded him of ancestral portraits lining the gallery at Ashford Hall—woolen breeches, and his own boots.

The hour was early, before dawn, when he entered the dining room, but Grace and her sister-in-law were already breaking their fast. Grace glanced up and nodded when he bowed; the older woman did not.

Fox had not seen Grace since their discussion the morning before. Even the message telling him she was ready to leave was delivered by one of the girls who worked for her. She was angry with him, he supposed, though he wasn't certain why. Or perhaps he did know why. He simply didn't know what he could do about it. Looking at her now, Fox wished things could be different between them. He wasn't sure how. But he did want different.

After her initial greeting she kept her eyes averted and ate little. Maude, on the other hand, couldn't seem to get the food into her mouth fast enough. The oat bread and eggs she quickly washed down with copious amounts of milk. As usual she was wrapped in her plaid, with very little showing but her face and hands.

Between bites she glanced toward Fox, her black eyes searching, but she said nothing.

What a puzzle she was. Fox would swear she didn't like him. But then there were times she stared at him as if she knew all about him. Even accepted him for what he was. Those were the times he wished he could force her to tell him . . . something.

Of its own accord Fox's gaze flicked toward Grace. He was drawn to her, of that there was little doubt. More than drawn. There was something about her that pulled at his heart. That made him want nothing more than to cuddle close to her and spend his days protecting, confiding, loving. Fox jerked his head to the side. What in the hell was he thinking? He was in no position to become involved with a woman, any woman. Especially not one who invoked such strong feelings. No, whatever spell it was she cast over him had to be fought, and fought well.

"Will you and Mistress MacCammon be taking a coach south?" Fox asked Maude.

"There be no coach," she replied, whereupon Grace added, "There are many stretches of road unpassable by more than a horse and rider."

"Which doesn't change the fact that we have no coach."

"Ye're right, Maude, it doesn't."

Fox watched the interplay between the two women with a sinking feeling. True, he'd expected accompanying a coach to take a great deal of time. But without one, well, how was the old woman going to manage?

Grace obviously tried to alleviate his concern. "We came from Edinburgh without a coach, and we shall return without one."

The castle courtyard, overgrown with the skeletal remains of last summer's bracken and heather, bustled with activity. Several of the servants had gathered to wish their mistresses "Godspeed."

"I can be coming with ye, even now, I could be ready in a wink." The old man who cared for the horses bowed respectfully to Grace as he spoke.

"Nay, Angus, I want ye to go to yer home. Ye can look in on the castle every now and then if ye would. Keep the vines from smothering the place and the moor from claiming it as its own."

"I'll keep Glenraven ready for yer return."

"And I shall be back. As soon as I can." She pressed a coin to his palm and folded large-knuckled fingers about it.

She did the same with each of the girls as they bobbed their curtsies.

Fox wondered about the other servants. He'd seen several women, and at least one man, a burly sort who looked more like he belonged in the fields but who had acted as more of a butler, at Glenraven. But none of them had come to the courtyard.

Angus, for all his talk of keeping the wolf at bay, could hardly manage a trip to the end of the overgrown garden. And the maids seemed anxious to be off. Whatever, it was not, could not, be his problem. He had too many of them at the moment.

Still, he could not resist a glance back as they galloped toward the moor. He noted Grace did the same, and wished he really knew what it was about Glenraven that kept her there. But then he wondered if it was not the castle so much as the moor that bordered it.

Or was that him? After all, he'd been the one lured back to Culloden.

They rode single file, Grace leading the way, the sister-in-law, to his surprise, sitting well and keeping pace, then Fox. His mount, the same one he'd borrowed on his ill-fated journey to Fort George was surefooted and stout. Steam spewed from his nostrils, mixing with the mist swirling about underfoot. The horse bore little resemblance to the magnificent animal he'd ridden to Scotland, but then Fox himself was hardly the same.

That was something he didn't care to contemplate. Not now. Time enough to think on that when he reached London, or so he tried to tell himself.

The air was chilled and the sun barely lightened the

eastern sky as they started off along the moor. South. Toward Edinburgh. Toward London. Toward normality.

He'd known the terrain once, studied it before the battle. It still seemed familiar. Perhaps because he'd lived the battle so many times, through nightmares and day sweats. Why, oh why had he come here? What demons had he hoped to flail?

Fox wished he could urge his mount into a gallop to leave this place behind. But prudence dictated they travel at a trot, and so he did, reins looped loosely through his gloved fingers. He didn't plan to turn his head, to stare out over the harsh, unearthly landscape, drifting in a sea of fog. But he had no choice. Lonely and brooding it seemed to call to him, its voice low, vibrating on the wings of the incessant wind.

Grace drew the woolen cloak more tightly about her. Leaving was more difficult than she expected. Though the air blew cold from the north, the chills racing through her flowed from the inside. She doubted a cozy chair by the fire would warm her, though she wasn't opposed to giving it a try.

But it would be hours, cold, bone-jostling hours, before they neared a hearth. Tonight they would sup and rest at an inn on the shores of Loch Gleven. Grace couldn't decide if thinking of the cozy chamber she'd share with Maude comforted or depressed her. They would be gone from the moor.

"He's not coming."

Grace shifted in her saddle. Had Maude said something, or was it the whipping wind playing tricks? When she glanced around, Maude merely pointed, back to where the Englishman stood, the wispy fingers of mist threading about his long cape. He'd dismounted, and though he still held the reins, he seemed oblivious to the horse, or anything else.

Grace couldn't seem to stop shivering as she turned her mount. When she was alongside Maude, she said, "Go along. We'll catch up to ye."

"Looks like he's not coming."

"I'm sure 'tis nothing," Grace replied as she urged her horse back along the trail. She had no idea if Maude did indeed continue on her way, for Grace didn't look around. Lord Morgan, Fox, was all she could see. oblivious to the horse, or anything else.

Grace couldn't seem to stop shivering as she turned her mount. When she was alongside Maude, she said, "Go along. We'll catch up to ye."

"Looks like he's not coming."

"I'm sure 'tis nothing," Grace replied as she urged her horse back along the trail. She had no idea if Maude did indeed continue on her way, for Grace didn't look around. Lord Morgan, Fox, was all she could see.

She was almost upon him before he turned, looking up to where she'd reined her mount to a stop. He watched, his expression one of puzzlement, as she slid from the horse's back.

"I can barely remember."

His voice, so eerily familiar, made Grace lean closer. "What can't ye remember? The battle?"

"Yes." He shook his head. "Nay, I remember the battle. The details. I can tell you whose division attacked when. It's the feelings, the emotions, that are fading." His shoulders slumped. "Why is that?"

She wanted to answer him. To reveal all the secrets of the universe to him and watch the crease between his brows fade. But she had no explanation, no reason for the way he felt. She was as confused as he.

Grace reached out. Her hand, pale in the morning light, touched his sleeve and he turned toward her. When they came together their embrace was comforting as a feather mattress.

In each others arms reality's sharp edges softened.

Chapter Eight

On the fourth night they stopped at a simple dwelling pressed along the banks of the River Tey. Made of divots, the hut had only two rooms. On either side, and attached to the main section were a byre, where horses were stabled, and a barn.

The hour was late, and the women's endurance, especially Maude's, continued to amaze Fox. They had traveled hard terrain, on little more than footpaths, resting only when the horses needed a break, and neither Maude nor Grace had yet to complain or fall behind. Fox doubted any of his soldiers would have been so stoic. Lord knew he was tired, anxious to sit upon something other than the plaid-covered saddle.

He didn't ask who lived here. So far, those who'd given them shelter and food had done so willingly, even cheerfully. Fox imagined by the looks he often received they did so despite his presence. Englishmen did not appear well-liked at the homes they visited, so he'd learned to keep attention away from himself as much as possible. That meant saying little. Since he spent most of his time alternating between reflection and brooding silence, this proved no hardship.

The sharp bark of a short-legged, sturdy dog heralded their approach to the hut. Fox began to dismount as the dog, tail wagging, circled his horse, but paused when Grace called his name.

"I'm not certain we will rest here tonight," she added, turning back in her saddle to face the front door.

Fox didn't ask why. If nothing else on this journey, he learned to trust her judgment in such things. A moment later the wattle door opened and a huge redheaded man filled the space. He squinted out into the setting sun, lifting a sword nearly as tall as himself as he did.

"I wish ye good evening, Alisdair McKinzie. 'Tis I, Grace MacCammon, come to ask for yer hospitality for the night."

At first the only sound was the nearby river chortling over rocks. The man said nothing, nor did he lower the claymore. Fox nudged his mount forward, till his horse was even with Grace's. She stopped him from pulling in front by lifting her hand.

It was then the man spoke, his tone belligerent. "I wonder ye'd expect a welcome here."

"I don't expect. I request."

The man appeared to think over what she said, then quickly let the broadsword drop to his side. "Ye're a brazen woman, Grace MacCammon."

"Nay, just a trail-weary one."

"Ye can rest yerselves here then." He twisted, yelling back through the door. A boy appeared, made his way over the manure pile, and took up Grace's reins.

Fox dismounted in time to help her down, then crossed to do the same for Maude.

The only light inside the kitchen came from the bluish glow given off by the smoky peat fire in the middle of the room. There were no windows, only a hole in the center of the blackened ceiling.

Angus motioned for them to sit on stools vacated by the brood of red-haired children as they entered. The stools formed a circle surrounding another that held a near-empty dish. With a nod, Angus motioned for a woman, his wife, Fox presumed, to fill the pewter dish with more food. Spoons were passed around and Maude made quick work of using hers. Grace glanced his way, then scooped a mouthful from the same dish. Fox followed her lead.

He couldn't say what he ate. It felt granular to his tongue and lacked a distinctive flavor, but seemed to fill his stomach. During the entire meal no one said a word. The boy sent to look after their horses entered the hut and took his place, kneeling behind the guests.

When a little more than half the gruel was eaten, Fox noticed Grace lower her spoon and touch Maude's hand. "Ye best watch ye don't eat too much and give yerself poor digestion," she said.

Fox had the notion that the sister-in-law wished to argue. But for once she didn't, and quietly laid down her spoon. Fox didn't need the green eyes turned his way for him to do the same.

"We thank ye for a delicious sup," Grace said as she stood. "It was most hospitable of ye all."

"There be more." The big Scot motioned over his shoulder toward a covered pot.

" 'Tis most grateful we are, but we could not eat another bite. We're more anxious for a place to lay our heads this night."

The man nodded. "Ye can have the ben. There be room enough for ye all."

The ben or sleeping room contained a built-in bed with

doors that closed. Several pallets were rolled up on the earthen floor. This room, like the other, had no windows, but there were a few chinks in the mud walls that kept complete darkness at bay.

Fox spread a pallet, consisting of a plaid and some linens, then stretched out, his boots in the dirt. He assumed both women would take the bed, so was surprised when Grace chose a pallet as well. Maude in the meantime had crawled into the bed and closed the doors.

The room was small, the pallets close. Fox tried to ignore her nearness as Grace settled down. She lay on her side, faced away from him, her red curls a mass of tangles. He had only to reach out to touch her.

Gritting his teeth, Fox shut his eyes. But the vision of her lying beside him would not fade. It was always so. He'd hear her voice, or see her smile, and feel it in his heart, keep it there. Lying beside her felt familiar enough to be commonplace. Nay, not commonplace, for he could not think of her in that way. But normal, as dear to him as breathing.

"We are taking their beds," Fox whispered, smiling to himself when she turned to face him.

"They'd be insulted if we didn't."

"I thought that might be the case." Fox squinted to see her in the near darkness, then realized looking upon her was unnecessary. He did not need to see her. He knew her. "How is it we came to spend the night at the home of Alisdair McKinzie?"

"It was late. His hut was close."

"True, but he did not receive us as the others have. Why is that?"

He heard her sigh in the night. " 'Tis a long story."

"I've told my share of long stories."

"Aye, ye have." She shifted. "I suppose ye'll be finding out as soon as we arrive in Edinburgh."

Fox strained to hear as her voice became even lower. "What is it?"

Grace hesitated, then began. "I mentioned to ye that my husband was involved with the Darien Project."

"Yes."

"He worked very hard . . . many hours. When it failed, he was devastated."

"Go on."

"Dugald used his influence to solicit money for the venture."

"And a great many people lost money."

"Aye," she agreed. "Some lost all they had."

"It's only natural a few people would resent your husband, that being the case."

"He understood that. However, there was more. It was rumored . . . Many, including the earl of Denbigh, accused Dugald of stealing some of the money for himself."

"Did he?"

She'd been expecting that question, realized it was perfectly logical to ask, yet still felt the force of it like a blow. Especially coming from the Englishman. But then he had no way of knowing what Dugald was capable of doing. She had known her husband as well as anyone, and even Grace couldn't say for certain. "No. I don't think so." She paused again. "I suppose it is possible."

"Was the earl one of those who lost money?"

"Lord McKinzie?" Grace couldn't help chuckling. "Goodness no. He was opposed to the project from the beginning. He believes strongly that Scotland's future lies with England."

"An enemy of your friend Alex, I suppose?"

"Aye. And a kinsmen of Alisdair McKinzie."

"And you still asked him for hospitality?" Leaning up on his elbow, Fox cupped his chin. "Should I be expecting our host to come barreling through the door any moment, sword in hand?''

"Nay. Despite it all, I know Alisdair McKinzie to be an honorable man."

"How do you know him so well?"

"I'm a McKinzie as well."

"The earl of Denbigh?"

"Is my uncle."

Fox hesitated. "Lord McKinzie? I've heard that name before."

"He's the man Alex mentioned as a friend of . . ." Yours? That did not sound right. Nor did saying he was a friend of Fox's grandfather. In the end Grace simply said, "Of Lord Morgan's."

His friend. Yet he'd never met the man. "We always seem to come round to this, this dilemma of mine, don't we?"

" 'Tis a difficult subject to ignore."

"I suppose it is." Fox rolled onto his back, stacking hands beneath his head. "I simply cannot accept it, the idea of it, as you appear to have done." Turning to stare toward her in the darkness, he asked, "How is it that you don't find the idea of me . . . of me being here, in this time, unacceptable?"

"I don't know for certain." Grace rolled to her side. "Wait, I do. As I see it, there are three possibilities. Ye are mad, which I don't believe to be true. The second is that ye're lying to me."

"I'm not."

"I did not think so. Which leaves the third likelihood."

"That I traveled through time."

"Aye. 'Tis not unheard of ye know. The ancients speak of it."

"Yes, well, I'm not an ancient. Or a Celt. Or a man who believes such foolishness exists."

"Ye will have to believe it sooner or later, I'm thinking."

"Believe the truth as you see it."

"Perhaps." He could hear her shift on the linens. "If ye are satisfied with yer truth, then so be it."

"You know I'm not." Fox sucked air through his gritted teeth. "I'm not satisfied with anything." When he reached out, Fox wasn't certain he would touch her. It had grown darker, and by this time he couldn't even make out her shape. But as they talked he'd been unable to escape the subtle scent of heather that clung to her like a gossamer veil. Every sound she'd made, every breath, honed his senses to her. When he brushed warm skin, it was as if his resolve to fight his need for her dissolved. "I can't stop thinking of you. Wanting you." The pulse beneath his fingertips quickened. "Tell me you feel the same."

"Do not ask me that."

"Why? Nay, don't turn away. Answer me. Please."

"Ye are known to me. Here." Her hand covered his, dragging it down till his palm covered her heart. "But I must not allow myself to forget the message ye bring."

"Is that why you've stayed away from me?"

" 'Tis the journey that separates us."

"We are not traveling now." His fingers squeezed. Lifting his head, Fox leaned toward her. She did not object when his lips pressed hers. He deepened the kiss, losing himself in her. When her arms wrapped about his neck, Fox moaned. It was then he heard the scratching sound. He jerked back, trying to control his breathing.

"What is that?"

Fox flattened a finger to her damp lips. "I don't know," he breathed. The noise came from the closed door bed. It was as if someone was scratching, trying to get out.

"Maude?" Grace tried to rise, but Fox kept her down.

"I'll see to her." Fox pushed to his feet, feeling his way the short distance to the bed. He found the rough knob, and gave it a pull. As the door jerked open, the noise stopped.

He almost expected something to leap out at him; a cat, or dog, or the old woman herself, fingers clawed. But there was nothing. No noise except his own ragged breathing. He couldn't tell if she slept or not, but she made no sound, and soon, Fox inched the door shut and felt his way back to the pallet.

"What was it?"

"I could see nothing. But the scratching seems to have stopped." Fox angled toward her, but this time she turned away.

"We must get some rest or we shall have hard travel tomorrow."

"We shall have hard travel regardless," Fox murmured, though he tried to follow her advice. But he couldn't. He lay awake, thinking on all that had happened to him since his awakening on the moor. As always, it was some logical explanation he sought.

As their traveling continued Fox lost count of the days. They slept, they ate, they rode. The landscape was mostly treeless and austere with the occasional rivers that needed to be forded. Bridges that had been in place since before his first trip to Scotland had disappeared. Roads were nothing as he remembered them. It was as if the military roads constructed by General Wade didn't exist. Or hadn't been built yet.

On the day he expected to enter Edinburgh, they stopped in the early afternoon at a palace on the Firth of Forth. Far grander than anyplace else they'd supped or rested, the manse was surrounded by manicured gardens and forested grounds.

Grace led them through the gate. Unlike Glenraven,

there were no crumbling towers, or weed infested court-yards. This castle had not been built to withstand siege, but to give the inhabitants comfort.

As soon as they reached the front a bevy of servants appeared, taking charge of the horses' reins and helping the ladies from their mounts. The center door opened, and Fox followed Grace and her sister-in-law into a sumptuously adorned hallway that reminded him of Ashford Hall.

Grace gave her name, and they were led across marble flooring to a pair of doors that opened into a large drawing room. When Grace glanced his way, all Fox could do was lift his brows. He continued to stand, even after port was served, despite the butler's instructions that they sit.

Perhaps it was the resemblance to his home, but Fox had a sense that he'd finally awakened from a nightmare. Things were as they should be again. And Grace was part of it.

His euphoria lasted till the double doors swung open and a short, plump man with dark ringlets brushing his shoulders appeared. If the wig wasn't proof enough that he, too, belonged to this earlier time, the coat and waistcoat of velvet and lace were. Fox felt the weight of unpleasant truth pressing all around him.

"Mistress MacCammon, Grace, how very delightful to see ye again." The man rushed forward on high-heeled slippers, capturing Grace's hands in his own and showering them with kisses. "I feared a trip to the netherlands of Scotland was needed to gaze again upon your fair face."

"How kind ye are." Before Grace dropped to a deep curtsy, Fox noted a blush that cast a pinkish glow to her face.

"Kindness has nothing to do with it, my dear. Up, up," he commanded before leading her to an elaborately carved and gilded settee. "Please rest yerself. And I see ye've brought yer delightful sister-in-law with ye." He minced toward Maude, who seemed perfectly amenable to his approach. "Dear, dear Maude."

When the man had the two ladies seated, his jovial face turned toward Fox. For an instant, their eyes met, and like a jolt of pain, recognition snapped through Fox. Anger, the urge to defend, surged through his body. Instinctively Fox's hand clasped the basket-handled sword he wore about his waist.

The sound of Grace, speaking his name, bore Fox from his deadly haze. He blinked, surprised to see Grace by his side. She touched the hand clutching the sword hilt.

Fox realized she had introduced the man, an earl, Hugh Archey, she had called him, the earl of Maymont. Fox bowed with a mumbled, "My lord."

"Ah, an Englishman." The earl's lips curved in a smile.

"Aye, Foxworth Morgan is from London, though he has been in the Highlands for some time now," Grace answered for him. Fox noted she said nothing of his title. "Mr. Morgan was kind enough to accompany my dear sister-in-marriage and myself to Edinburgh."

"Then I am most in your debt, Mr. Morgan. I could not bear the thought of something happening to my dearest friend. However, had ye but sent word of yer return to Edinburgh, I would have placed a dozen brawny escorts at yer disposal."

Grace's laughter sprinkled the room. "As ye can see, one brawny gentleman sufficed."

"Most certainly. But what of the servants I sent with ye, the lady's maids and Malcomb? Did they not return with ye?"

"How foolish of me." Grace lifted fingers to her forehead. "Of course, I should have traveled with them. There is no reason for me to keep them, none at all. Though I do appreciate yer generosity in lending them to me."

"Think nothing of it, my dear. I couldn't have ye going

into the wilds of the Highlands without a proper lady's maid, now could I?"

The earl offered refreshment and stayed by Grace's side as they drank claret. Then he sent servants to accompany each guest to a bedroom.

The rooms were large and lavishly decorated. Italian marble framed the fireplace in Fox's room. Above the mantel, in plaster relief, was the Maymont coat of arms. Draped over the walls were different tapestries. Brightening the room were tapestries of David slaying Goliath, hosts of angels, and pairs of animals entering the ark.

At the moment the amenity that appealed to Fox most was in the dressing room, where a large tub was filled with steaming water. Most mornings he'd managed to wash his face and scrape the whiskers from his cheeks with a bit of cold water and what passed for soap. But it had been days since he'd bathed, and the dirt of Scotland seemed embedded in his flesh.

With relish he doffed his clothes and sank into the hot water. A sigh escaped as the water lapped over his flesh. Knees to chin, he sat, soaking in the sensual pleasure of steaming-hot water.

He must be getting old, Fox thought, for never before, not even when he was in His Majesty's service, had a bath been so welcome. His head fell back, and Fox let his mind wander. He was tired of thinking constantly, of pondering. It was all he'd done for a sennight, and he was no closer to an explanation of what happened to him than he was at the beginning.

For now he would simply think of nothing.

Which is exactly when the answer popped into his head. Water sloshed over the side of the tub as he jerked up.

"My God."

Grabbing the soap, Fox swiped it across his chest, and under each arm. Tears blurred his stinging eyes because he wasn't careful enough to close them when he threw soapy water on his face. Cursing, Fox slid down till he could rinse the bubbles from his hair.

He left large wet footprints on the stone floor as he padded back to the bedroom, a scrap of linen tucked haphazardly about his waist. Damnation, where were his clothes? There'd been a servant in the room after he took them off.

After jerking the bell rope, Fox paced toward the windows and back. When the knock came, he growled a quick, "Enter." The expression on the young maid's face when she opened the door would normally have amused Fox. For now, though, he only wanted to talk to Grace. And damn it, he needed clothes to do it.

"I had a suit of clothing," he said, trying to soften the irritation in his voice. The poor girl seemed near swooning. Fox glanced down to make certain he'd covered the essentials. "My clothes," he repeated when she made no response. "Where are they?"

"Ummm." She swallowed, and Fox noted that her embarrassment appeared to lessen. "Freddy, musta taken 'em. He brushes 'em good, he does."

"I see. Well, could you get them back for me? Now?"

"Aye, sir." She bobbed a curtsy, then looked up at him through sparse, pale lashes. "But then, is there anything I can do for ye, sir?"

He'd heard that tone enough times from countless camp followers and whores to know what it suggested. For him it had usually meant a short-lived respite from loneliness, but he wasn't tempted now. "Just my clothes," was all he said, before turning away.

The chilled air had dried the beads of water covering his skin by the time a servant returned with the newly brushed grey jacket and breeches. Fox jerked on the fresh linen without help and rushed out of the room, pushing an arm into one sleeve of the jacket.

He had no idea what room Grace had been given. There were doorways all along the hall. As it happened, he didn't need the information. He caught a glimpse of her hair as she started down the staircase, and he hurried toward her.

She looked up with a smile, and Fox, as always, was momentarily taken aback. He knew she was no great beauty. At least his rational mind told him that. There was the hair, of course. And her eyes were a bit too widespread. Her brows too straight. Their journey, even with the limited sun they'd encountered, had multiplied the freckles once held in check across her nose. They now dusted her chin and forehead. Even her smile showed one tooth slightly overlapping another. Yet none of that seemed to matter.

Fox found her ravishing. The most devastatingly perfect woman he'd ever seen. It only took a moment of being apart from her for the truth of it to strike him afresh.

He smiled in return, lifting a finger to touch a flaming curl twisted atop her head.

"Lord Archey sent one of his daughter's maids to dress my hair."

"Lovely," he said, and was rewarded by the pinkening of her face. Fox took a breath and forced thoughts of continuing this flirtation from his mind. "I must speak with you."

"Of course. I'm on my way down to the drawing room now." She laid her mitted fingers on the wide, dark banister and took a step.

"Nay."

Startled, she looked back at him.

"I must speak with you now. And I must speak with you privately. Please," he added, when Grace still looked at him as if he'd sprouted wings.

"Of course. Come with me. There's a maze in the garden. Surely we can speak there." The hem of her emerald gown flared as she hurried down the stairs, Fox at her side.

They were almost across the hallway, when a jovial voice called out. "Ah, there ye are, Grace. And I see Master Morgan is with ye. Splendid. Come, come. Join me for a glass of claret."

There was nothing else to be done.

Fox bowed Grace forward, muttering under his breath as he bent forward, "Don't trust him."

"What?" Her eyes widened, then blinked. Turning, she faced Lord Archey, an innocuous smile brightening her countenance. "What is happening in Edinburgh? It's been so long since I've heard any gossip." With that she accepted Lord Archey's arm and moved into the drawing room.

Fox watched their chatter with an ever-darkening disposition. The awareness he'd had while bathing grew stronger every time he looked at Maymont. Their appearance was nothing alike, one sturdily short and dark, the other frail. But it was there, the sameness.

Fox shook his head, and drew Lord Archey's attention. "Dear Grace, I fear we're boring yer friend. Please, Morgan, do join us. We shall try to discuss something of common knowledge. Yer name, for instance. Last week Denbigh, yer uncle," he said with a slight tilt of his wigged head toward Grace, "entertained me at his home, and I met a man with the same surname. Lord Morgan, Earl of Clayborne. Have ye heard of him?"

Fox thought he might start laughing hysterically. With a great deal of effort, he kept his expression reserved. "I believe I have."

"A fellow countrymen of yers, of course. But very involved in Scottish affairs."

"So Lord Morgan is in Edinburgh?" Grace's eyes darted toward Fox.

"He is." Lord Archey leaned toward her conspiratorially. "Supposedly on a holiday, but I've heard differently."

"What have you heard?"

"Ah, Morgan has an interest in his kinsman."

"I doubt Master Morgan is related to Lord Morgan," Grace said.

"Nonsense. Aren't we all come from the same womb? Nay, I am simply teasing ye, Morgan. 'Tis obvious, the man is no relative of yers. For one thing, ye'd be no friend of our darling Grace, if yer leanings were that Royalist. But for Lord Morgan, 'tis said he is an envoy of the Queen herself. And loaded with Her Majesty's gold with which to buy friends."

The earl of Maymont talked more of Lord Morgan and the political clime of Edinburgh until they were joined by his daughter and Maude. If the latter had done anything to improve her appearance for the dinner, Fox could not detect it. The daughter, Margaret, was a girl of perhaps eighteen, pretty of face and form. She spoke of nothing else during supper than her impending trip to Paris.

Maude spoke of nothing, choosing to spend her time eating. Fox sat across from Grace, watching her. He wished there was some way to let her know what he knew. Some way for their minds to meld. But except for several times when their eyes met across the silver epergne, that didn't happen.

It wasn't till after they'd eaten, till Lady Margaret graciously acceded to requests that she play the harpsichord, that Fox had a chance to speak. He and Grace were seated on a settee, opposite the fire. Lord Archey stood near his daughter, seemingly hanging on every note she played.

"What is it ye wished to tell me?" Grace asked behind her fan.

Fox leaned forward, hopefully appearing lost in the music. "This man is not to be trusted."

"Lord Archey? That's ridiculous. I've known him for years. He was one of Dugald and the Darien Project's staunchest supporters. Even after the failure of the enterprise."

"Which didn't appear to leave him without a shilling."

"Not everyone lost all their money." Grace squared her shoulders. "Is that where ye find fault with him?"

Fox shook his head. "I know him."

"But how could ye? Ye said—"

"Not from this life. Not from this time. He lived when I did before . . . before the lightning struck me. In Ireland. He nearly killed me then."

Chapter Nine

She didn't believe him.

Fox sat across the polished table from Grace annoyed by the fact. She, who'd been urging him to accept the possibility that he'd traveled back to another time, was the true doubter. If she accepted that premise, and Fox still had trouble with it himself, then why couldn't she embrace the idea that Lord Archey was not who he said he was? Or perhaps he was . . . in this lifetime. But in 1747, this person wasn't Hugh Archey, Earl of Maymont. He was Sir Edwin White. A debauched killer, diseased and disgusting. A man capable of the most repugnant acts.

Unlike when he'd first awakened on the moor, Fox no longer doubted his memory. Things that happened a year ago sprang to mind as clear as the crystal adorning the earl's table. He'd been in Ireland in 1747, sent by the army to capture the elusive Rebel plaguing the English nobility there.

"A Robin Hood type," his commander said before Fox

set sail for the west coast of Ireland. "Loathed by the rich from whom he steals, but alas, loved by the Papist heathens. The damn Rebel ensures the locals' silence by scattering a few coins their way. But I've no doubt you can put an end to his reign of benevolence." General Poole had laughed then, a hearty, deep-bellied guffaw at his own wit.

Fox had accepted the challenge. What else did he have to do? Besides, it had made no difference to him that the army considered him somewhat of an expert at capturing elusive men. His reputation was not entirely won under false pretenses. He had hunted down and captured the Scottish renegade, Keegan MacLeod. Allowing him to live, to leave the country for the New World, Fox's sister in tow, did not change that. It did, however, cause Fox to question his own sanity. But then he'd helped MacLeod before, at least tried to. On the bloody, rainswept fields of Culloden. Because he'd felt a link, a bond with the man.

Discovering the Irish Rebel had been simple. Fox had known who he was as soon as he set eyes upon the foppish, dandy Lord Padraic Rafferty. Not that the disguise was not excellent. But Fox had met this man as well. Turning the Irishmen in had proved more difficult. And in the end Fox had helped save him. Helped send him off to the Carolinas. Helped keep Sir Edwin from killing him.

Fox glanced toward Lord Archey as their host leaned forward in his chair, his pudgy hands slicing the air as he spoke. He appeared ruddy and robust, and in a state of constant high spirits. Nothing at all about his appearance suggested Edwin White. But then Fox conceded the outward trappings of the man made little difference. But there was something there. Some innate core that held the essence of a person.

Organized religion meant little to Fox. Perhaps he had seen too much pain and death dealt in the name of God's word. Yet, soul was the only word that gave credence to what he saw. Lord Archey had Sir Edwin White's immortal soul. And it was black and pitted.

That soul was somehow linked with his.

Fox wondered if Lord Archey felt it, too.

Obviously Grace didn't. Her face sparkled with laughter as she listened to yet another of the earl's tales. Dressed in a gown borrowed from Lady Margaret, she shone brighter than the emeralds circling her fragile neck, the slender column of which almost took Fox's mind off the turmoil seething within. He wished he'd had more time to explain what he was feeling to her. A hasty, whispered warning hadn't been enough.

"Ah, Mr. Morgan does not appreciate the humor in my story I fear."

With a start, Fox focused on their host. He smiled, showing teeth, white and large.

"We are not being fair to my guest, dear lassies," he continued, glancing first at Grace, then his daughter, then Maude. "He has not been acquainted with us since birth as ye two have. Mr. Morgan does not know me as ye do"

Quite the contrary, Fox thought, though he decided to keep his own counsel for the moment. Lord Archey prattled away again, trying to explain to Fox who exactly his previous story was about.

"Lady Kilgore is a proud lady to be sure. All the more reason why the loss of her wig at such an inopportune time proved so embarrassing."

Laughter colored Grace's voice, but she held it in check. "I shall do my best not to give any sign I know of the episode if I should encounter Lady Kilgore in Edinburgh."

"Sweetness and light, as always, my dear Grace," Lord Archey said as he allowed a servant to pull his chair out. Coming around the table, he bowed over Grace's hand. "Let us retire to the drawing room, shall we?"

Fox was left escorting both Maymont's daughter, who

simpered and preened over his attentions, and Maude, who assuredly did not. He tried to hurry them across the drafty hall, for he could see that the earl's head leaned toward Grace in a posture of shared confidences, and he longed to hear what she said. But Lady Margaret would bear no negative response to her suggestion they view some of her ancestors in the gallery. Even Maude's reluctance to walk more than necessary simply called for a servant to escort her to the drawing room, or her bedroom, if she preferred.

As Maude muttered something under her breath, Fox took a good look at Maymont's daughter. She was tall, the top of her fontage nearly on his eye level, with an angular chin and nose. Hollows filled with rouge formed her cheeks. Despite her eyes being large, Fox could not make out their color in the light from the silver sconces lining the walls. His cataloguing of her features stopped, for he saw nothing more. No recognizable inner soul.

She must have noticed his survey, for she smiled invitingly. "I no doubt should not wander off with ye without a chaperone."

"Then perhaps we should join the others. I would not wish to compromise your honor." Which stood no chance of being compromised as far as Fox was concerned, but he tried to appear solicitous as he offered his arm.

She took it, but made no attempt to turn back toward the front of the palace. "I do feel safe with ye, Mr. Morgan. And would so like for ye to see the gallery."

The paintings filled the walls with ancestors. Fox did his best to appear interested as she prattled on about them. She did appear to have a great deal of knowledge concerning each one's place in history, which according to her was great.

When they reached a portrait of Lord Archey himself,

Fox did focus his attention. Out of curiosity he studied the painting, searching for any recognition like what he'd experienced when he met the man.

There was none.

"Interesting."

"I'm honored that ye find my father so," Lady Margaret said with a smile that showed a missing tooth.

"When was the portrait painted?" Fox asked, disappointed, but not surprised to discover the date. Sixteen ninety-two.

Despite the lady's pouting objections, Fox managed to steer them back toward the drawing room. He didn't like the idea of leaving Grace alone with Lord Archey. Even if Maude had elected to join them, he doubted the older woman would offer much protection.

Relief swept over him as he viewed Grace, obviously unharmed, sitting near the ornately carved fireplace. She glanced around when he and Lady Margaret entered, her expression contrite. Lord Archey's first words told him why.

"I understand, Mr. Morgan, that ye have grave concerns for Scotland's future if there is a union with England."

Fox's gaze flashed toward Grace. How much had she told the man? Settling into the chair across the game table from Lord Archey, Fox chose his words carefully. "I hardly think my misgivings are unique to me."

"Certainly not, sir. Do ye play?" Short fingers fanned across the chessboard."

"I have on occasion."

"Excellent. I'm always searching for a worthy opponent. Shall we?" He smoothed his thumb down the ivory queen's carved gown.

Behind him Fox heard Lady Margaret's giggle. "Ye had better be sharp, Mr. Morgan. Papa fancies himself omnipotent at the chessboard."

A fair warning Fox decided several moves later. He'd played chess frequently when in His Majesty's service. It was a pleasant enough diversion to while away endless hours of boredom. But it was obvious the earl was a far more serious student of the game. He appeared to anticipate Fox's moves, perhaps as many as three of them, in advance. The white queen was in danger before Fox could gather his defenses. Fox studied the board, hard-pressed to save her.

"Grace tells me ye think there may be resurrections among the Highland Scots if the union comes to pass."

"What?" It took Fox a moment to realize that the game was not the earl's main concern.

"She insinuated the Stuarts may try to keep Anne's legitimate successor from the throne."

Fox breathed deeply and tried to ignore the part of him that saw only Sir Edwin when he looked at Lord Archey. "I would imagine it's a possibility."

"More than a possibility, perhaps?"

Fox watched the earl of Maymont move his knight back to black territory, loosening the noose from about the white queen's throat. Had Lord Archey not seen the threat he posed? Fox lifted a straight, dark brow. "If you're implying I'm privy to some plot—"

"Goodness no." Lord Archey laughed aloud. "Grace dear, did ye hear yer friend? I was simply asking yer opinion. For an Englishman's view. I may be risking a great deal by telling ye this, but I'm very wary of a union with England."

Fox castled, a move that made the earl nod his head in approval. "And why is that?"

"I fear I'm a patriot. Grace can tell ye that, can't ye, Grace?"

Fox glanced toward Grace, where she sat by the fire, her

needlework forgotten in her lap. She met his stare and kept it while answering Lord Archey in the affirmative.

"Aye, Scotland is the land of my birth. I would do anything to protect her." He shook his head, brushing ringlets across the shoulder of his puce jacket. "The failure of the Darien Project was dreadful. Though our dear Grace's husband did all he could to stave off disaster," he added, sending her a fatherly smile.

"Did he?" Fox took the offensive, capturing a black bishop with his queen. " 'Twas my understanding there's some doubt about whether or not he stole money from the investors." Fox didn't look but assumed the gasp of surprise came from Grace.

"Sir, I find yer words repugnant, especially in light of Grace MacCammon's presence. I must ask ye to—"

"Forgive me." Fox bowed toward Grace, who didn't seem impressed by his apology, then toward Lord Archey. "It was foolish of me to repeat vicious gossip. I am deeply sorry if I offended."

The earl appeared to settle back in his chair. His expression showed acceptance. "Ye are a guest in my home, sir. Certainly we understand ye misspoke." He cocked his head. "I feel as if we've met before, Mister Morgan," he said as he moved a pawn protecting his king.

"I don't think that possible." After sliding his queen diagonally, Fox glanced up. "Checkmate."

He slept little that night, spending most of the darkened hours thinking. Thinking. It seemed all he did anymore. But at least now, he no longer tried to make sense of a senseless situation. He accepted his plight. At least recognizing Lord Archey had done that much for him.

Still, the larger question loomed.

Why.

Simple enough, but an answer refused to come.

By the time dawn pewtered the sky, Fox was out of the bed, pacing. Lifting the heavy draperies, he caught a flash of color in the garden below. Red hair. Grace.

Dressing quickly, Fox hurried out the door and down the wide staircase. The house servants were just beginning to stir as he hurried out through a side door and made his way back to the kitchen garden.

She sat on a bench, her slippered feet propped on a stone border near freshly tilled soil, staring out across the park. He didn't call her name. Nor did she glance around. Yet Fox was certain she knew he was there.

"I didn't tell him where ye came from," she said, as he slid onto the bench beside her.

"You mean when I came from, don't you?"

She turned her head, starting his day with the sunshine of her smile. "Whichever. Anyway, I did not share that with Lord Archey."

"And the Stuarts' attempt to regain the throne?"

"I did mention that, but certainly not that ye had any firsthand knowledge of it. After all, that is why I came to Edinburgh. To warn those who might be able to do something about it."

"And you feel Lord Archey is one of those people?"

Her eyes, green as a spring pasture in the early morning light, searched his. "I'm not sure what ye were trying to tell me yesterday, but I've known Lord Archey most all my life. He was my father's friend. Dugald's friend. I don't know how ye can think he'd—"

"He let me win the chess game last night."

Her smile was tentative. "Is that such a bad thing?"

Fox leaned back, stretching his legs, planting his boots in the dirt. "I had the feeling your friend the earl wasn't playing against me, so much as with me." He caught her eye. "Like a cat might play with a mouse."

"Surely ye don't see yerself as a mouse being batted about, knocked from paw to paw by a feline Lord Archey?"

The visual picture that conjured was amusing. Fox shook his head, chuckling. "He did have me beaten, and withdrew. And I've a strong feeling he knows me as I know him."

"Tell me again how ye know him."

" 'Tis not easy to explain, but I know him. From my real life. He was an evil man then, and I can see the same evil in him now."

"Yer real life."

"What?"

Grace shifted on the narrow seat till she faced him. "Ye called it yer real life. I'm wondering what ye think of this time as? Of me as?"

Fox tilted his head toward the morning sky and shut his eyes. "I don't know what to think. Sometimes this . . . now . . . you . . . seem like a magical dream. A dream from which I'll awake." His head rolled till he could see her. "Then other times I think I never want the dream to end. Not if it means never being with you again."

"I can't say I wish for the end of yer dream either."

Lifting a hand, Fox caught the tip of a red curl on his finger, then reluctantly let it go. "I don't think we should stay here any longer."

"Lord Archey sent servants yesterday to ready my house in Edinburgh. I doubt they've had a chance to air it out yet."

"Does it matter?"

"I suppose not." Grace bit her bottom lip.

"What is it?"

"Couldn't ye be wrong? About Lord Archey, I mean. I feel as if I've known ye, too, but I cannot see goodness or evil in ye."

"I'm not wrong, Grace. For your sake I wish I were."

* * *

It wasn't fashionable to build outside Edinburgh's walls, so the city expanded upward. Nearly every building was tall and narrow. However, not all the homes were as richly appointed as Grace's. Built of stone with well-sashed windows, the structure rose five stories above the stench of the streets.

Lord Archey's servants had been hard at work, for the furniture and floors smelled of wax, and the draperies and linens were as dust-free and fresh as the confined air of the city could make them. There was even a dinner waiting for Grace, Maude, and Fox when they arrived.

Potted pigeons and roasted lamb filled the serving dishes beneath the stuccoed ceiling in the dining room. Fox raised a brow as he surveyed the heavy silver and crystal adorning the table. This was not the home of someone who'd lost everything in a failed enterprise.

Grace must have noticed his appraisal, for she began chattering on about the fine wood carving throughout the house being done by some of Cromwell's soldiers. As usual, Maude said very little, but ate heartily.

When the meal was over, Maude left the room, and Grace excused herself. Fox wandered through the first-floor rooms, the drawing room, the library. The latter's walls were lined with books; however, the room was small and furnished modestly.

The desk was old, the top scarred. The candles, in plain pottery holders, were fat with dripped wax, as if they'd just been doused. The drapes were threadbare, the leather chair worn. Even the air seemed different somehow, smelling slightly stale, but not unpleasant.

Fox ran his finger along the leather book spines, reading the titles he could. Some were in Latin and French. Fox could stumble through those. The Celtic and Greek titles he didn't even try.

"These were my husband's."

Fox turned to see Grace standing in the doorway. She had changed from her borrowed gowns into one of the simple ones she had brought from Glenraven. Though Lady Margaret's gowns were lovely on her, Fox found he preferred the look of her now. Unadorned, the quiet beauty of the woman shone brighter.

She entered the room, moving toward the bookcase, and touching, as Fox had done, the worn leather spines. "Dugald loved these books. These and Scotland were his main passions."

Fox didn't point out the obvious. That he'd obviously had a passion for collecting beautiful things, expensive things as well. But, though he said nothing, Grace seemed to read his thoughts.

"We lived very quietly when we first married. Dugald was a third son of a clan chief. He became a merchant, and a very successful one, long before we wed. But he did not flaunt his wealth." Grace sighed. "I know what ye're thinking. The silver, the rugs, the expensive fabrics."

"It is quite different from Glenraven."

"Aye. When I left this house, I hoped never to return. I charged Lord Archey with selling it for me and splitting the profits among those most hurt by the failure of the Darien colony."

"He obviously didn't."

"Nay. I asked him about it yesterday. All this time I assumed it was gone, that the money was where it should be." She sighed. "He said he'd tried, but felt in his heart that someday I would return to Edinburgh."

"As you have."

"But not to live here." The sweep of her hand seemed to dismiss the house. "I want no part of this."

"Is that why you went to Glenraven when your husband died?"

Her gaze met his. "In part, aye. Here I was surrounded by reminders of what Dugald . . ." She shook her head. "Of what some said he did." She moved across the room, lifted the dusty curtain, and stared out the window. Fox knew the view was of a cramped garden, but she appeared to see beyond. "But there was something else. Something I cannot explain. Not to myself." Dust motes danced in the air as she dropped the curtain and turned back toward Fox. "I had a need, nay, a compulsion, to live at Glenraven."

Fox took a step toward her, then another. The air felt charged, as if he were on the brink of some wonderful discovery. He was close enough now to catch the subtle scent that was hers alone, to see the prisms of light in her eyes. He asked only one question. The question that haunted him always. "Why?"

She parted her lips to answer, but the commotion in the hallway seemed to break the spell between them.

Fox looked around as Lord Alexander MacDonald strode into the library. He appeared robust and annoyed. His eyes were for Grace and Grace alone, as were his words. "Grace, for God's sake, why did ye not let me know ye were coming to Edinburgh? I could have sent an escort for ye. Or come myself. Lord knows, I'm doing little or no good sitting every day in Parliament, listening to the likes of yer uncle singing the merits of a union. But no, ye don't tell me and ye come by yerself, and I have to find out ye're even here from Lord Archey."

"I was going to send ye a message, Alex. And as ye can see, I'm perfectly fine. I did not make the journey alone."

"I came with her."

For the first time Alex appeared to allow his focus to slip from Grace. When he noticed Fox, his lips tightened.

"What is he doing here? I thought him gone from our lives."

"He has a story to tell ye. One I think ye should listen to."

"I'm not interested in any stories . . . or lies . . . this one has to tell. Grace, I thought we agreed that everything he said was untrue."

"Alex, just listen."

"Nay! I won't. I will not listen to another thing he says. Nor shall ye." His right hand swept the sword from its scabbard. With a flourish he pointed the tip at Fox's chest.

"Alex, no!"

As if from a distance Fox heard Grace pleading with Alex. There should have been fear, for Fox had no weapon on him. But anger was all he knew. Anger at Alex for being so unreasonable. So impulsive. Just as he always had been. No, worse than he usually was. Much worse.

Without thinking of the consequences, Fox stepped forward. The sword tip caught on a layer of ruffles cascading from his neckpiece, but Fox didn't care. "Stop being so foolish," he said, his voice taking on the tone of one used to command. "You will listen, and you will try to understand. Impulsive behavior is something you must learn to curb, Padraic."

The sword swept downward. Grace screamed, and raced toward Fox. But there was no blood, nor even cut clothing. Alex had simply let the sword drop. He stared at Fox now, his eyes narrowed.

"What did ye call me?"

Fox blinked, then blinked again. "Padraic. Oh my God," he gasped. "It is you."

Chapter Ten

"What in the hell are ye doing?" Alex twisted his head as best he could toward Grace. "What is he doing?"

But Grace couldn't answer. Her eyes were wide as she looked on in amazement. Fox had his arms locked around Alex, imprisoning him in a giant hug that pulled his legs off the floor.

"Put me down, Englishman, or I swear I will run ye through. Englishman, do ye hear me?"

Apparently he didn't, for it took more yelling and kicking on Alex's part before anything appeared to faze Fox. Then with a mumbled, "Sorry," Fox let him down.

He felt utterly foolish now that the initial shock had worn off. Brushing at Alex's jacket earned Fox a steely-eyed look, so he simply waited for Alex to straighten his own coat and wig, and for the questions he knew would follow. He didn't have to wait long.

"Now, will ye tell me what the devil is going on here? And who in the hell is this Padraic?"

"Perhaps ye should sit down, Alex." Grace motioned toward the leather chair behind the desk. She wasn't sure herself what had happened, but by the expression on Fox's face she imagined Alex was going to have some problems with it. "Would ye like some claret?" she asked, not waiting for an answer before splashing liquid into three glasses. Then she settled into a chair by the hearth.

When they were both seated, and staring at him, Fox found himself baffled as to where to begin. He glanced toward Grace, lifted the tumbler to his lips, and took a gulp. Then another.

"Is this what I think it is?" Grace asked. When Fox emptied his glass and nodded, she continued, addressing this question to Alex. "Ye remember how we found Lord Morgan?"

"I recall finding the man who claims to be Lord Morgan, aye."

"It was like he'd come from nowhere."

Alex crossed his arms, and Grace hurried on. "Well, 'tis very possible that he came to us from another time."

"Another time?"

"I know it sounds ridiculous," Fox interjected. "Believe me, I've had trouble enough with this in my own mind."

"With what?" Alex pushed to his feet. "Neither of ye are making any sense at all."

"I traveled through time. From my time to yours," Fox stated, his tone firm.

When Alex just stared, Grace nodded toward his glass. "Drink yer wine."

"What ye're claiming is impossible," Alex declared, yet he'd settled back into his seat. "No one can do such a thing."

"I didn't plan to do it, I assure you. I still have a hard time accepting it. But there seems no other explanation."

"Explanation for what? Are ye both mad?"

"Tell him of the battle, Fox."

Fox began describing Culloden. The slaughter and its aftermath. He could tell Alex wasn't believing a word he said. "It was there, near the dry stone fence beside the road where I first met you."

"I never—" Alex shot a look at Grace.

"You were wounded, in a great deal of pain." Fox watched as Alex's hand instinctively reached for a spot near his knee. "I didn't know it at the time, but you were not really a British soldier."

"God, I should hope not."

"You were actually Irish, a privateer, or smuggler of sorts. I believe you were at Culloden to rescue Prince Charles. But, of course, you didn't."

"This is a fine tale, Englishman, but I don't believe a word of it. And ye, Grace. Can't ye see he's nothing but a fabricator of the worst sort?"

"There was another man. Two actually. A laird and his son. You saved the son's life by shooting an English soldier."

"There, finally ye've said something that makes sense."

Fox chuckled. "Of course I didn't know that then, or I would have had to kill you myself, despite the feeling I had of knowing you. I felt the same connection with the Scot, Keegan MacLeod was his name. I tried to save his father, but ended up being responsible for the laird's death, at least the Scot felt as much. He was sentenced to hang, for his deeds, but escaped."

"And tried to kill ye, I'll warrant."

"He did. But ended up kidnapping my sister, Zoe, instead. But that's another story." Fox clasped his hands behind his back and continued. "I had contact with you once. I arranged for you to take my sister and some Scots to the New World."

"After ye'd killed the MacLeod, I assume."

Fox shrugged. " 'Twas the way history recorded it."

"Aye, well I doubt a word of this is true."

"I came across you next when I was sent to Ireland to capture the Rebel. You tried to fool me with a disguise—you make a very convincing fop, by the way. But unfortunately for you, we had this bond of sorts, and knew each other immediately."

"So, did ye turn me in?"

"What do you think?"

"I think this is so much foolishness. Perhaps I resemble this Irish fellow in some way, but—"

"You don't. Not at all. Except perhaps for your impulsiveness."

Alex's eyes narrowed at that. "Well if ye plan to think ye know every man who dares to be a bit rash—"

"I don't."

"Then how in the hell can ye say I'm this Padraic if we share but one character trait?"

Shaking his head, Fox lifted his hands palm up. "If I could explain all that has happened to me, all that I know, I would. Suffice it to say, I know. It is as if I recognize a part of you, your soul, from my other life."

"I know 'tis difficult to accept," Grace said.

"Impossible, ye mean." Alex stepped toward Grace. "Don't tell me he has ye believing this."

"Legends speak of visitors from other times."

"Legends, Grace."

"Can you honestly say you don't feel it?" Fox asked.

Alexander twisted about. "Feel what, Englishman?"

"A bond. A feeling that you've known me before?" Fox lifted a brow in inquiry.

Alex stared . . . and stared. "Hell, what if I do? It means nothing. Ye just remind me of someone, 'tis all."

"Who?"

Focusing his attention back on Grace, Alex shrugged. "I don't know who. What does it matter?"

"Because you may be remembering me from before."

"Before what?"

"Before this lifetime."

"There was nothing before this lifetime, Englishman."

"I would have thought the same of my life . . . before this happened," Fox said quietly.

For a long while Alex said nothing. He glanced at Fox now and then, shaking his head one time, as he moved back to the leather chair. When he'd seated himself, and leaned back, arms folded, he sighed deeply. "I'm not saying I believe any of this foolishness."

"Alex, please—"

Fox held up his hand, quieting Grace. "What are you saying?"

"I'm saying, I'll listen to what else ye have to say, Englishman."

Which Fox supposed was as good as he could expect given the circumstances.

They sat in the library long after a servant came in to light the candles and add peat to the fire. Grace tried to convince her friend that Fox had come to them for a reason. To her way of thinking, that reason was to change history. To do what they could to keep the bloody rebellions from polluting Scotland's shores.

Fox wasn't as certain as Grace about why he was here. Or even if there was a reason beyond some horrible cosmic blunder. Finding Alex, or rather discovering who Alex became, gave some credence to Grace's theory. And then there was Lord Archey. Even if he were evil, which Fox didn't doubt, the earl didn't seem to be doing anything wrong. According to Grace and Alex, Lord Archey had always been kind and helpful, even publicly denouncing those who would blacken Grace's husband's name.

"Ye have a powerful poor memory for history," Alex complained, and not for the first time.

"I never claimed to be a scholar."

"Then why in the hell did the Powers Above send ye, I'd like to know? Where there no historians available for the journey?"

Fox drained the French claret from his glass, then chuckled. "I doubt too many people remember how every member of the Scottish Parliament votes on the union issue. Besides, can't you pretty well tell where the members stand?"

"If they were honest perhaps." Alex sliced a piece of cheese from the hunk on the silver platter a servant brought. "But so many say one thing, then do another." He chewed thoughtfully. "Of course there be no question where members of the New Party stand. Andrew Fletcher sees to that."

"How is Andrew? I have missed seeing him."

Alex's expression fell. "He is well."

"He still blames Dugald." Grace didn't bother to phrase it as a question.

"Ye understand how committed he was to the Darien Project."

"As was Dugald," Grace said defensively.

"Aye, and I know that." Alex expelled air forcefully. I will send a note round to Andrew mentioning yer presence in Edinburgh."

"We shall need him." To Fox she added, "The original idea for Darien was Andrew Fletcher's, or rather the notion came from a man he met at The Hague, William Paterson. They both came to Dugald, asking his help to raise money."

"Andrew invested much of his personal fortune."

"As did Dugald," Grace insisted, though she couldn't meet either man's eyes.

"Is Andrew blamed for what happened?" Fox wanted to know.

"He's considered a traitor by those who want the union, and a national hero by some."

"A rallying point?"

"Aye, but one with powerful enemies."

"And very few strong allies?" Fox asked.

"I suppose ye could say that. 'Tis hard to unite such a diverse people, even though they may agree on certain fundamentals."

"Isn't there something we can do, Alex?"

"I don't know, Grace." Alex refilled his glass. "Even if I believe this craziness the Englishman is saying, which I don't," he added quickly, "there just doesn't seem to be anything that can be done to stop passage of an act of union. England has us backed into a corner with the Alien Bill," he said, tossing a hard look at Fox. "If Dugald were alive, and if . . ."

"If he weren't suspected of stealing," Grace finished for her friend.

"Hell, Grace, ye know I don't believe a word of that."

"It doesn't matter," she said.

Despite Grace's words, Fox could tell it did matter.

Later, after a still-skeptical Alex left, Fox broached the subject again. The hour was late, Maude had retired hours earlier, not long after Alex took his leave. Fox and Grace had settled into the drawing room: Grace, her head bent over her stitching, Fox, looking through a pile of personal papers he'd taken from the library.

"Admittedly, I'm not well versed in reading financial papers," he began, waiting to gain Grace's attention. She glanced up and smiled, and Fox could not help doing the same. Sitting with her like this, it almost seemed as if they'd been together for years. Despite their solitary endeavors, he'd enjoyed knowing she was near.

"I never really took charge of Ashford Hall," Fox continued. "I was on my way there when I decided a detour was in order."

"To the moor?"

"Yes." Fox took a moment to absorb the domestic appeal of her. "As I was saying, I haven't had much experience with this sort of thing." He gestured toward the papers piled on the table beside his chair. "But I can find no evidence of wrongdoing by your husband."

Grace retrieved her needle and took her time weaving the point through a single thread. "Do ye suppose Dugald would leave such evidence around for someone to find?"

"I don't know. Would he?" Fox slouched down farther in the chair, then pinched the bridge of his nose between thumb and forefinger. When she didn't answer, Fox glanced back toward her. "Grace?"

"I don't know. He may have. He certainly made no pretense of hiding anything else."

Fox straightened. "Like what?"

"The furnishings." Grace lifted her hands. "The silver. The expensive clothes."

"I don't understand."

"Do ye think we always had such things about?" Grace shook her head. "We didn't. It was as if the worse the outlook for New Caledonia, the more elaborately we lived." Gathering her skirts, Grace rose. "There were times Dugald even accused me of spending money we didn't have."

"Why would he do that, when he himself was doing the same?"

Grace stretched her shoulders. "I don't know. Things would simply appear. A silver vase. Crystal glasses. Velvet gowns. He bought what he wished. Apparently he even forgot what he purchased. Once he noticed a silver tray on the table and accused me of purchasing it."

"And you didn't."

"Nay. This was after we'd learned of the colony's failure. Besides, Dugald was a merchant. He always ordered what we needed from France or England. I rarely did more than approve fabrics."

"But he said he hadn't bought the tray?"

"He denied buying most of the silver and furnishings in the house. Denied decking the servants out in new livery as well. Oh, and the coach. He insisted he hadn't ordered the new conveyance. But it was one of the most extravagant coaches in Edinburgh, and it was ours."

"Yet he said he didn't buy it. And you didn't either."

"I didn't. But obviously someone did. So it had to be Dugald." Grace leaned against the mantel. "I refused to ride in it. We had an argument." Flame-colored curls spilled forward as she shook her head. "He assured me he felt the same. Yet, I saw him in the coach. Riding from Holyrood. How he would think that no one noticed all these new riches is beyond my comprehension."

"It almost sounds as if he were flaunting his newfound wealth."

"Aye, as if he wanted people to think the worst of him."

"Is that why you left Edinburgh?" Fox stood, and moved toward her as he spoke. "Because people thought the worst of him . . . and you."

"I left Edinburgh for many reasons." Grace held her ground as he approached. "That was one of them."

When his hand cupped her cheek, Grace turned her face toward his palm.

"It must have been hard for you."

"Please. Must we speak of such things now?"

The heat from her breath dampened his flesh. "Nay." Fox let his lids drift down when her tongue touched him. His fingers curled into her hair, and his free arm pulled her near. "I've tried, Grace," he whispered. "But I can fight this no longer. If you would have me stop—"

"That is not my desire." Before Grace had finished the words, his lips pressed hers.

The kiss was long and sweet, a coming home.

Until the moment her arms lifted around his neck, Fox still thought he could control his actions. He was no longer a starry-eyed lad. He'd had command of himself for years. Making love was something he did lightly or not, depending upon the circumstances. But obsession was not in his vocabulary.

Until now.

Fox pulled away long enough to drink in the dewy-eyed splendor of her face, before his open mouth devoured hers. The sweetness now grew hot and bubbly, like sugar left to boil in a copper kettle.

It was as if he'd had her before, known her intimately, every tender bit of flesh, every misty fold, and he could not wait to have her again. Her throat, the pale skin dusted with faint freckles, teased his tongue with tantalizing tastes.

Remember, his mind seemed to say as his senses filled with her.

"Grace." His voice, husky, intense, shocked him. Dragging air into his starved lungs seemed more than he could handle as he grabbed her shoulders, forcing space between them.

It took her a moment to focus through the gossamer folds of desire. But when she could see him, really see him, a splash of cold dread swept over her. "What is it?" Her voice was near as breathless as his. "What has ye looking as if ye've seen a spirit?"

For a long moment he could say nothing. Fox just continued to stare, searching. His fingers dug troughs into the silky fabric of her bodice. When he finally spoke, his voice seemed to come from far away. "You too."

"What are ye talking about?" Grace twisted her shoulders. "Ye're scaring me. And hurting me, too."

"God, I'm sorry." His hands sprang away from her as if she were on fire. "I didn't mean to—"

"It's fine, really." Grace touched tentative fingers to her left shoulder. "Ye were scaring me more than anything." Her gaze met his. "What is it? I thought we . . ."

The groan seemed to start low in Fox's belly. He grabbed his head, flattening both palms over his temples, and turned away. When he gained control of himself, Fox looked back to see Grace looking as bewildered as before. And why shouldn't she be?

Even he wasn't sure exactly why he'd done what he did.

"You know that I knew your friend Alexander? And Lord Archey?" Fox asked as he made his way across the room to the serving table. His hands shook as he splashed port into a goblet. His silent offer was met with a curl-loosening shake of her head.

Shrugging, Fox upended the glass. "When we were kissing," he began, only to stop. "Perhaps I should say, that almost from the time I first saw you there has been something . . . something pulling me toward you. An attraction that transcends any I've known before."

"I've felt the same," Grace said, deciding there was no place here for coyness.

"Yes, well, not that I wish to outdo you, Grace, my dear, but I'd be willing to bet mine was stronger."

"Do ye mean . . ." Grace took a step toward him, a smile deepening the dimple beside her mouth. "Do ye recognize me from someone in yer other life? I've been wondering if 'tis true. Och." She stopped in her tracks. "I'm not some evil person, am I?" " Her hands flattened over her ears, and she turned away. "Nay, don't tell me if I am. I couldn't bear it."

"Grace." Fox's hands covered hers, then gently pried them loose. "You couldn't possibly be anything but good."

"Yet, I'd swear the same true of Lord Archey."

Fox kissed the knuckles of each hand before letting them go. He shook his head. "I only know what I feel, and I feel you are all goodness. However, I have no memory of you in my life."

"But ye said . . ."

"I know. You are known to me. But not from the time before the lightning."

"If not then, when?"

Fox shrugged. "I don't know. But you are not someone I knew before." He grinned. "I would have remembered."

Her skirts billowed as Grace settled into a chair. "I really don't understand."

"Nor do I. But you are not someone I recognize from London, or Ireland, or even Scotland. Nay, there is no one."

"Yet ye say that—"

"That I know you," Fox finished for her as he dropped to his knees in front of her. "And I do." His eyes searched hers. "I just don't know from where."

When his lids lowered, Grace laid her hand on the rough silk of his hair. Dark and glossy smooth, it waved about her fingers, bringing a smile to her face. It only took a little pressure for him to lay his head in her lap. His arms bracketed her legs. The heat of his body surrounded her and Grace allowed her fingertips free play in his hair.

Her body tingled with awareness—some remembered from their earlier kisses, others garnered from his vulnerability.

The hour was late, long past time for him to seek his bed. Yet Fox slumped in a chair, his back aching, his mind reeling. With his right hand he grasped a tumbler. Occasionally he'd lift the glass to his lips, but the French brandy did nothing to clear his head.

He'd been sitting thus since Grace retired. Fox squinted toward the clock on the mantel, trying to decipher the time in the feeble light radiating from the near-gutted candle.

Half past four. Even at his most debauched, he'd managed to find a place to lay his head by this time of night. Setting the glass atop the elaborately carved table at his side, Fox scrubbed both hands down his face. His eyes felt gritty, his cheeks rough with whiskers. From outside the closed window came the screech of cats.

Which was probably why he didn't hear the click of the door opening, or notice that someone had entered the drawing room until Maude spoke.

Fox barely kept himself from calling out in fright when he looked up to see her looming over him. "God, woman," Fox said, doing his best to calm his voice, "you should wear a bell about your neck."

" 'Tis late, Traveler."

Fox straightened, stretching his back. "Why do you insist upon calling me that?"

"We both know why."

"Yes, well, I don't like it."

"That I call ye that, or that ye've traveled so far?"

Fox snorted, then lifted the glass and downed the brandy in one swift, burning gulp. He doubted she referred to distance traveled. His eyes watered when he glanced back toward her. "What are you doing haunting the rooms at this time of night?"

Her expression, or what Fox could see of it within the folds of her plaid, didn't change. "One could ask ye the same."

"I have reason enough not to sleep."

"Ah, of course, self-pity."

Fox's lips thinned, but he said nothing to deny her assessment. She backed toward the door, and Fox congratulated himself for not responding. At least he was getting rid of her quickly enough.

But from the shadows, her voice took on an eerie quality as she spoke. "Ye think too much, Traveler. 'Tis yer feelings ye should follow."

Chapter Eleven

Mist floated, swirling, sending tiny tendrils to lap about her gown. Imprisoning her. Nay, 'twas not the mist that held her hostage. 'Twas her heart. Her heart that brought her out this day before the sun. To the moor. To her love.

Pulling the folds of her cloak more tightly about her, she hugged herself, trying to keep warm. Trying to forget how long she'd stood surrounded by the surreal, waiting.

He would come.

She knew he would. Yesterday he'd managed to get a message to her. Three words. Only three words, but she'd known what it meant. She would see him again. Touch him. Soon. The very thought made her heart sing. It had been a chore not to smile at everyone she saw.

And that would never do. Rodrick suspected her as it was. Closing her eyes, she thought again about what she was doing. Her behavior was irresponsible. And more. Much more. Yet there was no thought of turning back. Not even when the sun inched its way over the moor.

"He will come," she whispered to herself over and over, a litany.

She only paused when the muffled clomp of hoofbeats echoed through the drippy air. "He will come," she said again, and again, not turning toward the sound.

Behind her a horse skidded to a stop. A rattle of metal, and her shoulders were seized. Then with one violent jerk she was in his arms, and his open mouth swallowed the last of her chant.

Heat as she'd never known it engulfed, consumed. His tongue plunged, conquering any defense she had.

When he pulled her down, down into the swirling mist, she went readily, eagerly. His hands tore away the woolen cloak, then her gown, exposing her flesh to the damp chill. But she felt nothing but warmth as his battle-roughened palms rubbed over her body.

His weight pressed her into the spongy ground. The earthy smells of peat and her own desire intoxicated. When his fingers found her core, she cried out, consumed by quivery waves she could not control.

"Grace."

"Oh." Grace blinked, then shook her head. Her hands gripped the wooden sill of her window so hard they ached. Slowly she loosened her hold, and turned away from the darkened view outside her window. Nothing but a minute garden and the silhouette of houses beyond. But from the corner of her eye she thought she caught a glimpse of the moor.

"Grace, are you all right?" Fox moved toward the puddle of candlelight bathing her in an otherworldly glow.

"I'm . . ." Grace tried to shake the remnants of those other people from her mind. The lovers. But when her gaze met Fox's she knew it was impossible.

"What is it? Tell me." His arms wrapped about her, and she fell into him with such force he took a backward step before lifting her up. As gently as he could Fox laid her on the bed, then brushed loose strands of red hair off her face. "Grace?"

"I can see us so clearly." When his eyes narrowed, Grace licked her lips and started again. "I was dreaming, though not. Oh, 'tis so confusing."

"Perhaps you should rest. I came to speak with you, however—"

"Nay, I don't wish rest. 'Tis not what I need." As she spoke Grace lifted Fox's large hand in both of hers. His hand grew pliant and she spread the fingers, then pressed them to her breast. She'd prepared for bed, removing her outer bodice and stays. Naught but soft linen separated his flesh from hers.

For a moment, a brief breath of time, he did not move. Their eyes locked. Then with a growl that seemed to begin deep within him, Fox squeezed his fingers. Then his open mouth was on hers.

The kiss seemed to suck all from her. Grace clutched at his broad shoulders, trying her best to hold on to reality. But it was so hard. Her body seemed not her own. Every touch, every breath she took was his.

The sound of tearing fabric rent the air. She cared not. Anything, anything, to feel his touch. His hands were rough and aggressive, stealing all from her.

His hair draped over them, torn loose from its binding by her eager fingers, cocooning them. It would have been so easy to close her eyes and let the power of their passion overwhelm. But Grace could not. She continued to stare wide-eyed as he rolled to the side, stripping his own clothing as quickly and uncontrollably as he had hers.

When he was atop her again, Grace grabbed his head, bracketing his face as he entered her. The first thrust was deep, forcing her eyes closed. But she opened them quickly, needing to see him as they both raced toward completion.

Hers came first, wild and consuming, splintering her senses, yet strangely grounding her in reality. When he reared up, neck taut, broad chest straining, Grace dug her fingers into his hair, and called out his name.

"Fox."

But the word seemed to echo back through the centuries.

"Did I hurt you?"

Grace sighed, then let her lips turn up at the corners before lifting heavy lids. She could barely focus as she looked up at him. "Nay."

"Are you certain?" Fox rested his weight on one bent arm and used the other hand to brush the web of fiery curls from her face. "I can't imagine what came over me, to act like that."

Giggling, Grace let her hands run down the side of his cheek. "Can't ye?"

"Well, I can, but I usually try to keep a modicum of control. Which . . ." Fox let his gaze drift across the garment littered bed. "I didn't seem to do. Wait. What is it? I did hurt you. Grace, look at me."

Resisting the pull of his hand, Grace gave her head a quick shake, but kept herself facing the wall. " 'Tis nothing, really."

"Nothing hell. You're crying." He shifted, using more force, turning her cheek till her tear-sparkling eyes again stared up at him. "What is it?"

"I was remembering the others."

"What others?"

"My dream." Grace blinked as a tear rolled into her hair. "I was dreaming when ye came to my room."

"You were awake."

Grace shook her head. "No, I couldn't have been. I was—"

"You were standing by the window, staring into the night. I called your name."

"But I must have been dreaming." Grace licked her lips. "But it was so real." She swallowed, her eyes opening wide. "It was us, ye and me, only not us. Nay, say nothing. Just listen. Let me remember. We were on the moor. No, first I was on the moor waiting for you. When you came we . . ." Despite that she still lay beneath him, their bodies joined, Grace felt a surge of embarrassment. "We made love."

Fox couldn't help smiling. "I'm not certain I understand, however—"

"Ye and I, only it wasn't us, not exactly. We were different. There was a war, a feud . . ." Her brow wrinkled in thought. "I don't really know what it was, but there was more keeping us apart than simply my husband." Grace sucked in her breath before clamping her hand over her mouth.

"Husband?"

"My God, Fox. I was married, and I performed an adulterous act."

"Grace. Grace!" Fox rolled off her, pulling her to her side to face him as he did. "Stop it. It wasn't you that did this."

"Ye're wrong. It was me." Her stare pierced his. "It was me. And it was ye. And we were killed. Slaughtered by my husband's men."

Fox shook off the tingle that ran down his spine. It was harder to ignore the burning sensation in his entrails. But he still tried to make light of her talk. "Don't be silly, Grace."

"Silly, am I? 'Tis not me who comes from another time. We both know 'tis true. Just as I know what I know."

Fox let his head flop back against a pillow. For a moment all he did was lie there, his breathing shallow. When he began to speak, it was as if the words came from someone else. "You wore a saffron gown when I first saw you. It nearly matched the gold in your hair. You sat at the head table beside your husband. I couldn't take my eyes off you.

"I'd been sent to work out a truce between our two clans. It was what I did best, I'd been told. Talk. But you stole the breath from me. My tongue would not move. I bumbled my greeting to your husband, the laird, and you smiled at me. I smiled back, and I knew then, there would be trouble."

Grace pushed away from Fox. Turning, she sat on the edge of the bed, her legs, one still covered by a clocked stocking, hung over the side of the bed. "How can this be?" she asked, not looking back at him. "How can we both have the same dream?"

"I've had it for years. It simply comes to me as I sleep. It's been part of me for so long, I can't recall when it began."

"I used to fear that Dugald would know my thoughts. Or that I might call out in my sleep. It was always so real to me."

Fox lifted his hand, then let it fall back over his eyes. "What is happening to us?"

"I don't know." When Grace looked around at him there were tears in her eyes.

Fox reached for her shoulder, ignoring the slight shake she gave. "Come here," he crooned, as his hand moved up to caress her neck. When she lay back down, he cradled her body, pulling her close. She shivered and he managed to situate them under the woolen plaid covering the bed. And there they slept, bound by they knew not what.

* * *

Fox strode down narrow, dust-clogged High Street toward Edinburgh Castle. He'd awakened this morn, having dreamed of the saffron-clad woman again, having tasted the fear of his own death. For some reason he'd never allowed his dream to run that far before, always settling in and lingering on the sexual, always waking, hard and frustrated. But last night, cuddled against Grace's soft flesh, replete from their lovemaking, he'd moved on.

He'd heard the pounding of horses' hooves, felt the vibrations through the soft earth. He'd tried to fight them, pushing her behind, trying all he could to keep her safe. But they'd been alone on the windswept moor, hopelessly outnumbered, with no place to hide.

The trial, if it could be called that, was swift, the punishment final. He'd been an envoy of his clan, offered hospitality that he'd abused. Abused with the laird's wife, no less. The days between his sentencing and the day of his death passed in a blur of pain and self-recrimination.

How could he have done such a thing? He was a rogue, true. A man who took what he wanted and dared not look back. Surely when his clansmen learned of his death, few would be surprised, except by his stupidity. His ways with women were known. But this had been different. So different. And no one would ever know.

He'd learned of her fate the day his life was forfeit. She stood beside her husband, her beautiful face expressionless, her hands bound by a leather thong, as he was brought forward. She was to watch as the sword sliced through her lover's entrails. Then she was to receive the same fate.

The jarring of his body jolted Fox's attention to the present. He focused, finding himself knocked against a man, near as tall as himself.

"Idiot! Scoundrel!" the man yelled, shoving Fox, becoming even redder-faced when Fox didn't budge. "How dare you wander into my path, you knave."

Straightening himself, Fox considered answering in kind, but the man was obviously drunk, smelling sweetly disgusting, a mixture of whiskey and sweat. Deciding, too, that he very well could have walked into the man's path, Fox bowed and stepped to the side.

However the other's drink-soaked mind refused to think straight. He reached out, grabbing hold of Fox, twisting the fabric of his jacket. "Did you not hear what I called you, you Scottish pig?"

As he'd spent most of his time in Scotland feeling uneasy because of his obvious Englishness, Fox found this slightly amusing. But the man's actions lost their ability to entertain when he refused to let go his hold.

Still hoping to avoid a fight, Fox shoved just enough to loosen the grip. "I've no fight with you."

"Aw, do you hear that, lads," he called to the assemblage who'd gathered about them. "The Scot has no fight with me. 'Tis what they all say, I'm thinking. A more miserable lot of cowardly savages I can't imagine." He turned away, only to twist back around as he whipped a sword from its scabbard. "Now you shall pay for your lack of respect toward your betters."

The flash of steel sent Fox, unarmed as he was, leaping to the side. The crowd gathered about them seemed to meld into a circle that kept the two surrounded.

Fox was sidestepping another swish of the sword when something cold and hard was slapped into his open palm. He glanced over to see a burly Scot, face and head nearly covered by curling red hair, grinning at him. "Few would miss that one if he were to depart this world," the Scot yelled as Fox's hand clutched the sword's basket hilt.

It was no contest. Fox knew it the moment he forced the drunkard, stepping lively, back through the crowd. A cheer rose, and Fox turned to acknowledge his swordsmanship. A salute sent the crowd into another round of huzzah.

"Damn you, Scot," the man yelled as he stumbled forward. "I'll have your gizzard ripped from your body for that."

"Ah, but you must catch me first," Fox said, warming to the idea of playing with the fool. He needed something such as this to relieve his mind of all its worries. As the Englishman dived forward, Fox gave his rear a swat with the broad of the sword. The drunk man's cry proved the sting found its mark.

Fox had never been known for his swordsmanship, but compared to the drunken dandy, he appeared a master. Yet Fox soon tired of the game. With one flick of his wrist, he sent the dandy's sword clattering to the stones. Fox kicked the sword aside when the dandy stumbled to his knees.

"That's enough," Fox said as he turned to hand the borrowed sword back. The Scot stood back a bit from the rest of the crowd, his powerful arms folded across an equally powerful chest. Fox guessed his age to be well past what most considered prime, but there was none of the softening about him that often comes with age. He reached for the sword, and in that instant Fox felt a surge of recognition that left him speechless.

It also left him still grasping the basket-handled sword, which as it happened was a good thing. He didn't know who called out the warning, but Fox whirled about in time to see the drunken dandy lunge toward him, dirk in hand.

Lifting the sword was instinct.

What happened next took only seconds, but for Fox it seemed as if each subtle movement froze, as if an artist captured each nuance of motion on a canvas and lined them up for Fox to peruse at his leisure. Not only could he see the paintings, but he could smell the stifling scents of rotted fruit and chamber pots captured in the close-quartered streets. He could hear the crowd, the bloodlust in their collective voices, as they screamed for him to kill the English bastard.

Which was exactly what he intended to do. The dandy's bloodshot eyes bulged with terror as even his rum-soaked brain comprehended the course his cowardice had put in motion.

"Kill him! Kill him! Kill him!"

The drunken dandy was a breath away from the sword tip when a name yelled by someone in the crowd pierced Fox's consciousness. Frantically he tried to twist the sword away, but it was too late. The sickening feeling of ripped flesh and sinew vibrated up Fox's arm. Blood spurted. The crowd cheered. Fox tossed the sword to the stones, hearing it clatter as he lunged to catch his victim.

As if all his bones had turned to porridge, the dandy slumped against Fox. His eyes seemed to roll back in his head, and the long curled wig, which was cockeyed from the start, slipped off the smoothly shaved skull.

"Help me. For God's sake help me," Fox yelled as he heaved the man over his shoulder. The crowd, anxious to witness the English dandy's last breath surged forward, blocking Fox's path. He turned about, trying to get his bearings, wondering how in the hell he was going to disentangle himself from the masses, when the burly Scot stepped forward.

Lifting his arms, he uttered something in a language Fox didn't understand. His next words were in English, and they ordered the crowd to go about their business. Then he nodded toward Fox, who rebalanced his load, and they both started off up the street toward Holyrood.

Fox wasn't sure when the Scot veered off. He was too busy trudging as quickly as he could toward Grace's house, wondering if the man dripping warm, sweet-smelling blood down his back was dead or alive. He stumbled over an uneven stone in the roadway, nearly falling to his knees before regaining his balance.

All around him people went about their business, jostling through the narrow street clogged with carts, sedan chairs, and coaches. But no one seemed to notice him. Not till he climbed the stone steps and pounded on the front door.

The butler sent by Lord Archey opened the door, then nearly slammed it in Fox's face. If not for the boot Fox insinuated inside, he would have. As it was, the man demanded to know what was going on as Fox shouldered through into the hallway.

"Where can I put him?"

"Sir, I hardly think—"

"Find me a place, damn you."

"Fox!"

Glancing toward the sound of her voice, Fox saw Grace hurry down the stairs. "I need—" Fox began, only to have Grace turn toward the back of the house, with a cryptic, "Follow me."

Only one cook was in the kitchen at this time of day. She looked up, eyes big as the onions she peeled, when Grace and Fox burst into the room.

"Get Maude," Grace ordered the hapless girl as she used her arm to swipe the thick-boarded table clear. "Here. Put him here."

With a grunt Fox complied, hefting the weight off his shoulder, thankful that Grace took the wounded man's head, cradling it so it didn't bang onto the table. His burden gone, Fox leaned over a chair back.

"Oh, my God, Fox." Grace's hands were on him, his face, his shoulders. "Ye're bleeding. Where are ye hurt?"

"No, 'tis not my blood. Really." He straightened, realiz-

ing how he must look to her. "Really," he repeated when
she seemed skeptical. "His blood."

"Of course, 'tis his blood, Grace. Look at the man."
With those words Maude pushed into the room and toward
the table. Behind her the cook's helper, whose face was
so pale her freckles seemed to stand out in bold relief,
carried a large basket of woven grass.

After a cursory look, which included a bit of sniffing,
Made straightened. "What happened to him?"

"Stabbed by a sword," Fox said.

"Whose sword?"

"Not mine. But 'twas my hand that wielded it." Fox felt
Grace's gaze on him. "Will he be all right?"

"If ye're asking if he's dead, the answer's nay. There's
still a bit of blood in him."

That information made Fox's knees weak. "But will he
live?"

"I'm not a seer, Traveler, just a healer. Come, girl, bring
me my herbs. And I've no time to pick ye up from the
floor, so don't think of fainting away on me."

He obviously wasn't going to get any more information
from the old witch, so Fox backed out of the way, till he
leaned against the stone wall near the bake ovens. Occasionally he was called upon to do something, like scoop
boiling water from the iron kettle hanging over the flames
in the hearth. But for the most part he watched while
Maude and Grace, with reluctant help from the cook's
helper, toiled over their patient.

His clothes, smelling of whiskey and fear, and drenched
with blood, were stripped away. Fox tried to ignore the
blackish wound while he noted the similarities. Long torso,
broad shoulders, trim waist. Even the arms and hands
looked familiar. Long, thick-wristed, with flat palms, and
narrow fingers.

"Traveler! Did ye not hear me? Grind these seeds."

Fox took the hollowed-out stone bowl and began doing as he was told. But his eyes never left the wounded man's chest. He could see signs that he breathed, however shallowly. When Fox handed back the ground seeds he caught Maude looking at him. At least he thought she was by the glitter of her dark eyes in the shadow of her plaid. "He has to live."

"Seems ye should have thought of that before ye skewered him on yer sword."

"It was an accident." The words sounded ridiculous, even to Fox's ears. Turning away, he added, his voice gruff. "Just see that he doesn't die."

The blood on his jacket had dried and hardened, when Maude finished her ministrations and pulled a fine linen sheet to her patient's chin. "Well, Traveler, he isn't dead yet."

When she started from the overhot kitchen, Fox gave up his seat among the copper pans. "You aren't leaving him, are you? What if he wakes up?" *Or dies,* Fox finished to himself.

"Ye'll be there to watch, now won't ye, Traveler. This one's important to ye." Then, with a cackling laugh, she disappeared out the door.

"What does she mean?" Grace tossed the bloody contents of a bowl of water into the alleyway, then dried her hands down the front of a towel she'd used to cover her gown.

"I know this man," Fox said, as he walked slowly toward the table.

"What happened? Why did you fight him? I awake, thinking to find ye in my ... to find ye beside me, and then the next thing I know ye're bursting into my house, scarlet with blood."

When her lip quivered, Fox abandoned his place beside the table and went to her. He gently pried the earthen bowl from her hands, motioning for the cook's helper to take it and leave the room, which she was only too glad to do. "I'm sorry," Fox began. "It was thoughtless of me to leave this morn, and this . . ." With the arm not circling Grace's narrow shoulders, he gestured toward the man lying unconscious on the table.

"I have no excuse, except confusion. Which is what happened with him. I wasn't watching where I was. We collided, and he would not accept my apology. Before I knew it, swords were whipping through the air. Then he pulled a dirk." Fox paused to take a deep breath.

"But who is he, and why is it so important to ye that he live?"

Fox's gaze met hers. "Without him, I'd be dead. Or perhaps never born." When her head cocked to one side in confusion, Fox continued. "That man lying there, the man I nearly killed, is Lord James Morgan. My father."

Chapter Twelve

"The worst possible thing has happened," Alex announced as he threw himself into a chair near the hearth.

Grace glanced up from her needlework, another muted moor scene, a quizzical expression on her face. She'd hurried down to the drawing room when Alex was announced, expecting to entertain him for a quarter hour or so. But she hadn't expected his dejected manner, or his announcement.

"The earl of Clayborne's son has been kidnapped or murdered, no one seems to know which." He sat straighter. "What is it? Did ye hurt yerself?"

"Mmmm. Just a pinprick," Grace said, pulling her finger from her mouth. " 'Tis nothing really."

"Ye should be more careful." Alex stretched toward her. "What is that anyway?"

"Drummoissie Moor," Grace said, with a longing look at her needlework. "Why should it concern ye so about

Lord Morgan's son? I thought ye had no good for the man.''

"I don't. Nor does any true-blooded Scot, I'm thinking." His eyes narrowed. "Where's that Englishman? Grace, ye really should not have him staying her with ye.''

"He's . . ." Grace waved her hand. "About, I suppose. And, Alex, I do believe we've had this discussion."

"Aye, but ye never had my approval."

"Which, as I recall, I don't need." The hurt in his eyes had Grace feeling sorry for her tone. "Alex, I explained that Maude was here.''

"Maude," he began, only to mumble something Grace couldn't hear, and thought probably best.

"Tell me, Alex, why is it so important to ye about Lord Morgan's son.''

"Not just to me, Grace. The fop's disappearance is causing an uproar in Parliament. The Royalists are blaming the Country Party. They're saying the barbarian Scots have taken the lad to use as a bargaining tool. So now they are refusing even to discuss anything about the Act of Union until he's returned. Andrew Fletcher thinks the entire thing might be a ploy by the Royalists to break off negotiations."

"Oh my.''

"Oh my is right. A fight broke out this afternoon between Patrick MacVee, and Sir Randolph Wallace. Certainly they are both hotheads, but it was right on the floor of Parliament. The Commissioner had to call for a recess.''

"And all because of James Morgan?''

"Aye." Alex stood and began pacing the room. "That Englishman is not still claiming to be Lord Morgan is he?''

Grace stuck her finger again, but this time made no reaction. "Why do ye ask?''

"Well, I can't help thinking there might be some connection. Perhaps he wants Lord Morgan and his son dead. So he can claim the title for himself.''

"I'm sure that's not the case. Foxworth would not want the two men dead.''

Alex shrugged, dismissing the thought. He stretched his legs, then straightened, taking a deep breath. "Have ye thought any more about my proposal to ye?''

"Alex, for goodness sake.''

" 'Tis not as if I didn't ask ye before.''

"I know. But this just isn't the time.''

"Why not? Because of the problems in Parliament? They should be resolved as soon as the young Morgan is found. That is, if he's alive.''

"He is.''

"What?''

Grace squeezed her eyes shut, unable to believe she actually spoke the last out loud. She'd been sent downstairs to see Alex MacDonald gone, but by the look on his face, he was not about to leave. Not that he was before either. Why had she allowed him to harbor any hope that she would marry him?

"What did ye say about Lord Morgan's son? Ye know something, don't ye? Tell me, Grace.''

"I don't—''

"He's here. In the back bedroom,'' Fox said as he entered the room. He glanced toward Grace. "There's no reason he can't know.''

"Reason I can't know? For God's sake, what is going on? I should have guessed ye were somehow behind this, Englishman.''

"Ye did guess as I recall.''

"Ye were listening?'' Alex shot to his feet.

"Alex, settle yerself,'' Grace said as if she were speaking to a naughty child. "If Fox heard anything, I'm certain it was only because he was in the next room. With his father.''

"His—" Alex fell back into his chair. "Not more of this nonsense."

"You wondered if I'd want to hurt James Morgan," Fox began, ignoring any pretense of not hearing Alex's earlier conversation. "You seem to forget that he's my father."

"More than one man has practiced patricide when a title was at stake."

"True. But would they also be practicing suicide?"

"What are ye talking about?"

Grace rose and moved toward Fox where he stood by the door. "James Morgan is a young man. Unmarried. And he's yet to father a child. At least not one that we know of."

"Not my brother, or myself," Fox added. "Having limited knowledge of time travel, I can't be certain. But it seems to me, that my father is needed to sire me."

"I don't believe this."

"Think of it logically," Grace said.

"Logically? I can hardly fathom ye two would dare use the word."

"Alex." Grace sighed. "Ye aren't listening to what we say. It all makes perfect sense."

"Time travel makes sense? Surely ye jest."

"Come along." Grace grabbed up Alex's hand and dragged him from his seat. He sputtered once in disbelief, but gave no further protest as she led him toward the back bedroom. Fox followed.

Maude was departing as they reached the doorway. She glanced up, her deep-set eyes shining in the shadows, but said nothing before moving on down the hallway. Once inside the darkened room, Grace let loose Ale's hand and moved toward the window.

"What is that smell?" Alex asked, bring a perfumed handkerchief to his nose.

"One of Maude's tonics no doubt," Grace responded

as she pulled open the draperies, allowing light to stream into the room. "See for yerself."

Alex stepped toward the bed and uttered a curse. "My God, it is Morgan." He looked first toward Grace, then Fox, who was leaning against the doorjamb, arms folded. "What did ye do to him?"

"He was wounded."

"I ran him through with a sword," Fox said, overriding Grace's vague explanation. "It was an accident, or at least I did not intend to harm him."

"How can ye stab someone without intent, I'm wanting to know."

"For goodness sake, Alex, that's not important. Look at him."

"He appears alive. Just barely."

"Aye, though Maude seems to think he'll survive. But I want ye to study his face. His hands. There, closer. Who does he look like?"

Signing in disgust Alex bent over the bed. He recognized the man as Lord Morgan's son, though he'd only seen him fleetingly. He was nearly as white as the linens beneath his close-cropped head. His eyes were closed, his breathing regular. What in the hell was he supposed to be seeing? Alex turned back toward Grace, who stabbed her finger toward James Morgan, signaling for Alex to examine him further.

All right, damn it. High forehead beneath shaved head. Aquiline nose. Square jaw. Well-defined mouth. He was obviously tall. And had the look of an Englishman about him.

Alex's mouth dropped open. He jerked his head around to look at the Englishman, Morgan he claimed to be, then stared back at the man asleep on the bed.

"When he wakes, ye'll find his eyes a dark blue, almost black," Grace said.

"All right. I grant ye they look a bit like each other."

"We're father and son. Though in this case the son is older than the father," Fox said. "I've seen portraits, and should have realized immediately who it was."

"How seriously is he hurt?"

"Maude seems to think he'll be fine. 'Tis the alcohol consumption he's sleeping off now."

"I should visit my grandfather. Let him know his son is alive," Fox said.

Alex grabbed Fox's sleeve. "Are ye mad?"

"Perhaps," Fox answered dryly. "However, I doubt this would prove it."

"Ye have no idea how volatile emotions are in the city at this moment." Their gazes met, and Alex let his hand slide. "Talk of the possible union is on everyone's lips. Now this with Lord James."

"All the more reason to let someone know he is alive."

"Ye say he'll recover. Why not just wait and let him go himself, though Lord knows he'll have his father's wrath down on ye then as well." Alex turned toward Grace. "And on her."

"Maude said it may be days before he's well enough to be up and about. You needn't worry yourself. I shall take care that no harm befalls Grace."

"Ye? Brave words to be sure, but how will ye protect her while imprisoned in the castle, I'd like to know."

"Stop it, both of ye." Grace stepped between the two men, staring at one then the other until they relaxed their belligerent expressions. "Fox will not be jailed."

"Nay, perhaps he'll be killed straight out."

"Alex, please." Her tone held less fire, more exasperation. "We shall accomplish nothing if we continue this arguing. Frankly, I resent the two of ye thinking one or the other must take care of me."

"Grace, I only meant—"

"Enough, Alex." The spark was back. "Of course Edinburgh is in an uproar. The entire country is, or will be. That is precisely why we must do something to change what will happen. Do not roll yer eyes at me, Alex."

A muffled snore from the bed had all three of them looking toward Lord Morgan's son. After making certain that he still slept, Grace herded Alex and Fox from the room, closing the door gently behind her.

"I think Fox is right. He should tell his . . . Lord Morgan that his son is safe."

"Gracie."

"It would also be an excellent opportunity to discuss this planned union with Lord Morgan."

"This is insane. He'll never see ye."

"I've already sent a note to my uncle, Lord McKinzie."

Inside the rented sedan chair Grace peered out the window and took a deep breath as the carriers lowered her in front of the grand town house. Stepping out, she tried not to allow the nerves fluttering in her stomach to show.

This was her uncle she was visiting, not some unknown ogre. Her favorite uncle. At least he had been until he chose to believe the worst of Dugald . . . and her.

He had sent her a post then, when things were bleakest, telling her he wanted no more to do with her. Accusing her, accusing Dugald, of betraying all for the lure of gold. To this day Grace remembered the feel of the parchment between her fingers, the scent of the wax impressed with the earl of Denbigh's seal, as she read the clipped note.

And she remembered the anger she felt at Dugald for putting her in such a situation. It was still there.

Taking another calming breath, Grace entered the front

door. She expected to be kept waiting, was surprised when she was ushered into her uncle's private sitting room.

He'd aged in the five years since she'd seen him. Always a handsome man, or at least she'd thought as much, with thick red hair and sparkling eyes, it appeared as if an evil artist had washed the canvas with grey. His hair, his skin, even the light in his eyes.

Grace dipped a curtsy, blinking away the tears stinging her eyes.

"Grace, ye are looking well."

She'd chosen her gown with care, finally utilizing the talents of the lady's maid Lord Archey insisted she keep. "Thank ye."

"Please sit." When she was settled in a small chair across from him, Lord McKinzie leaned back in his own chair. "I must admit to being a bit surprised by yer note. I did not know ye returned to Edinburgh."

"It was only recently, and I do not intend to stay."

He shrugged. "It is yer choice, I assume."

"But my presence was an embarrassment to ye before."

He cleared his throat. "I never wished to believe ill of ye or Dugald, Grace."

"Yet ye did."

"There was naught to prove otherwise."

"Is that how it is, then? I must prove myself innocent to ye?" When he said nothing, Grace looked away. "Would it mean anything if I said that I was? Innocent, that is."

"Is that what ye're telling me?"

"I am. I never knew anything about extra money."

"Yet I was told, and shown, I might add, all the things ye and Dugald were buying. And this when others were losing all they had."

"Dugald accused me of the same. But I never did." She saw his eyes narrow as he let his gaze scan the silk gown she wore. "Would ye have me wear rags to visit ye, an earl?"

"Nay. And I hardly begrudge ye fancy clothes. But 'tis rumors I heard of yer coach and silver, that caught my attention. And 'twas more than just hearsay."

He was right. There was a coach. One had been ordered and paid for with sterling. She'd accused Dugald of doing it. He'd blamed her. But she hadn't. And she told her uncle the same now.

"Dugald's death makes him unable to speak for himself."

"That is true, but I swear to ye, I've not lied. After he died I sold the coach, ye must know that. And gave the money to investors."

Lord McKinzie looked down at his hands, where they lay on his lap. "Ye know my feelings on that entire episode. I never kept my views a secret."

"Our opinions often were at odds, Uncle Angus." Her old name for her uncle slipped out without thought, and Grace was happy to see he made no attempt to correct her. Instead, he actually smiled, showing a bit of his old verve.

"True enough. Ye were always a bit headstrong."

"Which was often as not attributed to being yer kin."

Lord McKinzie's expression sobered. "I never wished to believe ill of either ye or Dugald. Despite our differences, I did admire yer husband."

What could she say to that? She'd always admired Dugald as well. Not loved him. At least not in the way she did the Englishman.

Grace sucked in her breath at the realization of what she was thinking. Did she? Could she love the Englishman? Foxworth Morgan. A man who believed he was of another time.

Her uncle's voice interrupted her thoughts.

"I'm glad ye sent me the note, Grace. Glad we've had this time to talk."

"So am I, Uncle Angus. But I must admit, I had another reason for wanting to see ye." Grace regretted having to say the words when she noticed the way the lines around his mouth deepened. "Ye know I love Scotland. 'Tis a McKinzie legacy. And I know we differ on what we think the best course for her is."

"Grace, I did not invite ye here to discuss politics."

" 'Tis not politics. 'Tis the future of Scotland's people for which I speak. No good can come if the present course is taken. The union—"

"Scotland's union with England will happen, Grace. There is naught ye nor anyone can do about it. Yer husband and those like him tried with their Darien scheme, and only made matters worse."

"Aye, 'tis true. I admit it. Still, there must be another way."

"There isn't." Lord McKinzie pushed to his feet and began to move restlessly about the room. "Do ye think I haven't thought this through? I'm a wealthy man. 'Tis not more gold I seek. I am not settled in an Englishman's pocket."

"I never thought that, Uncle Angus."

"Without England, without her markets, Scotland is doomed."

"Scotland, or at least her people, are doomed anyway."

"What are ye saying, lass?"

"I agree the union will be signed. But there will be many Scots unable to accept an alliance with England. Many who will not embrace a German king. There will be riots and battles, and attempts to restore the Stuarts to the throne. Finally there will be an insurrection that will slash Scotland, killing her citizens and dooming those that remain."

When she finished speaking, Grace realized that she,

too, stood. Letting her arms drop, she turned away, drawn to the window. For several minutes the room was quiet except for the ticking of the clock on the mantel.

When Grace finally glanced around she saw her uncle staring at her, his eyes narrowed.

"Ye speak, Grace, as if ye know what ye're saying."

"I do."

"But there is no way for—"

"There is. Uncle, I came today because I wish ye to meet someone. A man who can tell ye more than I."

"Grace—"

"Please," she said, moving toward him. "If I ever meant anything to ye, just do this for me. Too many lives depend upon it."

Their eyes met and locked. "Who is this man? I've already met with Alexander MacDonald and Andrew of Saltoun."

"He's not a Scot, but an Englishman. And if I told ye his name . . . or his title, ye wouldn't believe me anyway." When he didn't answer, Grace continued. "I would never do anything to harm ye. Please believe me."

"When do ye wish me to meet this man?"

Grace let out her breath. "Today. As soon as possible."

"This afternoon then."

"Could ye have yer friend Lord Morgan here as well?"

"I doubt he's in much mood to discuss politics. His son disappeared. Why do ye wish to see him anyway?"

"It's because of his son. Nay, I really can't say more. But please, do yer best to have him here."

They'd settled on a time, and Grace had managed to avoid answering any more questions. She knew her actions were suspicious, and she respected her uncle all the more for being willing to meet with Fox under the circumstances.

She rode home through the crowded noisy streets. The weather was dry and calm, warm for this early in the year, and Edinburgh was in need of a good wind to blow away the stench that settled inside its walls.

Back inside her house Grace delivered the news to Fox, finding him the first place she looked, in his father's room.

"Has there been any change?"

Fox glanced around from where he stood looking out the window to the tiny enclosed garden. When he saw her, he smiled, and Grace felt a warmth spread through her. Aye, she loved him. Despite the feeling she had that naught good could come from it.

"He awoke earlier."

"Oh?"

"He was not in the best of moods. He didn't recognize me as the man who wounded him. I imagine his brain was fairly pickled at the time. But he ranted and raved about his discomfort."

"It is a nasty wound."

"It was more his head that drew the brunt of his rage. Although he did threaten to kill us all and leave."

Grace let her gaze slip toward the sleeping man, whose appearance echoed Fox's. "He appears fairly calm now."

"Maude gave him a brew. Put him right to sleep. But she says we won't be able to keep him quiet much longer."

"We meet with his father at half past three."

"We?"

"Ye didn't think to go by yerself, did ye?"

"I did."

" 'Tis I who arranged the meeting. 'Tis my uncle who'll be there."

"What if Lord Morgan does not take this news of his son well?"

"What if he doesn't?"

"Gracie," Fox said as he started toward her. "I'm not of Alex's mind that I'll be murdered on the spot." His hand curved about her cheek. "However, there could be repercussions, and I don't want ye involved."

"But I am." Grace tried to ignore the way her bones suddenly felt soft, unable to support her weight. "From the moment I found ye on the moor, I've been part of this." She forced herself to turn away from him. His dark eyes mesmerized her. "There is more to this then simply informing Lord Morgan that his son is safe."

"Predicting the future," Fox said, and shook his head.

"We're not predicting, and ye know it."

"Maybe I do. And maybe you do. But not another single person does, including Alex."

"He may complain and bluster about, but I believe in his heart he knows the truth."

Fox gave her a look that implied he wasn't as sure.

"What of Lord Archey?"

"What of him?"

"Did ye not feel he knew who ye were and where ye came from?"

"You mean when I came from. And yes, I had a feeling. But I don't believe either yer uncle or my grandfather are going to care much about that."

"Possibly not. But we have to try."

"Do we?" Fox walked toward the door. "So far I've embroiled you in a controversy. Nearly killed my father. I'm wondering if my best course of action isn't simply to disappear. Hell, maybe I can even manage to find my way back to my own time."

Chapter Thirteen

His continued suggestion that he go alone to meet his grandfather and Lord McKinzie were ignored. Fox was finding that Grace could be a force to be reckoned with. She had this idealistic notion that she could change history for the better.

Impossible.

At least that was Fox's take on it. Of course, he'd have said time travel was impossible until recently.

Giving his jacket one final swipe with the silver brush, Fox turned toward the door to his room. There was just enough time, before leaving, to look in on his father and try to reason with him if he was awake. Grace had retired to her room earlier, and Fox had a strong urge to knock on her door.

Simply to make certain she hadn't changed her mind about going to her uncle's, Fox tried to tell himself. But he knew the truth. Once inside her room, he wouldn't be able to keep his hands from her.

She was becoming an obsession with him. He could think of little else. And last night, loving her, holding her in his arms, had done nothing to slacken his desire for her.

What in the hell was he thinking?

His life was in turmoil. Not his own. Not even his own time. Hell, he had no idea what was going on anymore. He'd fought with and wounded his own father, for God's sake. His own father, who was younger than Fox. How very strange was that?

And in the midst of this, he found himself falling in love with a woman who called to his soul.

Grace.

Her very name sang to him.

Perhaps the notion, a little romantic for his taste, blurred his hearing. At any rate he was nearly to the bottom of the staircase when he heard the noise. As Edinburgh, and the house were hardly quiet, Fox didn't know why this particular sound affected him so.

But he was scrambling up the stairs, nearly bumping into a linen-carrying maid, before he stopped to think. Grace's door was locked. It took him two attempts of throwing his weight against the thick paneling before he heard splintering wood.

The third time his shoulder slammed into the door it shattered, hurling Fox, off-balance, into the dressing room.

In his mind's eye ran the vision of Grace sitting at her dressing table, a quizzical expression on her face, as if to say "What are ye about bursting into my rooms?" But that's not what he saw.

Furniture was overturned. A chair. A small wooden chest.

Then from the other room, the bedroom, where he'd made love to her last night, he heard a muffled cry.

"Grace."

Fox caught sight of her as she landed on the mattress,

facedown. Before her assailant could pounce, she'd turned, her hands up to defend herself. But there was no need, for Fox had grabbed the man by his shoulders, barely missing the knife swiped his way.

"Damnation."

Fox chopped at the man's arms, sending the knife clattering to the floor. Fisting his fingers, he then socked him in the jaw. The feather mattress absorbed some of the blow, for though blood erupted from the man's torn lip, he remained conscious.

Fox pulled back to punch again but he wasn't fast enough. The man brought his knee up, sending it toward Fox's groin. Fox twisted, but only in time to deflect the blow. There was a moment of hesitation as nausea swamped him, and the man scrambled to his feet.

Fox glanced toward Grace, who was pushing up, staring at him wide-eyed, then he twisted after the assailant. The attacker started toward the door to the hallway but, seeing Fox about to cut him off, jerked around toward the open window. He bracketed the sash as he leapt onto the wide sill.

Hands out, Fox leapt toward him, intent upon keeping him from escaping. The man twisted, his elbow connecting with Fox's jaw, just as Fox grabbed for him. Fox clawed for substance and got flimsy fabric instead.

The wool ripped, and, with a scream, the man fell rather than jumped from the third-story window. The sound of him hitting the brick walkway below echoed through the air.

Fox stood, his hand still out as if to catch the assailant, when Grace rushed to the window. "Are ye all right?" she asked. After Fox nodded, she looked toward the garden below.

"I don't think he is though," she whispered.

"Nay, it doesn't appear as if he is." Fox clutched her

shoulders, pulling her back inside the window. "My God, what was he doing? Wasn't he one of the servants?"

"Aye, 'twas William." She glanced out the window again. "Is there any way he's not dead?"

"None, I would say." On the pavement below, William's head was attached to his body at an odd angle. "He might have made it, if he'd jumped, but . . . ." Fox shook his head. "What was he doing in here?"

"Exactly the question I asked when I awoke from a nap to see him standing over my bed."

"What did he say?"

"Nothing. He simply tried to grab me. We struggled. I managed to get out of bed and ran for the door. Ye came in about then."

"I thought I heard you call for me." Fox curved his hand about her face. "Are you sure he didn't hurt you?"

"Only frightened me. Really." Her hand closed over his. "I tried to call for you, but he kept a hand over my mouth most of the time."

"And you've no idea why he would try to kill you?"

"Nay. I've known William for years. Since before Dugald died. He's always been completely trustworthy. Very good with horses, I was told."

"By whom?"

"I don't recall. Shouldn't we do something about him? He's just lying there."

"In a moment." A movement below grabbed Fox's attention. "There's Maude. She'll take care of things, I wager." There was a gleam in his eye when he looked back at her. "Wait a moment. You say you knew William before your husband died, yet he wasn't with you at Glenraven. At least I don't remember seeing him."

"He wasn't there when ye were. He'd already come back to Edinburgh."

"You sent him here?"

"Not exactly. He actually works for Lord Archey. He was one of the servants his lordship lent Dugald." When Fox's brow arched quizzically, Grace continued. "Lord Archey thought we needed more help. It was during the time when we learned of the colony's failure. We had the new coach. Apparently Dugald ordered it without thinking of the need for more staff."

"You had no coach at Glenraven."

"Aye, but there were horses, though not enough to keep William busy. Lord Archey must have sensed that, for one day a messenger arrived, asking me if I would send William back to Maymont. I did, of course."

"And then he showed up here."

"He was here when we arrived. Fox, shouldn't we do something about him?"

Fox gently pulled Grace away from the window. Several servants were below readying William's body to be hauled away . . . making certain nothing of value remained on his corpse.

"It's being taken care of, Grace." Taking her into the sitting room, Fox upended two chairs, and settled her in one. Her hands still trembled, and he wanted nothing more than to cuddle her against him and assure her nothing would ever frighten or hurt her again. But how could he, a man who through some twist of fate found himself dumped into this time, assure anyone of anything? Every time he woke, every time he turned a corner, he felt as if some cosmic force might realize its error and snap him back to his own time.

So instead of holding her, of reassuring her, of even pretending he had some control over her fate, and his, he tried to reason through what had happened.

It didn't make sense that a servant would want Grace dead. He might wish to steal from her, but then why enter her room while she was there? How much easier pilfering would be if he'd waited till she was out. Besides, Fox glanced about the room. Chairs were overturned, linens spread about. It was obvious there'd been a struggle.

But the jewelry box on top her chest didn't look disturbed. William hadn't been there to steal. He'd been trying to kill Grace.

Fox wondered if this was the first time.

Pulling his chair close so that they were knee to knee, Fox grabbed her hands. They were cold, and he enveloped them in his own, warming as he absently rubbed. "Grace, I want you to think carefully. Was William still with you when you had that dream?" Her shining head cocked to one side, and Fox explained further. "The one you told me about the first night I met you."

"Where I dreamed someone tried to kill me? Oh, Fox, ye don't think . . . Ye can't think—"

"Just try to remember."

"Nay, he was long gone back to—" Grace pulled her hands free and sat straighter. She wet her suddenly dry lips. "He was there, though I'd already received the message from Lord Archey. I remember now wondering if I should mention my dream in a post to him and have William deliver it."

"Did you?"

"No." Grace shook her head, sending wisps of red hair swirling about her head. "I decided I was being silly. Seeing evil where there was none."

Fox wasn't so certain there was none. "What of when the chandelier fell? I was at Glenraven by then, so I suppose William was gone."

"Aye. What are ye thinking?"

"What?" Fox shook his head. "Nothing really." He forced a smile then, hoping to reassure her, when he felt anything but reassured. The more he thought on this, the stranger it became. And the more he feared there was more to this than met the eye. Much more. But it wasn't something he wanted to discuss with Grace now.

First of all, he had no desire to frighten her if he were wrong. And he very well might be.

Secondly, well, secondly, she might not believe him.

"We should be leaving for our meeting with Lord McKinzie, should we not?"

"Of course." Grace brushed a hand over her hair, realizing the elaborate style was hopelessly mussed. Curls spiraled down her back, the silver pins probably scattered all over the room. "I'll need just a moment to ready myself." Grace let her hand drop when she saw Fox move toward her.

His eyes seemed very dark and intense beneath lowered lids, and a half smile curved his lips. Her heart, which had nearly slowed to its normal beat after her brush with death, began to pound faster. He did that to her. Always. Thinking about him. Seeing him. Catching his scent. All were enough to send goose bumps spreading across her body.

But when he looked at her like he was doing now, as if he, too, felt the pull between them, it was almost more than Grace could bear.

Her breath caught when his fingers sifted through her hair.

"Are you certain it wouldn't be better if I just went myself? I hate to drag you through all this."

"Ye know I must go." His fingertip grazed her ear, and her voice faltered. "I'm as much a part of this as ye."

"Not exactly." Fox smiled. " 'Tis not your father, younger than you yourself, lying in the other room, wounded by your own hand."

Grace's laugh helped ease some of the tension. But not much. "That's true. But ... oh. That feels wonderful." Grace tried to pull herself together. His palm now caressed the side of her neck, bringing memories of last night cascading about her. "I was saying, I have a stake in this, too. Lord McKinzie is my uncle. And 'tis my country, my countrymen who are to suffer."

"It's not your fault, Grace." Fox's hand cupped her head. "You didn't cause the Darien colonization to fail."

"I know ye're right." Grace didn't protest when he brought her head to his shoulder. "But I can't help feeling somehow responsible . . . at least now that I know what will happen." Her face lifted, and green eyes met his. "Can't ye understand why I must do all that I can?"

"I do." His lips grazed hers. "And I admire you for your stand, even as I wish you not so courageous."

"I'm not brave, Fox. Not at all. If I were, I'd be out in the streets right now trying to convince others of what I know. Trying to make them see what has to be done." Her bronze lashes lowered. "Instead I'm hoping my uncle will speak for me."

"Grace." Fox paused. "Look at me." When she did, he continued. "You think I'm not frightened? Every morning I awake, wondering what is going to become of me. Wondering why I'm here, and if I'll ever return to my own time." His voice softened. "If I want to return to my own time. And knowing all the while that people will never believe me."

"I—"

"Yes, I know. You believe me. And for that I'm grateful, though it still bewilders me that you do. But I should be the one out on the streets telling anyone who will listen what I know."

"We'd make quite a pair."

Fox bent his forehead to meet hers and chuckled. "Till they had the constable lock us up." He kissed the tip of her nose, his expression growing serious. "Nay, we may not be brave, but we are clever, at least as clever as we can be under the circumstances. Convincing your uncle and other influential men is the best way to go.'' Forcing himself to let loose his hold in her hair, Fox rested his hands on her shoulders, forcing some distance between the two of them. "As much as I love holding you, I think we best stop this or we'll never make our appointment with your uncle. Besides, I think I best see to helping Maude with William's body and give you a chance to ready yourself."

After sending several servants to Grace's room, to straighten the furniture and help their mistress, Fox went looking for Maude. He found the old woman in the kitchen bent over a table covered with dried herbs and grasses. She didn't look up when he entered, yet Fox sensed she knew of his presence.

"Is the body gone?"

"Cleaned and disposed of, though no thanks can be given to ye for it, Traveler."

"Grace was upset. He tried to kill her."

She glanced up now, her face deep within the shadows of her plaid. "Why would he do that?"

"I thought you might know." Fox reached for a dried bit of something that looked like a weed, only to have her bat his hand away.

"Well, I don't," she rasped.

"And you wouldn't tell me if you did."

"Didn't say that. Didn't say that at all."

"I hope you're telling me the truth. When I burst through the door William was about to stab your sister-in-law."

"Then it's a good thing ye burst through the door, eh Traveler?"

Shaking his head, Fox turned to leave. He could get more information from a tree, he decided. She either didn't care about Grace, or refused to act as if she did.

Fox hoped it was the latter. He started from the room,
surprised when she called him back. He turned, ready to
see nothing but her well-wrapped form, startled by the
sight of her lined face. She'd pushed aside the plaid, and
her sunken eyes seemed to hold him captive. She began
to speak, and Fox could swear an icy wind off the North
Sea swept into the kitchen. The fire in the stone hearth
bristled and spit.

"Ye will take care of her, Traveler, or ye'll have me to
answer to, and I swear it."

Her words haunted Fox as pace by annoyed pace, he
measured the richly appointed anteroom. Lord McKinzie
had him waiting for nearly a half an hour now, a half hour
that Grace was out of his sight. Granted, he'd allowed her
to come here this afternoon alone, but that was before a
servant tried to slice her open.

Fox strode to the door, and was just reaching for the
handle when it turned. The liveried footman who led the
way toward an upstairs drawing room kept his gait sedate.
When the double doors were thrown open Fox searched
the room for Grace, finding her seated on a chair near
the hearth. She sat there, looking beautiful, and fragile,
like the heather of the Highlands in her gown of deep
lavender. But like the heather, Fox knew she was not near
as fragile as she seemed. She caught his eye and gave a
slight nod of acknowledgment before Fox let his gaze shift
toward the other people in the room.

Her uncle, Lord McKinzie, stood near Grace. The family
resemblance was notable even if the time had dimmed the
brilliant red hair. Fox bowed, then turned toward the man
who spoke, the clipped tones of his English accent sounding foreign after weeks of hearing naught but soft Scottish
burrs.

"What word do you have of my son?"

Fox turned to look into eyes the same deep, deep blue as his own.

"Out with it. Is it coin you wish? If so, I'll pay."

"Thomas, let the man speak. Grace said this was no kidnapping. Sit, young man. Would ye care for some refreshment?"

"He likes claret, as I recall."

Fox turned at the sound of the voice he hadn't heard for some time. From the shadows stepped Lord Archey, a genial smile on his face. A smile that did nothing to soften the instant trepidation Fox felt.

His bow was stiff, his voice the same. "I didn't expect to see you here, my lord."

"Really." He took a sip from the goblet he held. "I would have thought Grace had told ye her welfare is my constant concern."

"Did she tell you someone tried to kill her?"

"Foxworth, please." Grace stood, wishing she could do something to keep him quiet. This wasn't supposed to be the topic of conversation this afternoon.

"Is what he says true, Grace?" her uncle asked. "My God, are ye all right?"

"I'm fine. And yes, he is telling the truth."

"What does this have to do with my son?" Lord Morgan asked, annoyance lacing his tone.

Turning toward his grandfather, Fox shook his head. "Nothing. I came to tell you he is safe and healing well."

"Healing?"

The stance, one leg straight and slightly forward, head held high and at an angle, were just as he'd been painted in later years. How many times had Fox stared at the portrait in the library of his London town house and wondered at the arrogance of the man? And been irritated when his sister Zoe teased that Fox was his double. To see him now in the flesh was surreal. Fox tried to pull himself together.

"Your son was drinking, picked a fight with the wrong person, and ended up wounded. Nothing life-threatening. However, a day or two of rest is in order."

"This person he fought? It was you, I assume?"

"It was."

Thomas Morgan nodded and walked toward the carved mantel, under which burned a warming peat fire. "I would also guess, knowing my son's lack of sense, that you had the ability and opportunity to end his life if that were your wish."

"Yes."

"Then I'm both grateful and possibly vexed with you, young man. Though as a father, I feel gratitude is the proper emotion. However, James is hardly the son I would have wished." He paused then, as if seeing Fox for the first time. "Your name?"

What if he told him? Simply opened his mouth and spit out the truth? Fox could possibly recite enough family history to at least make the old man, who wasn't an old man at all, wonder.

No, chances are he'd never get far enough for that. He'd be considered mad and shoved aside, and that would be the end of it.

But there was no way he couldn't give his real name, not with Lord Archey here.

"Foxworth Morgan," Fox said, hearing the soft intake of Grace's breath even though she stood separated from him by nearly the entire room.

"Morgan?" Fox's grandfather cocked his head. "You're English I assume."

"I am." Fox paused. "From Devon."

His grandfather appeared to take that in . . . Fox could almost see the process as his mind went over all the families he knew from Devon. "Foxworth? A notable name, yet I don't recall any Morgans from Devon called such. Who is your father?"

"I'm—"

"Please excuse me for interrupting," Grace said. "However, let me say, I can vouch for Mr. Morgan's word. Your son is safe and will return to ye soon. In the meantime, there are compelling circumstances that must be discussed."

"Such as?"

Grace took a deep breath then turned toward her uncle. It was obvious her interruption had done nothing to quell Lord Morgan's curiosity about Fox. Couldn't he see the resemblance? But that couldn't be her concern at the moment. Scotland was.

"Uncle Angus," she began. "I know how much ye love Scotland. And I truly believe in my heart ye'd do nothing to hurt yer countrymen. Which is why we must discuss the possible union with—"

"Grace, for God's sake, this is none of yer concern."

"I disagree. It is everyone's concern. The union will bring devastating results. Wars, the death of hundreds of our countrymen. The end of Scotland."

"Grace dear, don't be so melodramatic. The end of Scotland," Lord McKinzie repeated, his tone sarcastic. "As ye very well know," he said, his eyes boring into Grace, "Scotland can survive quite a lot."

The guilt swept over her, almost blocking her ability to speak. But there was too much at stake. "I realize what ye think," her focus broadened, "what ye all must think about the Darien colony. But I tell ye now, I had nothing to do with its failure."

"Of course not, Grace dear. No one blames ye." Lord Archey's tone was honey-sweet. "Ye're a woman after all.

A gently bred woman with tastes and needs that we all understand.

"Tastes and needs?" Grace heard her voice turn shrill and wet her lips. "What do ye mean by that, my lord? For if ye mean what I think ye do, I shall have to take insult from it."

"Grace dear, I would never, never do anything to hurt ye. Who stood beside ye when no one else did?" Lord Archey let his eyes flick toward her uncle. "I've always believed ye an innocent pawn in the entire sordid affair. However, any man, and yer husband was just a man, Grace, will succumb to the wishes of the woman he loves." The earl lifted his hands and shrugged. "Who can blame him?"

"So that's what ye think? That I begged for beautiful clothes and fancy coaches, and Dugald got them for me the only way he knew how?" Grace turned toward her uncle. "And is that what ye think as well?"

"No one blames ye, Grace."

"No one blames me?" Her chin lifted, and her hair seemed to bristle with fire. "Well that's comforting, especially since I am not to blame. I never needed extra coin, nor did Dugald for that matter. He was a true patriot, who despite yer contention would not have chosen me over Scotland." She took a fortifying breath. "Never chose me over Scotland."

For a moment silence reined. Lord Archey stepped forward to squelch it, no doubt with another statement meant to make Grace and her late husband seem guilty. But before he could speak, Fox took the initiative.

"The matter under discussion is the union of Scotland and England, and what it will mean to the Scottish people."

Chapter Fourteen

"They wouldn't even listen."

"Did you really expect them to?"

Grace sighed and shook her head before climbing the five steps to her front door. "I suppose not. They both wish the union. Yer grandfather, of course, doesn't care about Scotland, really. He's English, like ye."

"What do you mean by that?" Fox covered her hand with his before she could reach for the doorknob. "Do you think I don't care what happens in Scotland? I've lived through the worst of it, if you recall."

"I do. But then it wasn't really ye who was being hunted down like a beast, was it?"

"Nay, it was I trying my best to stop it. And living with the fear that I could have done more. Haunted by the cries of the wounded till I sometimes wish it had been me lying on the moor at Culloden."

Turning her hand, Grace linked her fingers with Fox's. "Please forgive me. Of course, I know how ye feel. It's just

I do not know what to do." Her voice softened. "And it is painful for me to know what people think of me, even though I try to tell myself I don't care."

"For what it is worth, I believe you." Fox brought their joined hands to his lips. Her angelic smile was his reward.

"We make a strange pair, Fox," Grace said with a laugh. "I believe ye are from another time, and ye believe me when the whole of Scotland thinks me worse than a traitor."

"Your uncle doesn't see you that way."

"He doesn't wish to." Grace entered the house. "But he does. How can he not?"

"How can who not?" Alex asked as he strode out from the drawing room into the hall.

"Alex! How long have ye been here?"

"Long enough to wonder what ye were about. And to look in on yer prisoner."

"He's hardly that," Fox said pushing past Alex. He walked toward the side table and poured himself a generous splash of brandy. "How is my father?"

"He seems to be rather enjoying his role of patient. For some reason he's drawn to Maude, if ye can believe it. Spends most of his time complaining to her of this and that."

"A trait he will not outgrow," Fox mumbled as he poured more liquid into his glass. His father had always been one to grouse about things. It was either too rainy or too dry, too warm or the bone-chilling cold bothered him. His sons were too compliant, unable to think or make a decision for themselves, or in Fox's case, headstrong and ungrateful.

They'd never got on. Even as a young lad, Fox's memories of his father were tarnished by dislike. And it had been mutual.

His grandfather, though, was a different story. Fox didn't

remember him well, at least not a litany of facts, but the feelings evoked by thoughts of him were warm. Walking beside him, Fox's hand nearly swallowed by his grandfather's. A half-forgotten image really of sitting upon a lap, the scent of tobacco and brandy cocooning them. And his grandfather's voice, clipped, intelligent—the same voice he'd heard today.

Fox jerked himself back from thoughts of his childhood. He'd been four, maybe five when his grandfather died. Certainly it seemed strange to see the man now, younger than when he'd known him before. Strange, weird, totally unbelievable. Yet true.

The hand on his arm had Fox stilling the glass midway to his lips. He looked down into Grace's soft green eyes. Sympathetic eyes, that seemed to reach out to him through time. "This isn't the answer," she said softly, and Fox followed her gaze to the decanter on the inlaid table. It had been nearly full when he entered the room, and now was well below the halfway mark. How much had he stood here and drunk? His mouth and throat tasted bitter, and he wished for a moment to clean his teeth.

Instead he lowered the glass and gave her what he hoped was an apologetic grin. As he left the room, he ignored Alex.

He found his father sitting up, pillows bunched behind him, playing cards scattered on a silver tray perched on his lap. He glanced up, waving Fox in with his right hand. His left arm was wrapped in bandaging.

"She tells me you're the one who wounded me."

Fox peered into the corner to see Maude roosting on a stool. "I am," Fox said, wondering where in the hell this was going.

"Well, I don't like it one bit, this tear in my arm. It hurts like hell. Damn it, man, have you ever been wounded?"

"Several times."

"Well then." He lifted his arm and moaned. "Hand me that glass there," he said, then waited for Fox to do his bidding. "She also tells me you are responsible for my being alive." Thomas Morgan sighed deeply, as if the idea of admitting this disturbed him. "Is that true?"

"That's something you need to determine for yourself."

"Well, I can't, you see. My memory of events is shadowy at best. There was a tavern. Not a decent one, mind you, but one of these damn Scottish hovels. Barbarian lot, these Scots. Anyway, I may have drunk a bit too much. Can't recall much after that."

"You took exception to my being on the street, decided a fight the only way to solve the problem . . . swords," Fox added when his father lifted a brow.

"Ah, I'm quite an accomplished swordsman."

"Perhaps a bit less so when drunk."

He smiled then, a smile Fox saw often in the mirror. "So you chose not to kill me."

"Saw no need."

"And you brought me here to . . . this your house?"

"A friend's."

"A lady friend's. Yes, I've seen the fair Grace, is it?"

"Grace MacCammon is a lady."

"I'm certain. As a matter of fact, the delightful Maude has been telling me the same thing. Anyway, I shall need my servants brought to me here, at least my manservant. Clothing." He glanced down at the borrowed nightshirt. "I can hardly be expected to wear this about. And some decent food. I'll need a coach of course."

"Is he well enough to leave?" Fox directed the question to Maude, who'd made no move to say anything to this point.

"Aye, 'twas the drink more than the baby cut ye gave him that's keep him bedbound."

"Baby cut," Fox's father said with a laugh. "She's always

saying something clever like that. What a gem she is. You wouldn't think of letting me have her, would you?"

"Maude is Mistress MacCammon's sister-in-law."

"I see. Well, then. Do you suppose I might have something stronger than watered-down ale to drink?"

"The clever Maude seems to be taking care of your needs. Ask her. Now if you'll excuse me, I must be off. Take care of yourself." With that, Fox left the room.

He was being foolish, he knew. This man had no idea who Fox was. How could he? If he noticed any resemblance, he would think little more than that they were distant relatives. Cousins perhaps. Father and son? Never.

Still, there was something in Fox that wished for that recognition. Who wanted his father to look at him with eyes of love, and know, just know, who he was.

Utter foolishness.

Fox strode down the hall and out the front door.

"They aren't willing even to listen to me, Alex. I feel so helpless." Grace glanced up as she heard footfalls in the hallway. "Fox. Fox!" Laying her stitching aside, she rose just as the front door closed behind him.

She looked back at Alex, who only shrugged and continued to leaf through a book he'd picked up off the table.

"Where do ye think he's going?"

"I have no idea."

"He hasn't been the same since seeing his grandfather."

Alex rolled his eyes. "For God's sake, Gracie, he's always been strange. Strange? Hell, the man thinks he comes from a different time. He thinks I'm some fellow named Padraic who's a grand friend of his, and—"

"Alex!"

"Oh, hell." Alex dropped the book onto the table with a bang. "I suppose ye want me to go after him?"

"He does consider ye a friend. As do I."

"Aye, but ye think of him as more, don't ye? No, no, don't look at me with those soft eyes of yers and try to think of a way not to hurt me. Believe it or not, 'tis ye I worry bout." Alex grabbed up his plumed hat. "Did ye ever think what will happen to ye if he does come from another time and he has to go back?"

"Ye love him, too, don't ye?" Grace said as she accompanied Alex to the door.

"Hell no. He's a nuisance. Which way did he go?" Alex stood at the top of the stairs and looked out over the swarm of people milling about High Street. He started down the stairs, elbowing through the fishwives and merchants, after seeing a dark head above the crowd.

"Fox! Damnation, Fox, slow down. I know ye hear me."

Fox kept his pace steady for two more steps, then stopped, allowing the flow of humanity to stream about him. What in the hell did Padraic, no, not Padraic, Alex, want with him? He didn't want company. But it looked as if he was going to get it. He could hear Alex rushing toward him.

"What's wrong with ye?" he said, sounding a bit winded when he finally caught up. "Ye must have known I was calling yer name."

"What if I did," Fox said as he began his steady stride again.

"Listen, it wasn't my idea to come lumbering after ye."

"Grace."

"Aye, Grace. For some reason known only to her and God above, she fancies herself in love with ye. Nay, don't say a word. Just listen to me. Damnation, where are all these people off to?" Alex asked no one in particular as he bumped into a giant of a woman with a basket of wool held in front of her.

"Anyway, as I was saying, Lord knows why, but she loves ye and ye had better be good to her."

"What if I can't?"

"What?" A group of children, each louder than the next pushed their way between Alex and Fox. "What did ye say?"

Fox stopped in his tracks. "What if I can't be good to her? What if something happens and—"

"Ye mean ye're tossed back where ye belong?"

Fox snorted. "Something like that, yes."

"I don't— Hell, follow me." Alex led the way to a tavern off one of the alleys. The darkness within took a moment or two of adjustment. When their eyes had reacted, Alex led them to a table in the corner, away from the crowds.

"We call this Patrick Steele's Club. It's a haunt for members of Parliament, of the New Party persuasion, of course. We might even see Andrew Fletcher if we're lucky, though he keeps pretty much to himself." Alex ordered a bottle of Madeira and two glasses. Uncorking the bottle, he filled both glasses, then with a quick salute set about to empty nearly half of his. "What were we talking about? Ah, yes, Grace, my dearest love. The woman that loves ye."

"She'd be better off with you," Fox conceded before tossing the contents of the glass down his throat.

"Of course she would. I have power and influence. I can protect her from those fools who think her capable of cheating anyone. And I adore her. You, on the other hand"—Alex motioned with his glass—"are a nobody from nowhere. Oh, don't get in a huff. Even if ye are who ye say ye are, it does ye no good. This isn't 1748, or whenever ye say yer time is. It's the here and now, and ye don't belong."

"Don't think I don't know that?"

"Well, there ye have it. Grace should be with me. We're all agreed . . . except Grace. And damnation the woman seems to have a mind of her own. She wouldn't let me help her before, just ran off to that godforsaken Glenraven with Maude." Alex shook his head. "What's a man to do?"

"I don't know."

"Well, of course ye don't. It was a rhetorical question. But here's one that isn't. Do ye love her?"

"I said she'd be better off with you, didn't I?"

"That's not what I'm asking. Aye or nay. Do ye love her?"

"Aye." Fox barked the word. "There. Does that make you happy?"

"Actually, it does. Mad as it seems, I want her happy. And she wouldn't be if ye didn't feel for her as she does for ye." Alex poured them each another drink, then paused, studying his companion. "Ye're telling the truth, aren't ye?"

"What, do you want me to jump on the table and yell it. I love her, I tell you."

"I'm not talking about that, right now. The time thing. Padraic. It's the truth."

Fox took a deep breath. "Yes."

"Hell."

"Did you think I was lying all this time?"

"I don't know. I was hoping ye were. So tell me, in this next life of mine, what am I like? Handsome, I suppose, and brave?"

"Braver than I've seen you so far in this one."

Alex jerked to his feet, then slapped both palms on the table, and laughing, returned to his seat. "I can understand why we're friends."

Fox shook his head. "Yes, I suppose we are." He leaned against the chair back. "You have many of the same characteristics as the Rebel." At Alex's quizzical expression Fox explained. "Your, or rather Padraic's, other self. A masked man who stole from the rich and gave to the poor. Anyway, even if I didn't 'know' who you were, I'd be reminded of Padraic."

"Hmmm. So I wear a mask."

Fox chuckled. "A black silk one. As a matter of fact, you dress all in black. Even ride a black horse."

"Interesting, I've always been partial to black horses."

"Proof enough in my mind," Fox said with a laugh.

"Ye realize how difficult this is for people to believe. I mean if we could remember something, anything about another life, then maybe."

"I've had moments, flashes of something before this happened to me. I never considered them anything, but now I wonder. Have you never met someone and thought you knew them? Or had something happen to you and think it had happened before?"

"Aye, but it was merely a coincidence. Wasn't it?"

Fox shrugged, and Alex remained silent a moment. Then his lips thinned. "Everything *else* ye said is true, too. Isn't it?"

"I'm afraid so."

"Damnation." Alex leaned back in his seat. Off to his right a patron lifted his glass in a toast, and the others at his table joined in. But Alex only continued to sit, his eyes lowered, his shoulders drooping. "I've tried, but there simply aren't enough votes to block the union. Some of our own members, men who were against the very idea of an alliance with England, are going over to the other side. And truthfully," he said, lifting his face, "I can't blame them. Oh, not the ones who are doing it to fill their own pockets with English coin. They can be damned for all I care. But there are those who see no other way out. Not with England holding all the cards, damn them."

"Trade runs the world, it seems. And from what I know, it only gets worse."

"I suppose if anyone can see the future, it's ye." Alex divided what was left in the bottle between the two glasses, then called for another.

"Only so far, and only long-range. My own future is as much a mystery to me as yours is to you. More so."

"True. Maybe we're not supposed to know what happens. Lord knows even those who can control their own fates don't do a good job of it."

"Someone has control?"

"Well not really, I suppose, but I was thinking of Dugald."

"Grace's husband." Fox found his words slurring a bit and wondered if he should stop drinking.

"Aye. Granted he was disgraced, but he only made things worse for his wife."

"What are you talking about?" Thirsty, Fox decided to empty his glass.

"When he shot himself. Few doubted his guilt then, and he left Grace to flounder for herself."

"Grace's husband killed himself?" Fox sat upright in his chair, brushing aside Alex's attempt to refill his glass.

"Aye. Didn't she tell ye? He shot himself while we were out, leaving Grace to find him. He was my friend, ye know, but at that moment, seeing her face, I could have killed him myself."

Fox looked into Alex's earnest face, and for the first time since he recognized the other's soul, saw only Alex. True, in his next life he would be Padraic Rafferty, the Rebel, but for here and now, he was Alexander MacDonald, and he had his own share of troubles and triumph.

As did Grace. In the here and now.

Fox closed his eyes for a moment. When he opened them he stared straight ahead. The heavy-lidded effects of drink seemed to lift, and the world, the smoke-filled tavern, seemed clearer. "I have to do something," he said, gaining Alex's attention.

"What are ye talking about?"

"Don't ask me what, for I don't know yet. But I must do something about Scotland. About myself. And about Grace."

She'd been playing the hostess for near an hour now, wondering when Alex would return with Fox. At first, when the visitors had arrived, she had assured them it would be mere moments until Fox's return. At this point as she offered them more tea, she began to fear they never would. What could have happened to them?

"Perhaps we should leave, and return later," the young woman said. Her name was Elsbeth MacLinn. She'd accompanied her father, Grace's other visitor. He was a large Scot, Highlander by the look of him, and he'd come to see Fox. They'd met before, according to him.

Grace had nearly asked if it was this lifetime or another where this acquaintance was made. At any rate, they were interesting company, especially to someone who usually lacked it. But Grace was beginning to feel uncomfortable as the mantel clock ticked away more minutes.

"I really don't know what could be keeping Mr. Morgan. He must have been detained."

"Think nothing of it," the man said. "It has been time well spent getting to know ye."

The three of them rose, Grace to accompany them to the door. They made it as far as the hallway, when the front door burst open and Fox, his arm about Alex, nearly fell through the opening. There was little doubt both men were deep in their cups. And absolutely no doubt the callers couldn't miss them.

"Grace, darling," Fox said, stumbling toward her, "I've

spent a delightful time here with my good friend Padraic, er, I mean Alex. I really must stop calling him that other name, don't you know. I even wish I could forget about that other life. I want to stay here with you." His hand curved around her head, and he would have pulled her into a kiss if not for Alex's words.

" 'Tis the MacLinn," he said, awe coloring his words despite his drunken slur. "My God, 'tis the MacLinn."

"Who?" Fox forced himself to straighten, then turned, a smile spreading across his face. "I know you. The sword. You gave me the sword during my fight with my . . . with Lord Morgan's son."

"Aye. And I've come to see how both of ye are."

"I'm fine as you can see, and so is my—" Fox brought a finger to his lips. "No, mustn't call him that. James Morgan."

"That's good to know. His disappearance has caused a bit of a stir."

"Don't worry. That's been taken care of." Fox grinned, then his eyes narrowed. "I know you."

"Aye, we just discussed that I lent ye my sword."

"No. No. I know you," Fox insisted. "From before."

Grace reached for Fox's arm, but there was no stopping him. He stepped closer to the laird, examining him as if he were a rare jewel.

"Fox, please, think about what ye're doing," she pleaded, but he paid her no mind.

"You're Keegan MacLeod, by God. Keegan MacLeod."

"Oh my." Grace watched with trepidation as Fox circled the man, repeating his name. For his part the laird seemed not to have any idea what was going on. He twisted his head, watching Fox. There seemed to be nothing Grace could do.

Except . . .

"Alex, do something." He'd obviously done his part to

get Fox drunk. Surely he could see what was going on. But as she looked toward Alex she realized he'd be no help. For he seemed to be struck speechless. All he could do was stare, eyes bright, silly grin upon his face, at the laird's daughter.

Chapter Fifteen

The roles were reversed.

It was now Grace and Fox and Alex seated in a drawing room, waiting. They had ridden a few miles out of Edinburgh to the castle where the MacLinn was staying.

"Do we look good enough?"

Grace let her gaze drift over Alex, who'd asked the question, and Fox, who always looked nearly perfect to her, and nodded. "Certainly better than ye did yesterday."

"I apologized for that, Gracie," Alex said, straightening his jacket yet again. "How was I supposed to know the MacLinn would come calling?"

"It was my fault," Fox interjected. Yesterday he'd allowed himself succumb to self-pity. Poor Fox, tossed about into a strange universe where things were not as they should be. Forced to meet both his father and grandfather. Forced to know the future. Forced to fall in love with a woman he feared could never truly be his. He'd allowed himself to dwell on all that and more.

The result was a headache that wouldn't go away.

"Rather than placing blame, I think it best we work to amend any bad feelings. We need the laird's support if we are to save Scotland."

Fox rubbed his forehead, wishing the pounding would stop. When it didn't he looked up slowly, catching Grace's eye. "We must accept that changing history may not be possible."

Before she could respond, a door opened, and Duncan MacLinn strode into the room. He offered no greeting to either Alex or Fox, but did smile and nod toward Grace. "Pleased, I am, to see ye again, Mistress MacCammon." Then almost reluctantly he added, "And welcome to ye, gentlemen."

"It is my honor to meet the MacLinn. I have sought an audience with ye since ye arrived in Edinburgh."

"I've been aware of that."

Taken aback, Alex cleared his throat. "My party would very much like to count on yer support during these important times."

"Ye mean while ye and the others are wagging yer tongues, trying to decide what to do about England?"

"Well," Alex floundered, obviously not knowing exactly how to answer, " 'tis what we must do. The Parliament, I mean."

"Hell, boy, that is no way to deal with the English. Certainly even ye know that."

"What do ye consider needs to be done?" Grace asked, gaining the large man's blue-eyed stare.

"The answer is not what we will do, but what we will not allow to be done."

"English rule?" Now it was Fox who had the Scot's attention.

"Ah, the swordsman."

Fox chuckled. "Hardly that." His eyes narrowed. He

was doing his best not to make a fool of himself as he no doubt had yesterday. But it was hard not to confront this laird with what he knew. Especially since Fox thought the MacLinn recognized something in him.

"Aye, English rule is not acceptable to Highlanders, as I doubt ye would accept Scotland invading yer country."

"A union would hardly be an invasion."

"Ye don't think so?"

Fox shrugged. What could he say to this man? *Accept it. The union will come whether or not you like it. All your protests will come to naught, and will only bring death and despair upon your beloved Highlands.*

Fox glanced toward Grace and realized she wanted him to do just that. He cleared his throat. "You may dislike the idea of a union, however, if it is to come, it may bring prosperity to Scotland."

"Prosperity at what cost?"

"Perhaps it will save innocent lives, then," Fox countered. "I fear that if there is a union, and if men, honorable men, continue to oppose it, there will be much warfare and unhappiness."

"Ye sound almost as if ye can see the future," came a feminine voice from near the door. Fox turned to see the laird's daughter, a pretty girl with brown eyes and dark hair. " 'Tis a future I do not wish to see, Lily," he said, not realizing until she began to laugh, what he'd said.

"Lily?" she said. "Why would ye call me that. My name is Elsbeth. Granted, ye most likely don't recall our earlier meeting—"

"I remember." Fox couldn't help the smile that crossed his face. He glanced toward Alex and saw the same expression of besotted bewilderment he'd worn the first time he saw the girl. And now Fox knew why.

"Elsbeth, my dear, I wonder if I might prevail upon ye

to show Mistress MacCammon the gardens. And perhaps Master MacDonald would care to join ye.''

''Of course, Papa. I'd love to acquaint Mistress MacCammon, and''—her eyes lifted shyly— ''Master MacDonald with the fine array of flowers my aunt grows. She has one of the loveliest display of roses in all of Scotland.''

Grace hesitated, glancing toward Fox as if to ask what the laird could possibly want with him. But Alex was already by Elsbeth's side, great flower lover that he was. With a lift of his brows, Fox let Grace know he had no idea what the MacLinn wanted, but that he'd be careful.

When they were alone, the older man motioned toward the table, where several bottles of French brandy and wines were displayed. ''Help yerself if ye want something to drink.''

''I believe yesterday cured me of that for the time being.''

''A bit of overindulgence has a way of doing that, I suppose.''

''What is it you wish to see me about?'' Fox asked, deciding the direct course the best.

''Ye intrigue me, Fox Morgan.''

''How is that?''

The MacLinn laughed, a bit self-consciously. ''Ye know, I'm not certain. When I first saw ye, there was something about ye that reminded me of my wife.''

''Your wife?''

''Aye, Rose, a true beauty she was, and that's not to say I'm calling ye such,'' he added. ''She was the light of my life, but alas, she was a fragile thing. Rose passed on ten years ago. She did leave me Elsbeth.''

''A charming girl.''

''Aye.'' Duncan appeared to pull himself back to the present. ''As I was saying, when I saw ye on the street, ye reminded me of Rose, or perhaps of the son I never had.''

''I'm flattered.''

" 'Tis why I lent ye my sword."

"For which I'm truly grateful."

The laird shook his head. "That young pup was lucky 'twas ye he chose to insult. Many another would have run him through and thought nothing more of it."

Fox answered something inane, wondering when the laird would get around to the real reason he wished to talk to him. It came moments later.

"Yesterday when we met ye kept calling me by another name."

"Keegan MacLeod."

"Aye, that was it. Why?"

"I was deep in my cups I'm afraid."

"That much was obvious. But I felt as if ye were speaking the truth as ye knew it."

Fox shrugged. "Perhaps you remind me of someone."

"This Keegan MacLeod?"

"Yes."

"Who is he?"

Fox took a deep breath and leaned back in his chair. How to answer. The truth? Was this man able to hear the truth? Fox didn't know, and he wasn't willing to lose all credibility to find out. Alex felt any attempt to keep peace among the Lowland and Highland Scots, between the Royalists and Jacobites depended upon this man. Grace believed the same.

"Keegan is a Scot, like yourself. A Highlander. A patriot."

"Strange I've never heard of him."

"There is much in this world that cannot be explained."

"Like what it is about ye that reminds me so much of Rose."

Zoe? Fox wondered if this man's wife could be his sister. In another time and place Fox would have thought the idea ludicrous. Now he wasn't so certain. But he would never know since Rose was dead.

Fox nodded. "Yes, exactly like that."

"And I remind ye of your friend in the same way?"

Was he trying to tell Fox something? Did this man believe?

"Tell me more about yer friend."

"What do you wish to know?"

"He was brave?"

"Very. But there is no reason to speak of him as if he had already lived his life."

"Then he is alive?"

"I believe so, yes."

"Ye are a strange man, Fox Morgan."

"Not so strange, really." Fox leaned back in his chair and crossed his arms. "Scotland could become a battle-ground."

"It's a land long accustomed to the sound of clashing claymores."

"It could be worse, much worse. England will get its union."

"Are ye speaking now as an Englishman?"

"I'm speaking as a man who knows." Fox stood and walked to the window. "There will be a union, and there will be bloodshed and destruction for those of you who cannot or will not accept."

"That sounds like a threat."

"Believe me it is not."

Their eyes met and held, and Fox felt as if he could see back through time. They'd known each other more than this lifetime. More than the one to come.

The laird was the first to break the contact. His breathing was heavy and he swallowed hard. "Who are ye?"

"I've told you may name."

" 'Tis not yer name I'm after." Agitation dogged his

steps as he crossed the room and paced back. "Are ye a seer, then? A mystic?"

"Nay."

"Yet ye claim to know the future."

Fox said nothing. There was nothing he could say.

"What do ye want from me?"

"Reason. A mind open to possibilities and compromise."

"Capitulation, ye mean," the laird growled.

"Nay. I mean a chance to discuss what is to become of Scotland. Aye that's what I want. You to be willing to meet with men you might consider your enemies. To meet and talk, and try your best to work out an agreement that all can live with."

"Ye ask a lot of me."

"I know. But it is because of the friendship we will have that I feel I can."

Duncan MacLeod stared at him then, a long, hard stare. "Ye are like my Rose. No one else has ever been able to change my mind once it was settled. Her methods were more of the feminine nature, but she taught me to never say nay."

"Does that mean you will come to a meeting?"

"Have ye ever seen such a perfect smile?"

Fox and Grace shared a look, a smile that they each thought surely the most perfect, before Grace answered Alex. "Aye, she is lovely."

"Not that ye aren't, Gracie. Ye know I will always think ye the most beautiful of women."

Grace's lilting laughter rang out above the pounding of hooves. They rode three abreast, Grace in the center, along the path leading from Castle MacLinn to Edinburgh. "I hold no grudge against Elsbeth, Alex. I think her a marvelous woman, and one certainly worthy of my good friend.''

"I think she's perfect for you as well," Fox added. As a matter of fact, he knew she was, but decided that didn't need to be said.

"She does seem partial to me, don't ye think?"

"Oh aye, more than partial," Grace agreed. "I could have been a ghost for all she cared as we toured the garden."

"But she was gracious, don't ye think?"

"Most gracious," Grace agreed. "I only meant she seemed very taken with ye."

"I thought so, too," Alex agreed, a smile splitting his face. He opened his mouth to say something else, but before he could a shot rang out, sending a covey of doves exploding into the air.

"What the hell!" Fox tightened the reins, gaining control of his mount, then reaching to help Grace do the same.

"Where did that come from?" Alex asked, just as another blast rang out, one that left no doubt the shots were aimed at them.

The horses stomped, pulling at their reins. Fox gave Grace's horse a swat before yanking his pistol from his jacket. "Let's get out of here! And stay low."

The third shot sent fire tearing through Alex's arm. He called out, but managed to keep his seat as the black jacket sleeve turned crimson.

Fox jerked his head around, trying to see their pursuers, but the thick fog of dust camouflaged all. He could hear pounding hooves, but couldn't tell who they belonged to. Another shot rang out, zinging past his head. "Damnation."

Squinting, Fox searched the road ahead. Maybe a half mile up the road was a stand of trees. He'd noticed them on their trip to Castle MacLinn. It was a long shot that they'd even make it that far, but if they did . . .

The horses pounded, straining. "Keep going," Fox called to Alex. "Get her inside the town's gates."

Fox thought he heard a question, something about what of you, but he ignored it. "Just ride," he yelled as he jerked his mounts head toward the trees.

Fox plowed through the underbrush, scraping against tree bark, slapping limbs before he could halt his horse. He slid to the ground, sending the horse off again with a whack to his rump. Running back toward the road, Fox pulled out his other pistol and aimed.

It was mere minutes till two horsemen came thundering down the road. They were in hot pursuit, seemingly unaware of Fox's having left the chase. He had no time to make a plan, he merely fired one gun, barely taking time to notice as a man slid from his horse. But the other culprit took note. He jerked his mount around, stopping him in mid-stride.

Fox found himself looking down the barrel of the man's gun. He lifted his own and both guns flashed at the same time. The horse whinnied, jumping to the side, depriving both men of a clear shot. Both balls missed their target.

As the smoke and brimstone drifted into the air, Fox saw the mounted villain reach inside his coat. Leaping forward, Fox grabbed his leg, jerking him from his horse. They fell to the road, grappling. First the horseman on top, then Fox. Fox lifted his arm, pounding the man's face with his fist. Blood spurted from his nose.

But he was a big man, burly, and a broken nose wasn't enough to keep him down. He jerked a knee, barely missing Fox, who had to wrench to the side to protect himself. The man's fist slamming into his head made lights dance before his eyes. He blinked, shaking his head.

Fox swore, then pushed to his feet and grabbed the

man by his jacket, yanking him up, only to plow a fist into his jaw. He lay dazed, and Fox pulled him up again.

The man's head lolled to the side, his eyelids drooped. Fox shook him as a terrier would shake a rat. "Why were you shooting at us? Who put you up to this?" Blood-tinged drool rolled from the man's mouth. "Damn it, answer me. Tell me who."

The man blinked, and focused, his mouth opening.

"Well?"

The report of a gun was the only answer. Fox looked up shaken as the man he held upright drooped farther. Blood spattered over Fox's coat, but it was not his. At least not yet.

He glanced around to see the other highwayman standing on the road. Blood darkened his left shoulder, but he obviously wasn't dead, though as Fox let the fabric fall from his fingers, he imagined his companion was.

The man facing him pointed a pistol at Fox. The explosion didn't surprise him. The fact that he didn't crumple to the ground in pain did.

Grace stared down at the smoking pistol in her hand, then toward the man sprawled on the ground. They seemed the only real things in her universe. Except for the fact that Fox was not dead.

There was commotion around her, but nothing fazed her until Fox pulled her off her horse. The feel of his hands on her made her body tremble. She couldn't stop.

"Grace. Grace darling, what's the matter?"

"I couldn't stop her, Fox," Alex said. "She realized ye weren't with us and jerked her horse around. Damnation I should have stayed here and helped ye."

"It worked out," was all Fox said as he continued to caress Grace's slender back. He had a feeling he knew what was wrong with her. Killing someone was never easy. And he imagined this was the first time for her.

When she finally looked up at him, her eyes were damp, like rain-washed moss. "He was going to kill ye," she said.

"Yes, and it's thanks to you he didn't."

She smiled then, her lips trembling, and pulled herself from his embrace. Fox noticed she didn't look at either dead man as she moved toward Alex. Wordlessly she reached for his arm.

" 'Tis nothing, Grace. A mere scratch."

"But we should have Maude look at it nonetheless."

Alex's face did wrinkle in pain then.

Alex's wound was slight, but he put up with it being washed and bandaged by Maude before he left. He and Fox spoke briefly of the incident along the road. Neither man recognized either highwaymen.

"Perhaps it was just a robbery attempt," Alex said. "The roads are full of miscreants just waiting to steal a purse."

"Then why didn't they confront us, ask us to stop?" Fox countered.

"Easier to kill? Hell, I don't know. But I can see ye have yer own theory."

"I think they were trying to kill us . . . at least one of us."

"Grace?"

"There have been a rash of people wanting her dead lately," Fox said, his expression grim.

"Why?"

"I think it's more who. And I don't know the answer to that." Fox clenched his fingers into a fist. "But I intend to find out."

Chapter Sixteen

"Ye don't need to keep watch over me while I sleep."

"You think that's why I'm here?"

Grace lowered the silver-handled brush, placing it on her dressing table. "I don't know."

"Let me assure you it is not." Fox stood in the doorway of her bedroom, leaning against the jamb. He'd been watching her brush her tangle of red hair, thinking how important she'd become to him. Now he straightened. "However if you wish me to leave . . ."

Grace turned on the stool to face him. "Why would I want that?" she said, a small smile lighting her face.

She looked so sweet, so vulnerable, Fox could not stay away from her. The door shut with a click. Then he was moving toward her. Kneeling in front of her, he took her hands in his and leaned down, pressing his lips to the tender skin on the inside of her wrist.

Having him near, touching her, Grace sighed softly. "So much is happening," she said. "There are times I wish . . ."

"Wish what, Grace?" Fox asked when she hesitated.

"I don't know." She bent to kiss the top of his head. The smooth black hair felt like rough silk beneath her lips. "That we could just return to Glenraven. Ye and I. Forget all this unpleasantness. Pretend we don't know what we do."

"I feel that way as well." Fox lifted his head from where it rested in her lap, and looked up at her. "At first I couldn't believe what had happened to me. Then I only wished answers. Why? How?" Fox paused, then wrapped his arms about her hips. "Now I simply wish to forget everything but you."

A perfect fantasy. "Except we can't."

His voice, muffled by the silk of her skirt, was resigned. "Nay, we can't."

"That's what I did before. I simply ran away and hid."

"You had reason enough."

"Perhaps," Grace conceded. "Yet, I wonder now what might have happened had I stayed." Her fingers played with a strand of dark hair. "I suppose I was afraid of what I might find if I'd questioned anything."

"Your husband's death?"

"Aye."

Fox waited for her to say more. When she didn't, he took a deep breath. "He killed himself."

"Yes."

"Why didn't you tell me?"

"I don't know. I suppose I never wanted to face it. His ultimate disgrace. Ye must understand," she said when Fox looked up at her. "I never believed what people said about Dugald taking money. Not even when the coach arrived. The silver. But the day we found him." Tears glistened her eyes. "How could I doubt his guilt after that?"

"Grace."

"And more," she continued. "If he was guilty, then so was I."

"That's foolishness."

"No. Oh, I had no idea how he got the money. But at first, when there were more servants to do my bidding, when gowns simply appeared in my wardrobe, I didn't protest. The Darien Project had taken nearly all our resources, and I was not overly fond of being poor. Surely Dugald realized that. Perhaps I said something. Or appeared unhappy. My father was very wealthy. He didn't wish me to marry Dugald because of his social standing. But he was rich before he invested all our money in the colony." Grace lowered her voice. "Dugald knew all this."

"So he decides because of you he must steal? Grace, you put too much upon yourself."

"I'm not the only one to come to this conclusion, Fox. Others have said as much."

"Your uncle?"

"Aye. And Lord Archey. Oh, he wasn't attempting to reprove me. He simply wished to let me know what others were thinking."

"How kind of him."

"You needn't use that tone. I know ye don't like the earl, but he made it possible for me to go to Glenraven."

"Aye, and gave you a servant who tried to kill you. Grace, for God's sake, 'tis more than dislike that I feel for him. I know him."

"From yer other life."

"Yes. Grace, I'm not mistaken about this." His gaze searched hers. "You do believe me, don't you?"

"Yes. I just don't wish to think about it right now."

His arms wrapped about her slender waist, and Fox was reminded of what had happened this day. To her. "I apologize. I didn't come here to argue with you."

"Why did ye come?" The question was asked without guile, and he decided to answer in kind.

His lips came within a breath of hers. "Because I cannot stay away from you."

His mouth touched hers once, twice.

"I don't want ye to." Grace leaned into him, meeting each bit of contact with eagerness.

Feathery kisses teased, driving them both to feverish heights. When his fingers dug into her hair, she moaned, more than ready for his onslaught.

His mouth was hard. Driven. Pressing her lips open to accept the firm thrust of his tongue.

Grace felt her knees quiver, then suddenly found herself lifted high against his chest. Lips still searching, melding, Fox carried her to the bed. They fell upon the mattress together, a tangle of legs and skirts.

Fox shifted, rolling on top of her, framing her face with his forearms. She lay beneath him, lips moist from his kisses, eyes heavy-lidded with desire, and Fox lost all semblance of reason.

"I've fallen in love with you," he said. "I never want us to be apart."

"Nor do I." Grace reached up, clutching his face with her hands. "Oh, Fox, it frightens me that we might be separated." She arched up, kissing his chin, the tip of his nose. "I couldn't bear it were ye to leave me."

"I'll never leave you," he said, pressing his face into the sweet scent of her hair. But even as he kissed her ear, running his tongue along the shell-like swirls, he feared it was not in his power to keep that promise.

Whatever powers ruled the universe had chosen to pluck him up and toss him about. He'd cursed them at first. But now, warm in the cradle of Grace MacCammon's beautiful body, he'd found contentment and an overriding love. He could not let himself think that this wondrous feeling might not last.

She was the only real thing in his world, and he reached out, holding her as tightly as he could. They rolled to their sides, touching, caressing, wishing now they'd taken the time to rid themselves of clothing before falling on the bed.

He wanted to touch her everywhere. Fox started with the flesh exposed to him. Her throat, long and delicate, tasted better than the finest wine. His mouth moved down across her breastbone, then lower, skimming the soft swells of flesh, delighting in her moans.

"I want you naked," he whispered, stirring the wispy curls of fiery hair beneath her ear.

"And I want ye the same glorious way." To prove it, she began pulling the tail of his shirt from his breeches. When a bit of hair-roughened skin emerged, Grace leaned forward, rubbing her face against him, breathing in the scent of him, manly and sensual. When he stiffened she grew bolder, using her tongue, the way he used his, wetting and tasting.

"Ah, Grace." Fox grabbed her hand, pressing it to the hard ridge beneath his woolen trews. "See what you do to me." Her fingers tightened, and he groaned.

"Turn around." Fox's voice was gruff with desire.

"I thought ye liked this."

"I do, too much. If something doesn't happen quickly to rid us of these clothes, I'm afraid I may embarrass myself. Now turn around and let me unlace you."

"Mmmm." Grace squirmed against him as she twisted about, to show him her back. His fingers played with the laces, trying to unhook them. He may have accomplished more faster, had he not stopped often to nuzzle the tender skin at the nape of her neck.

When the laces finally gave, the bodice gaping open,

Grace turned, offering him breasts already pebbled hard from wanting him.

The moist heat of his mouth, the teasing lick of his tongue, drove Grace even higher. She clutched at him, pressing his face into her breasts, trying to spread her legs over his body.

Fox jerked away, pushing to his knees on the center of the bed, pulling her up as well. He yanked her bodice down, till she was exposed to him to the waist. Then he swept his shirt over his head and pressed their bodies together.

And together they fell back onto the mattress. The rest of their clothes were discarded with more haste than finesse. The skirts and petticoats; Fox's boots proved especially troublesome, but they were determined.

Finally they lay on the bed, gloriously naked, their frenzied motions slowed. It was a loving hand that caressed Grace's breast, loving eyes that stared back at him and studied the strong contours of his face.

"We belong to each other," Fox said as he slid into the enveloping warmth of her body. "We always will."

"Always," came Grace's breathless reply. "Always."

Together their bodies moved, finding their rhythm, building. Each motion, every touch, took them higher, bound them more to each other. Their bodies melded, their souls became as one.

When they lay in each other's arms, replete, Fox knew he'd found contentment. He was home.

Beneath the woolen plaid Fox pulled up to cover them, he and Grace dozed and woke, only to doze again. They made love, cherishing the way their bodies responded to each other. They talked, not of the state of the world or problems, but of life.

Grace told him of her love of stitchery. "With a needle and thread I can begin with a blank stretch of fabric and create my own flower, as perfect or not as I choose. I can see the moor even when miles and miles separate me from it.''

"I envy your talent," Fox said as he absently lifted each of her fingers to his lips. Her hands were lovely, long, and tapered, an artist's hands. And he saw her needlework for what it was, her canvas and paints. The light was too dim to actually to see the wall hanging over the mantel, but his mind's eye remembered the vivid colors and fine detail that made him almost feel the wind sweeping across the desolate landscape.

"You love the moor, don't you?"

She hesitated a moment, thinking. Was it love she felt or a strange longing? "It is as if I need to be there," she finally said. "It calls me."

"We'll return soon, I promise."

"That would make me very happy. There was a time I enjoyed the bustle of Edinburgh, but no more." Grace sighed, as his lips moved to the sensitive skin under her wrist. He kissed her pulse, warming her blood. "But what of ye? Can ye be happy living so far away from people?"

"I'd have you," he said, and rolled her toward him, pressing her breasts to his flesh.

She dreamed then, after the loving, of those other lovers who met on the moor. Of their happiness and pain. Of their separation. Her dream was haunted and sad, a place of gossamer webs that rarely let the sun shine through.

And then it changed. In her sleep she smiled, and when Grace woke the new dream was still fresh in her mind. "It was me, but not me," she began after Fox asked her to tell him about it. "Have ye ever had that thought?"

"Aye," Fox whispered into the night.

"I could not tell what I wore, or even my name, though I know 'twas not Grace. But I was happy, and I was with ye."

"Then we were both happy."

Their fantasy world lasted until they woke with the dawn.

What is it about the light of day that brings reality crushing down? Grace wondered.

"We must do something to protect you," Fox said. He lounged on the bed, his head propped on bolsters. Grace lay by his side.

She sighed. "I know. The entire idea is just so hard for me to accept."

"Perhaps you should go back to Glenraven." Fox's fingers tangled in her hair.

"I can't go now." She lifted her head, staring into his eyes. "Ye may think me foolish, but trying my best to help Scotland is important to me."

"It's not foolish, Grace, but my God, I don't want you killed."

"I don't want it either." She smiled. "Life has become very precious to me of late. But ye must understand how I felt before. My father was a patriot. My whole clan. For people to think me capable of being a traitor to my country . . . it was almost more than I could bear."

"Who cares what other people think?" Fox growled. "Who cares about the entire mess?" He was being selfish, he knew, but he couldn't seem to help himself.

"Fox, my darling Englishman," she said, caressing his cheek. "I care. And so do ye."

He wasn't so certain. Damn, but he wasn't.

Fox wanted to think he cared about all those nameless Scots who would be cut down at Culloden. But it was Grace who filled his thoughts.

He hurriedly dressed, donning a new suit he'd had tailored to fit him. He glanced in the cheval mirror and stared in awe at the man looking back at him. He looked as if he belonged in these clothes. A gentleman of 1705.

And more, he was beginning to feel as if he belonged. There was no more mad compulsion to find his way back to his own time. Fox smiled. He was satisfied, nay glad to stay in the here and now, as long as he could be with Grace.

Which brought up the question of how to protect her. If she wouldn't go back to Glenraven without an attempt to reconcile the disagreeing parties in Scotland, then he would just have to do his best to see that they at least discussed their differences.

He'd already spoken with the MacLinn. Now it was time to revisit his grandfather and father. But first he had a stop to make. As it turned out Fox didn't have to seek out Maude. She stood outside his door, scaring him near-witless when he jerked it open to go find her.

"Damnation, Maude, what are you doing just standing there?"

"Ye wanted to speak with me, did ye not?"

He just shook his head. "I'm going out. I want you to stay with Grace, and keep her here till I get back."

"Where are ye off to, Traveler?"

"To see our former patient." He started down the hall-way, stopping before he reached the stairs. "Maude?" She still stood where he'd left her. "Were you home when your brother killed himself?"

"Who said he did?"

Fox lifted a brow. "Didn't he?"

"Dugald was not a coward. Only a coward would do such thing."

"He was under a lot of pressure."

"He knew he did nothing wrong."

"Spoken as a loyal sister?"

"Spoken as a woman who knows."

Fox retraced his steps. "Tell me."

"What do ye wish to know, Traveler?"

"If he didn't steal money from the investors in the Darien Project, where did he get all his coin?"

"He never had any." When Fox folded his arms, Maude continued. "Believe what ye like. It makes no difference to me."

Fox walked down High Street toward the Court of Session. The Scottish Parliament met twice daily except on Saturday and Monday. Today was Tuesday, and the members where filing out from beneath the hammer-beam-roofed building when Fox arrived.

He spotted Alex standing beside Andrew Fletcher of Saltoun and started toward them. "Have you seen Lord Morgan?" Fox asked when he joined them.

"He's over there with Lord McKinzie, but it will do ye little good to talk to either of them. I proposed a meeting with the Jacobites and leaders from the Country Party, and he nearly laughed me out of the chamber."

" 'Tis not the Tory way to compromise, especially when they have no need," Andrew inserted.

"Still, I think I shall see if there's anything I can do. Will you gentlemen excuse me?" Fox bowed, then made his way through the crowded courtyard toward his grandfather. The older man saw him coming, and said something to Lord McKinzie.

"Morgan," Lord McKinzie said, "is it true what I heard? Was there another attempt on Grace's life?"

"Aye, but she's fine for now. Though I don't know how much longer she should stay in Edinburgh."

"Perhaps she should stay with me. I know we've had our differences—"

"I doubt she'd be so inclined, though I will relay your

invitation." Fox expanded his focus to include both men. "I'm of the opinion she should leave, as well. At least until whoever is trying to kill her is found. However, she refuses."

"Refuses?" Lord McKinzie snorted. "She always was a stubborn chit. What keeps her here now?"

"Her love of Scotland," Fox said succinctly.

"Well," Lord McKinzie muttered. "We all love Scotland."

"Do we?"

"What kind of question is that, young man? I've devoted my entire life to the good of this country."

"Mr. Morgan, I believe you forget yourself." This from Lord Morgan, who hadn't taken his gaze off Fox.

"I meant no disrespect, sir."

"What do ye want from me, Morgan? What does Grace want?"

"A willingness to listen to all points of view. A willingness to compromise."

"I believe that's what we were doing this morning. What we will do again this afternoon. It is called our Parliament."

"Yes, and you are planning to vote it away. You and I know it will happen. But we also know there are those who oppose it mightily. Who will go on opposing it, with their lives and their sons' lives if necessary. The bloodshed will be overwhelming. The suffering severe. Is it too much to ask that you reach out to these groups and try to help them understand? Show them that you understand?"

"An impassioned speech, Morgan. But do you really think any of this would do any good in the long run?"

"I don't know. Possibly not. But if there's any chance, I feel it must be taken."

"And Lord McKinzie's niece feels the same?"

"She does."

"My niece is hardly the issue here," Lord McKinzie said.

"Yet you yourself agree she's risking her life by staying here."

"I agree to nothing but that she's being a foolish girl."

"Who believes in something very strongly, eh, Morgan?" Lord Morgan shifted, keeping his eyes on Fox. "I think the young man might have a good idea, Angus."

"But—"

"No, think on it. As he said, nothing will change, but it might be better to have more people in agreement about the union." He turned back to Fox. "If the Royalists' Party should agree to a meeting of sorts, how would we know the others would come?"

"I already have the word of the MacLinn." Fox ignored Lord McKinzie's sudden intake of breath. "And Andrew Fletcher and Alexander MacDonald have agreed as well."

"They're both obnoxious enough in Parliament. I see no reason to subject myself to extra meetings with them."

But though Lord McKinzie still sounded as if he were adamantly opposed to the idea, the earl of Clayborne seemed more amenable. Ignoring his Scottish friend, Fox's grandfather continued to converse.

"The meeting would have to be at a place of our choice."

"A neutral spot if possible," Fox countered.

"Yes, neutral." He nodded his head, shaking the ringlets of his dark wig. "Let me see what I can do," he said, and Fox had no choice but to agree.

Chapter Seventeen

True to the man's word, Fox received a message from Lord Morgan the following morning. It was written on heavy vellum, and sealed with a family crest Fox recognized immediately. The missive was short. *Call on me today at quarter past eleven.*

Fox tapped the folded parchment against his open palm, too deep in thought to notice until Grace touched his shoulder.

"What are ye thinking?"

"Ah," Fox smiled at her. It never ceased to amaze him as he looked at her, just how lovely she was. Like a breath of spring-scented air, or a soft comforter on a rain-chilled night. He couldn't think of enough metaphors to describe how seeing her made him feel. Like coming home.

"Is it the post?" she asked again, her tawny brows lifted.

"The letter? Nay." Fox schooled his expression, imagining he'd been staring at her much as a lovesick lad would. "It is from Lord Morgan."

"Yer grandfather."

"Aye. He's simply requesting I call upon him."

"Do ye suppose he's been able to persuade my uncle to meet with the MacLinn and the others?"

"Perhaps." Fox shrugged. "I hope so. But that's not what I was thinking about."

"No?" Grace sidled to his side. They'd spent last night together in each other's arms. Had made love earlier this morn, but knowing the bent of Fox's mind, Grace had every right to think him in an amorous mood again.

And he could be at any moment. Fox draped his arm around her waist. He sat on the chair by the lady's desk in her room, and absently caressed her hip beneath the panniers as he spoke. "Ye're a bold one, Grace MacCammon," he said with a chuckle. "Which I must admit to liking. But believe it or not, my mind was occupied elsewhere."

"Then perhaps I should let ye alone to think," Grace said with a laugh as she tried to pull away. Fox's grip tightened, causing her to giggle.

"You're going nowhere, lass," he said, before his tone grew serious. "I spoke with a merchant yesterday, a Mr. Henry McGreger. Does that name mean anything to you?"

Grace leaned back against his arm, and looked into his face, her brows beetled. "No, I don't believe so. Should it?"

"He's been in business for years. He imported a coach for your household five years ago."

"I see. Why would ye be talking with him?"

"Because of something Maude said yesterday. She's convinced her brother didn't steal any money . . . or spend any either."

Grace's smile faded as his words sank in. "And are ye convinced?"

"Aye, after speaking with Mr. McGreger, I am."

"Well, I don't know any Henry McGreger, and I didn't buy a coach."

Fox pulled a struggling Grace back into his embrace. "Wait a minute. I never said you did. It was not you I was checking on. I believed you from the beginning."

"But then . . ."

"It was Dugald I wasn't sure of. And now I am. He didn't order that coach. McGreger's memory is not all that keen, but he did recall this transaction because he thought it strange."

"Strange how?" Grace's movements slowed.

"The man who originally came in to discuss the purchase was not a gentleman, but a servant. A clever one, McGreger remembers. He asked for a coach to be brought from England. A fancy coach, as ostentatious as possible. And he wished it done quickly."

"I don't understand."

"He paid McGreger in sterling when it arrived and had it sent round to your residence and placed in the carriage house."

"I still don't see why this proves anything."

"Because McGreger found it strange and asked again if the man was certain that's where he wished the coach to go. You see, McGreger recognized the servant, and had assumed all along the coach was bought by this man's master."

"Who is?"

"Was, I'm afraid. If McGreger's description was right, I believe I killed the man when he flew through your bedroom window."

"William? But he was Lord Archey's servant." Grace's eyes widened. "Ye're not saying . . . But why would he pay for a coach for us? He was our friend, and he did try to help, but a coach . . . It doesn't make sense."

"Unless it wasn't a friendly gesture." Fox noticed she

pulled away then, walking across the room, putting space between them.

"I don't understand what ye're implying?"

"Simply this. You and your husband are well-respected Scots, obviously able to influence the populace. You said yourself that Dugald and Andrew Fletcher were the main impetus behind the Darien Project and that Dugald raised most of the funds."

"Aye. I'm not denying it."

"And what was your stand on Scottish politics?"

"Scotland first. Ye know that. We wanted to create a strong Scotland that had no need of a union with England."

"What if there were those who didn't agree with your ideas?"

"There are, certainly. My uncle is one of them."

"True, there are always two sides to every question." Fox noted the lift of her brows and added, "Even this question. And that's good, most of the time. However, problems arise when we deal with amoral people."

"I know ye think ye know Lord Archey from yer other life—"

"I *do* know him." Fox stood and dug his fingers back through his hair. "I don't understand how you can believe part of what I say and not all."

"I'm sorry." Grace stopped by the window and turned. "It's hard for me to accept the earl as anything but good. He and my father were friends. Lord Archey saved Father's life." She shut her eyes, then opened them slowly. Her expression was resolute. "Tell me the rest."

"It's a theory, Grace. I know that." Fox kept himself on the far side of the room purposely. If he got too close to her, he might be tempted to soften the ideas that had been running through his head. Better she hear all of it and either think him mad, or believe there was some merit to what he said.

"Say Lord Archey is such a man. Yes, yes, I know, he is a patriot and saint. But let's just say for the sake of argument that he isn't really. That he's a cold, conniving man who does a good job of hiding his true nature.

"Let's say also that he decides the best way to influence people is to play each side against the other. One group, the English, think he's sympathetic to them. The other side feels the same. Perhaps he even has some allegiance to one group or the other. It doesn't really matter. His final fealty is to himself."

"I can conceive of a man like that," Grace said. "But I still don't understand why he would buy Dugald and me a coach."

"Bear with me a moment. Let's say our person wants to cause havoc and really discredit one of the groups in our little drama. First of all, being a crafty sort, he realizes their chances of coming out on top are slim. And he wants to cut his ties with them without making enemies. Actually, he plans to do his best to keep them thinking he's on their side."

"While they disappear."

"Exactly." Fox gave her a mock salute. "This small but determined group of patriots devises a plan that has little chance of succeeding. However, through hard work and because the citizenry admires this group, the plan seems to be going well. But there's a setback. A disaster. Lives are lost. Fortunes, too. Now our villain understands the human heart well. At times like these men seem to stick together—especially if they are all in it together."

Grace nodded. "But let one of the suffering appear to not be suffering at all . . ."

"Aye, far from suffering, he's profiting, collecting coin for the project and keeping it himself. Unforgivable. Especially if that person was a hero before. Someone the people looked up to and admired.''

"But Dugald wouldn't have done that." Grace paced to the fireplace and back. "I admit there was a time I thought . . . well the evidence seemed so overwhelming. But I think I always knew he couldn't do such a thing."

"But it didn't matter. Unfortunately things are too often as they're perceived rather than as they really are."

"An expensive coach is delivered to us, naturally people believe we bought it."

"The same for the servants. The silver. Your gowns."

"Oh my God." Grace slid into the nearest chair. "Do ye really think Lord Archey did that? He had the opportunity. But to spend so much money. Surely there was an easier way to discredit us."

Fox shook his head. "I don't know. It seems a colossal waste of time to me, as well. It certainly isn't the kind of speculation I'd expect many people to embrace."

"But if it is or was Lord Archey who did these things, who made us appear as bad as traitors, why would he be trying to kill me? That is part of your theory, too, isn't it?"

"Yes. There are too many coincidences. William's presence at Glenraven. His obvious attempt here." Fox let out his breath. "But as to why, I haven't a clue. Unless . . ."

"Unless?"

"Could he fear you'd discover something? Perhaps something about Dugald's death?"

"I don't know. Do ye suppose Dugald didn't really kill himself? What if he were murdered?" Grace wrapped her arms about her waist, suddenly chilled. "Do ye think that possible?"

"I can't say. I don't know how he was found."

"With a pistol in his hand. Sitting at his desk." Grace's voice caught as she remembered the scene. The blood. "There was a gaping hole . . . here." She pointed to her temple. "I could hardly believe it, even though there he was. Dugald and I married more out of friendship than any great passion. But I had learned to care for him. He . . ." When Grace looked up her eyes shimmered with unshed tears. "He didn't deserve what I thought of him. He didn't."

"None of this is your fault, Grace." He did go to her now because he had no choice. What he'd told her had started out as a glimmer of a notion. A paranoid notion, to say the least. But as he'd spoken, the idea had suddenly taken on a life of its own. What had started as a far-fetched guess suddenly seemed as if it had really happened.

Fox held Grace in his arms, caressing the gentle contours of her back. He thought she was crying, expected she would. So much of what she'd believed for so long had been snapped from her. He did his best to console.

However, when Grace finally looked up at him, her spring green eyes were no longer misty. They were hard as glass.

"If this is true, he needs to be punished for what he's done. To Dugald. To Scotland."

"I agree. But first of all, we can't prove any of this. Remember, I said it was a theory only."

"Aye, but a theory that makes much sense." Grace pulled out of his arms. "I'm thinking of things that happened then, before Dugald died. It was a bad time. Our money was gone, and Dugald, all of us, were so worried about the Darien colony. Then when we found out it had failed . . . I remember thinking things couldn't get worse. But they did, and at first I couldn't understand. I should have spoken with Dugald more. If we'd talked about this and understood, maybe we'd have known that neither of us was spending money. But I was embarrassed. And I was willing to believe it was him, because I couldn't stand the thought of anyone thinking I had done anything wrong."

"Grace, anyone in your situation would have—"

"Nay, don't make excuses for me, Fox. I've always tried to think of myself as a compassionate person. But this . . .''

"Listen to me, Grace. If this is what happened, Lord Archey is the person responsible. Not you. And if he did do this, he isn't finished yet. He's still trying to kill you. We must figure out a way to stop him."

"Ye're right of course." Grace sank into a chair. "But that is something I don't understand. Why try to kill me? Dugald was the one who people came to, the one who held power. I don't. Especially now. I'm not even welcome in most society. Ye saw the way my cousin treated me. It's been the same since we arrived in Edinburgh."

"I don't know why he would want you dead. Why anyone would. But the truth is there is someone out there that does."

Fox arrived early at Lord McKinzie's impressive town house, expecting to wait. However as soon as he stepped inside the wide marble hallway a liveried servant led him up the staircase to Lord Morgan's apartments. Fox's grandfather sat in a gilded chair by the window, and he motioned Fox over.

"You're prompt. I must admit I admire that."

"Years of military training, I suppose."

"I see." He waved his hand toward a decanter on a nearby table. "Have some refreshment, if you care to. Then answer me this question. Who are you?"

"Foxworth Morgan."

"We are related somehow, are we not?" When Fox said nothing, the earl of Clayborne continued. "Ever since I saw you I've searched my mind for some liaison I may have had when I was young."

"Is this a way of asking if I'm your bastard son?"

"Are you?"

Fox shook his head in annoyance. "No, I am not."

"Yet your name is Morgan and you look so very much like my son. Me, too, for that matter. Surely there is some link."

"Perhaps there is; however, what it is is not important at the moment."

"And what is?"

"To me? Grace MacCammon. And doing what I can to eliminate decades of strife between Scotland and England."

"The union will see to that," Thomas said confidently.

"I know you think it will," Fox began only to pause. There was no way this man would believe Fox knew of the future. Despite his belief that they were somehow related, Fox could not imagine suggesting the truth. That they were grandfather and grandson.

Settling back in his chair Fox folded his arms. "The union will pass. I think we both know that. And there will be those who never accept it. That probably can't be helped. But there are men of more moderate, if decidedly patriotic attitudes, who might be persuaded to your way of thinking. If reason and compromise are used."

"So you want this meeting you suggested?"

"Yes, a chance for all to air their views."

"I believe we all know how we feel about this issue."

Fox used two fingers to rub his forehead. When he finally spoke, his voice was deep, and seemed to be coming from far away. "There will be wars. Battles will be fought. Many people, both Scottish and English will die. We must do what we can." Fox looked up then, his gaze meeting that of his grandfather's. "Future generations depend upon what we do here. Now."

*   *   *

There would be a meeting.

Fox returned to Grace's house on High Street confident the different sides would sit down and discuss the issues. After all, Lord Morgan had said he would arrange it. From all Fox knew of his grandfather, he was a man of his word. Lord McKinzie might balk, but in the end he knew his support came from England and the earl of Clayborne.

Fox felt pretty good about what he'd accomplished as he entered the front door. Until Maude descended upon him.

"What is it? Is Grace all right?"

"Aye, Traveler. Yer Grace is safe for the moment. But ye must know ye can't truly protect her."

"What are you talking about, old woman? I shall see that no harm comes to her."

Her laugh cackled. "Have ye learned nothing on your journey? Ye have no control over anything." She'd let the words drag out, slowly, for emphasis. "Surely ye can see that."

"I don't know what you're talking about."

"Don't ye now." The head wrapped in plaid moved slowly from side to side. "Ye can't even control where ye land in time. How are ye going to make certain Grace stays safe? What makes ye think ye can play around with history?"

"I'm only doing my best to fix it."

"It is what it is, Traveler. Do not forget that."

Chapter Eighteen

"I don't want you going."

Grace shut her eyes, then turned slowly on the dressing-table bench to face Fox. He stopped pacing the bedroom.

"For God's sake, Grace, you'll be walking right into his damn stronghold."

"I've never thought of Maymont as a stronghold before."

"Well you'd better start. And don't make light of this. You could be killed."

"Fox dearest," Grace stood and moved toward him. "I could be killed in my own bedroom. None of us can control what happens to us."

"Have you been talking to Maude?" Fox said, turning away from her. She was being irresponsible, damn her, and he wasn't going to allow her to take his mind off the matter at hand.

"What does Maude have to do with this?"

"Nothing." Fox shook his head. "She was just giving

me the same line the other day about being unable to control our own fates.''

"Well, we don't.''

"Hell, I know that. But it doesn't mean you offer yourself up like some sacrificial lamb.'' Fox stopped, then turned on her. "Is that it? Are you planning to offer yourself in some kind of rite of repentance? For if you are—''

"I'm not. Do ye think my life means so little to me?''

Fox ran fingers back through his unbound hair. "I don't know what to think anymore. Nothing makes sense to me. I want to take you away. Back to Glenraven. Forget all this intrigue.'' His hands cupped her shoulders, and he pulled her toward him into a hard embrace. "Damnation, I love you, Grace,'' he said into the soft curls of her hair. "As I've never loved anyone before.''

Her arms circled his waist, holding him as tightly as he held her. "I love ye, too, Fox. Sometimes it frightens me how much. 'Tis as if this one lifetime isn't enough to hold all that I feel for ye.''

"Oh God, Grace.'' Fox squeezed his eyes shut. "Don't leave me. Promise you won't.'' Even as he said the words Fox realized how foolish they were. It wasn't a promise she could make . . . any more than he could.

She was right. Hell, Maude was right. He had no control. He'd been shown that endlessly. At Culloden. With his sister Zoe. When fate grabbed him up, tossing him into another lifetime. Yet he still tried to act as if somehow he could command life.

"I'm sorry,'' he said, allowing a breath of space between them. "I shouldn't ask such things.''

"If it is in my power, Fox, I will never leave ye.''

Fox hooked her chin with his finger and lifted her face. Forcing a smile, he said, "I feel the same.'' Then, when another thought came his way, he smiled in earnest. "Perhaps we should wed. Hell, no perhaps about it. Marry me, Grace. Please. I love you so much.''

Marriage. Grace hadn't really considered it. Not after Dugald. But now the prospect of spending the rest of her life with Fox made her pull him closer. "Aye, I'll wed ye.''

"You will?'' Fox held her at arm's length, searching her face as she nodded her agreement. "When? Now. What of now? I'll find a clergyman.'' He let her loose and headed for the door. "Where should I look? Ah, yes, the church. That's what I'll do. I'll go to the first church I find and—''

"Fox. Stop. Please.'' Grace was near doubled over with laughter. "We can't do it now. And ye can't race around with yer hair all mussed running into churches.''

"Why not?'' He was at her side again, giving her a quick kiss, then a not-so-quick one. "I would do anything for you. Don't you know that?''

"I do,'' Grace said with a smile. "But we must be reasonable. We leave for Maymont in less than an hour. There just isn't time. Nay.'' She held her hand up when he would have interrupted. "Ye know there isn't. Besides, I don't want my wedding to be hurried. We have time. Let us wait till this business at Maymont is over. Yes, yes, I know ye don't wish me to go. But I must. It's important to me. Please try to understand.''

"Grace, you'll be in Lord Archey's house. Surrounded by people in his employ. We've already seen what one member of his staff was willing to do.''

"It's not as if I'll be alone.''

"Grace.''

"Please just think about it. The MacLinn and his clan will be there. And my uncle. If Lord Archey is the one who is trying to kill me. Nay don't look at me that way. I believe he is. Anyway, he couldn't possibly do it in front of everyone. Actually, I think I may be safer there than anywhere else.''

Fox stared at her a moment. "I will not leave your side."

Her response was a devilish grin. "I shall count on that, sir."

Fox laughed as she sidled closer. "Don't take my attention away from the matter at hand, lass. I'll only be protecting you, nothing more."

"Really." Her fingers brushed aside dark hair to play with his ear. "That's all ye'll be doing?"

"Witch." Amid screeches and laughter, Fox scooped her into his arms, strode the few paces to the bed, and dropped her in the middle of the feather mattress. He followed, pinning her down with his weight when she would have rolled off the bed.

"Let me up," Grace said between hiccupy bursts of laughter. "We haven't time for this."

"Ah, now she sings a different tune," Fox chuckled. "No more enticing me with your magical fingers?"

"Nay, nay, no more."

"Let me see." Fox manacled her wrist with his hand. She was delicate, with fine bones, and it occurred to Fox how truly vulnerable she was. He brought her hand to his lips, pressing her skin, loving her scent.

"When this meeting is over will you be satisfied?"

"That I've done enough?"

"Yes."

Grace's brows came together. "I think so. There's nothing else to do, is there?"

"I can't think of anything."

"Except perhaps find out what really happened to Dugald."

"You let me handle that."

Grace wriggled till she could see him better. "What are ye going to do?"

"I don't know yet. But something. In the meantime, I don't want you off trying to find out yourself. Do you understand?"

"Yes, sir."

"Don't be flippant with me, Gracie."

"I wouldn't dream of it, sir. After all, ye're to be my husband."

"Soon."

"Aye, soon."

"After the meeting at Maymont we will leave for Glenraven." Fox watched her face as he spoke, hoping to see agreement in her countenance. What he saw made him happy.

"Just as soon. But ye know I feel as if we are already wed," she said, insinuating her hand between their bodies to a spot over her heart. "In here."

Fox did, too. He felt as if they were one. Would always be one. But that didn't stop him from longing for the time when he could take her away. When they could go to Glenraven, to the moors, and be alone. Together. Forever.

Maymont was bustling with activity. Men arrived on horseback and coaches, and in the case of the clan MacLinn, on foot amid a colorful display of plaid and pipes.

"An attempt at intimidation," Fox whispered to Grace as they stood on the lawn watching the parade of sorts. "The MacLinn knows he has little to bring to the bargaining table, so he decided to sway what heads he can."

"There is something inspiring about the sound of the bagpipes, though, isn't there Fox?"

"Aye." He remembered the sound as if it were yesterday. "They are enough to make your blood run cold when they come at you in battle."

"I imagine," she said with a bit of pride.

Fox decided no good would come of telling her what the future held for the Scottish instrument. How after Culloden it would be outlawed. How the sound would disappear from the rugged landscape. It would disappear as would the wearing of the plaid, the possession of weapons. All this would happen if the next few days did not go well.

For Lord Morgan and Grace's uncle had only agreed to stay five days. Five days to work out an agreement that was acceptable to all. It hardly seemed possible. But then the English had little need for concessions. Coin was easier to use to regulate votes.

Fox saw Alexander walking toward them across the lawn and threw up his hand.

"Ah, there ye are. Well, what do ye think? A splendid spectacle, I'd say."

"Fox was just commenting upon how the pipes sound in battle."

"Especially when you're on the opposing side," Fox added.

"Well, there won't be any fighting here. At least not the kind where bullets fly."

"What do you think the chances are that any good will come of this?"

"Yer guess is as good as mine," Alex said. "I don't know how willing the Jacobites are to compromise. They want nothing to do with a union of any sort."

"As if ye and the Country Party do," Grace said.

"Well, I think we might be a little more open to compromise."

"Which I wouldn't expect a lot of from the Royalists," Fox added. "They have very little to lose."

"True. Someday ye'll have to tell me how ye got them

to agree to this. Now don't be modest, I heard Lord McKinzie say 'twas yer influence that got him here.''

"Well, you can be guaranteed it was not my plan to use Maymont as the meeting place."

"Why, it's perfect. Lord Archey is not known as a partisan on either side. Never sways too far in either direction. I doubt he even has a stand on the union issue."

"Not one that he would keep anyway," Fox said as he offered Grace his arm. The pageantry was over, the laird safely deposited within the walls of Maymont House. The clansmen who'd accompanied him now milled about on the south lawn, setting up a camp that would be their home for the next five days.

Grace and Fox were luckier. They had rooms in the main house, though they were in opposite wings. Fox wondered if Lord Archey really thought he would allow Grace to stay there by herself. Of course she wasn't truly alone. Maude had come. Her room connected to Grace's.

"Talks will begin in earnest after we sup. Andrew Fletcher is our party's representative; however, he's asked me to make the opening remarks," Alex said with a bit of pride.

"And will Elsbeth MacLinn be listening to those remarks, do ye think?"

"She will, though her father is not too happy that she even came. He doesn't care for me, I think."

"More likely your politics," Fox said, as they walked along a brick path toward the castle. "But if I were you, I'd pursue her."

"I intend to. As a matter of fact I believe the lady's affections are already won. It's her father."

"I'm not surprised she took to you, Alex."

"Nor am I," Grace added, giving Fox a strange look. "And ye to her. She's such a sweet girl. And beautiful. I couldn't be happier for ye, Alex."

"And now I'll stop pestering ye with proposals of marriage."

"I never considered them anything but flattering."

"I'm happy for ye, too, Gracie. Whatever happens over the next few days, ye've come a long way from the woman who went off to Glenraven."

"Not so very far," Grace said. "For I'm going back as soon as this is over."

"We're to be married," Fox added, a bit hesitantly since it seemed hardly any time ago at all that he'd wakened to hear Alex asking Grace to marry him, and her turning him down. But Alex appeared elated, even calling to his friend Andrew Fletcher, telling him the news. Before they knew it everyone seemed to know.

There were congratulations and backslapping, and for an instant Fox almost forgot why all had assembled. But by the time dinner was over and the principals and their audience had adjourned to the ballroom, reality came back to him. He glanced around the room, which had been furnished with a large polished table, wondering if he might find anyone else from his other life in the gathering.

He felt someone staring at him and turned around abruptly, calling for Grace when he saw Lord Archey.

"She's off with the ladies. I believe they're refreshing themselves before the evening entertainment."

Fox lifted a brow. It was hard to look at the earl and not see the dastardly Sir Edwin White from his other life. "Is that what you consider this?"

"Oh yes." He paused, lifting a finger to his cheek. "Don't tell me ye actually think some good will come of this meeting. Oh no." He chuckled. "I can see that ye do."

"Your own attitude surprises me, as I've heard you all but insisted the meeting be held here." Fox glanced about, wishing he would spot Grace. So much for keeping her at his side at all times. He hadn't even realized she was gone.

"Did I? I don't recall. But who wouldn't wish to host such a diverse and lively group?"

Fox nodded. "Yes, but people must wonder where you stand on the union business. It seems a volatile topic. Certainly you have an opinion."

"Ah, dear boy, I learned years ago to keep my opinions to myself. That way ye have few enemies."

"And fewer friends?" Fox questioned. If he expected to rattle the earl, he was disappointed. Lord Archey only laughed.

"That's far from the truth. Just ask yer lovely bride-to-be."

"I have. As a matter of fact, I've seen examples of your *friendship*. Now if you will excuse me, I must find Grace."

He found her, fan in hand, standing beside Maude near the doors leading to the terrace. "For God's sake," he said, coming up behind her. "Didn't I tell you to stick close to me?"

"Well ye were conversing so intently with Lord Archey I didn't wish to disturb ye."

"I'm serious, Grace. Maude." Fox turned toward the older woman. "Would you please tell her?"

"Ye're still trying to control, Traveler."

Fox swallowed an oath, then leaned toward Grace as she spoke. "I found out something interesting," she began, only to stop when Lord Archey stood at the head of the table and started to speak. "Later," she mouthed, and Fox found himself seething but unable to do anything about it. What in the hell was she thinking? She was not to be finding out anything, interesting or not.

Lord Archey gave a welcoming speech, that did a lot to show Fox why the man was well thought of. Not by Fox, of course. He knew what he really was. But the others laughed at his witty remarks, and grew serious, nodding when he spoke of the importance of these proceedings.

Then the gentlemen were introduced and each said a few words. Near an hour had passed before the serious position statements began.

Lord McKinzie spoke of the fine relationship forged, through mutual endeavors, between England and Scotland. He blessed their joint queen, and reiterated that a union was her fondest wish. Then he mentioned the trade benefits Scotland would enjoy as England's partner. Valid points all. He only brushed on the Alien Law passed by the English Parliament and what would happen to Scottish citizens in England and to Scottish enterprises if the union was not passed.

No word was spoken of the colony at Darien, or the financial woes now facing Scotland. There was no need. Everyone knew.

As he predicted, Alex stood and gave a brief overview of the Country or New Party's beliefs. The long-standing Scottish Parliament and how with one vote they could wipe themselves from existence. He spoke of patriotism, and loyalty, and Fox could understand why Alex was elected one of the Burgesses.

The MacLinn regarded England's choice of a successor to Queen Anne with scorn. He made no attempt to do otherwise. The laird praised King James, wanted him returned to the throne of England and Scotland, and appeared willing to fight to see it accomplished.

In other words, Fox decided, each group had their own scheme and their own strategy to advance their ideas. Lord McKinzie used reason, and Fox assumed he believed most of what he said. Alex appealed to Scottish pride, and did a damn good job of it. Fox was nearly ready to stand up and cheer when he finished his speech. And the MacLinn chief told it exactly how he felt. There would be no compromise. War was inevitable.

Acceptance of this was difficult for Fox. It was heavy as a hammer and suffocating as a damp blanket draped over his face. He had come, traveled from one time to another, for naught.

He would not change history.

The Rebellion of 1715 would take place. Culloden would scar the hearts of all Scots, and some Englishmen. It was all for naught. These men could talk until there were no more words, and the result would be the same.

It took Grace's hand on his arm to drag Fox from the despair he felt.

"What is it? Are ye all right?"

He smiled then, a forced smile, for he knew she would be as disappointed as he, perhaps even more so, when the talks proved fruitless.

But then he looked into her eyes, those soft green eyes that seemed to see him exactly as he was, and his hand closed over hers. This is what he'd come here for.

For Grace. His beloved.

After the opening statements the men got to their serious discussions. Most spectators were asked to leave, but as in the Parliament where space at the north end of the chamber was reserved for privileged members of the public, some were invited to stay. Fox was among them. However, he chose to leave the ballroom with Grace. There was nothing he could say to the representatives. Nothing they couldn't learn themselves by looking into the past. History seemed always to repeat itself, and Fox imagined would until mankind learned the art of compromise.

Perhaps steps would be taken today. But he doubted it, cynic that he was.

* * *

Grace waited until they were getting ready for bed before broaching the subject of William. She doubted Fox would like that she asked about him, and she was right. Crossing her arms, mimicking a stance he often used, Grace waited for him to vent his frustration. He ranted a bit about her safety. Reminded her repeatedly that she was to stay with him. And even lamented his need for a biddable wife.

During all this Grace tapped her foot. When he'd finished, she began again. "As I was saying, I told Lord Archey's daughter that my servant William had run away. She was familiar with him." Grace paused and her cheeks pinkened. "Apparently they'd been lovers at one time. Anyway, she seemed shocked that he would do such a thing because he was one of her father's favorite employees."

Grace waited, expecting him to say something. Anything. Instead he simply stared at her. "Well?"

"What if Lord Archey knows William is dead?"

"Even if he does, I don't believe Lady Margaret knew. But what of William being a favorite staff member?"

"Grace." Fox tried to remain calm, but thoughts of something happening to her never seemed far from his mind. "It's incriminating but unfortunately proves nothing. We most likely will never be able to prove my theory about what happened."

"Our theory," Grace said.

"Our theory then." He reached for her hand, drawing her near. "I'd love to be able to give back to you the years, the pain, this man caused you. But outside of him deciding to tell the story himself, I don't see that happening. I could simply challenge him."

"Don't be foolish."

"You don't think I could win a duel with Lord Archey?"

"Aye, ye could. But it's not what either of us wants."

"Let me handle this, Grace. I know the earl's mind. I've dealt with it before. And I think he knows it. I seem to make him nervous." Fox's lips thinned. "Grace, are you listening to me?"

"What? Oh yes, Fox." She'd been listening, and she'd been thinking. And what she'd been thinking was that getting Lord Archey to tell everything might not be as hard as all that. She thought she knew how, but she needed some time. Alone. And Fox didn't seem about to give her any.

Being as deliberately seductive as she could be, Grace turned her back on Fox. "Could ye unhook my gown," she said. "I'm ready for bed." When he touched the curve of her shoulder, Grace no longer had to pretend desire.

His hands traveled down her back, then up. He kissed her nape as his fingers slowly untied the ribbons holding her bodice together.

When he'd loosened the laces, and her gown gaped open, she turned in his arms, pressing her naked breasts to his chest. Together they fell on the bed.

Fox finished undressing her, taking his time, caressing, kissing as he went. Her skirts, her petticoats, the clocked stockings tied above her pretty knees with ribbons, all drifted to the floor. Her skin was silky, dewy wet from his lips. Inviting. It was all he could do to remove his breeches.

And then he was on top her, pressing her into the feather mattress. He'd made love to her often, but each time seemed new. It was almost as if he'd forget how perfectly they fit together; or how strong he felt being held in her arms.

They kissed, they touched, all the things that lovers do, but Fox knew what he felt for her transcended the here and now. Their bodies joined, strained and craved release, but it was their souls that soared.

"I want you with me always," Fox said as they lay in the bed drowsy and satiated. "Don't ever leave me."

She mumbled something against his chest, her breath cool against his still fevered flesh. But she was too near sleep for her words to be clear.

Sure they were what he wanted to hear, Fox sighed, then tightening his arm about her shoulders, fell asleep.

When he woke in the morning she was gone.

Chapter Nineteen

He was in the garden, tending his roses.

Grace had doubted even a history-making conference held within the walls of his home would keep Lord Archey from an early-morning round of his garden. And she was right.

She approached through a maze of sharply trimmed boxwoods, spotting the earl, scissors in hand, near a neat row of pale pink roses. Grace stopped to take a deep breath. She was not a brave person. At least she'd never thought of herself as such. She told herself there was nothing to worry about. Not really.

It was not as if she'd chosen to meet him behind a closed door. The garden was out in the open, observable from most of the south-facing windows of the castle. She could smell the campfires of the clan MacLinn.

And she'd left the note.

Her courage shored up, Grace continued along the brick path, stopping with a start when he jerked around.

"Ah Grace my dear, ye startled me. Are ye out for a walk this morning?"

"Aye, well, actually, I was hoping to have a moment to speak with ye."

"With me?" Lord Archey pursed his narrow lips. "Of course, dear. But I must keep moving. I prefer to prune my darlings before the sun gets too high in the sky." He motioned with the hand holding the scissors for her to lead the way. On his arm hung a large woven basket into which he dropped the spent blossoms he snipped from each bush.

"Roses are very interesting, Grace. Very much like people really. If ye aren't callous, nay ruthless," he said, shaking his head, "with pruning, the plant doesn't do its best." Pulling a stem toward him, he brushed his fingers across the velvety petals of a perfect bloom. "Take this rose for instance. Some would say it has reached its pinnacle of beauty, and after all, isn't that a rose's primary function on earth? To be beautiful?"

When she realized he awaited an answer, Grace nodded. "I suppose so. But they also offer a sweet scent."

He brushed her comment aside. " 'Tis beauty that we expect from a rose, Grace. Everything. Everyone must give what is expected of him." Then, with a sweeping motion, he snipped the blossom, sending it tumbling into the basket. He glanced up, smiling at the expression of surprise on Grace's face.

"But it was still beautiful," she said.

"From the zenith there is nowhere to go but down, my dear. Ye must remember that. There must be sacrifices for the good of the bush, of the whole."

"Was that what Dugald was? A sacrifice?" The words were out of her mouth quickly, leaving no time for thinking. This was not the way she'd wished to broach her accusations. But there it was. To his credit Lord Archey appeared taken back. His eyes opened wide, then narrowed, as he continued along the line of rosebushes.

"Dugald chose to take his own life. A tragic incident, true, but one that only he could control."

"Really? Is that what ye think?"

"I thought it was what we all thought. If ye care to delve into Dugald's state of mind when he took his life, perhaps calling it an accident is generous. However . . ." He paused to cut a rose. "I am a generous man."

"Yes, ye are." Grace stepped up her pace to stay abreast of him. "Servants, gowns, silver, even a coach. Most people would say giving those things to someone else was very generous."

He stopped for a moment, then moved on, becoming even less discriminating about the blossoms he cut. "I think ye're mistaken, my dear. I lent ye a few servants, nothing more."

"That's what I thought as well. And I was grateful, believe me, thinking ye a saint among men. Especially when so many others deserted both Dugald and me."

"Then I fail to see what the problem is. Perhaps ye think I did not do enough."

"Ye did too much. And I feel foolish for not realizing it. The gowns, the silver. Ye knew I would blame Dugald, and he would blame me."

"Dear girl, I don't have time for this . . . this fantasy of yers."

"It's no fantasy and ye know it. Dugald knew, and that's why ye killed him."

He stopped, jerking around and pointing the scissors at her, backing her along the walkway. Thorns snagged her skirts, tearing the silk. "I'll hear no more talk like that, Grace. Do ye hear me?"

The urge to flee overwhelmed her. She could turn and run, no doubt meeting Fox as he came looking for her.

They could ride to Glenraven. Hide there forever, safe in each other's arms. The logical part of Grace's mind urged, demanded, she do so. But she hadn't come this far to stop. He was close. Very close.

So she stopped backing up and faced him, her chin up, her eyes as hard as she could make them. "He told me."

Lord Archey pushed around her and walked briskly along the path, stopping to snip the heads of roses, not even bothering to drop them into the basket. The blossoms fell to the path to be trampled by Grace as she hurried to keep up with him.

"He wrote me a letter, telling me all of it. Leaving proof," she improvised, because though the earl was obviously agitated, he had ceased to take her seriously.

It worked. He looked around at her, hate twisting his usually genial face. "There is no proof."

"Well," Grace said, feeling more comfortable with her charade, "perhaps not enough to prove what ye did. But I imagine enough to make my uncle, perhaps even the Crown, take notice."

Lord Archey seemed to ignore her at first, carefully examining several more rosebushes, clipping and fondling. Grace moved along with him, trying to keep a bit of distance between them.

But when he finally jerked around, she realized how little space there was.

"What do ye want?"

"The truth."

His eyes narrowed. "I thought ye already had that."

Grace felt her stomach sink. Perhaps her mind didn't run toward intrigues and lies, but she held her ground. "I want to know how ye did it and why."

"What will ye give me for this knowledge? A trip to the gallows? I think not."

"I'll give ye what Dugald left for me to find. Ye see, he

never thought that I'd go off to Glenraven. He assumed I'd stay in Edinburgh, and that I'd look in the secret place that we used to exchange notes. It was a romantic notion of my husband's," Grace lied, inventing this part of the story as she went. "We often left things for each other behind a loose brick in the fireplace. I didn't think to look until I returned to Edinburgh."

"What's to keep ye from telling someone about this?"

"I'll leave. I want nothing more to do with Edinburgh anyway. I've already made arrangements to go back to Glenraven. And ye have my word."

"What proof did he leave ye?"

She hadn't expected that, though Lord knows she should have. For a moment Grace floundered, then she remembered Fox's talk with the carriage importer. "Dugald suspected something was wrong. He knew he hadn't ordered the coach, and he believed me that I hadn't." Grace wished this last had been true. "So he spoke to the merchant who brought the coach from London. Mr. McGreger named ye as the person who ordered it through a servant." Grace took a breath. "From there Dugald did some investigating. He talked to people, to the servants. He figured out everything. And he put it all in a packet for me."

"Which ye plan to show to your uncle?"

"Yes, unless ye tell me everything."

"My dear Grace, go right ahead. I shall simply deny it. Or perhaps I will admit to buying my dear friends a coach." He paused at the foot of the stairs leading into an outbuilding. "There is nothing wrong with that."

"There is if ye got the money by embezzling it from the investors in the Darien Project."

"So Dugald told ye that, did he?"

"Aye." Grace was still making it up.

"Now I know ye're lying." Lord Archey entered the

stone building used to house the gardening tools, with Grace close on his heels. "Because Dugald hadn't figured that part out," he added, reaching behind Grace to shut the door. "I did tell him, of course, but only moments before I killed. So ye see, my dear, he wouldn't have had time to leave that bit of information for you in a note."

Fox only took the time to yank on breeches, stomp into boots, and toss yesterday's shirt over his head, before he raced from the room he'd shared with Grace.

What in the hell was she thinking?

He clambered through the hall and down the stairs, passing a maid and nearly flattening her. She carried a silver tray laden with chocolate pot and cups, and the china still rattled as he turned around and grabbed her shoulders.

"Where's the rose garden?" he yelled into her startled face. "The rose garden?"

"Outside, sir," she finally managed.

"Hell, I know that. Where outside? Front? Back? Damnation, girl, have you no tongue," he finally said, when she simply stared at him.

Continuing down the stairs he ran across the marble-floored entrance hall, and through the front door. His head jerked left, then right, but he could see nothing that looked like a rose garden. But Maymont's lawns were parklike and huge.

Fox ran toward the side of the castle, calling to the several clansmen as he passed. No one answered him. He tore through the kitchen garden, stomping onions and herbs beneath his boots.

To the right was a maze of boxwood and, showing no concern for the well-trimmed bushes, Fox fought his way through. To the rose garden. Fox sucked in his breath when he saw it, then rushed up and back through the rows of flowers.

"Grace. Grace!" Fox could feel panic surging through him. He heard voices and veered to his left, forcing his way between two plants into an open area where a fountain gurgled, and three men sat on a bench.

Without thinking Fox lurched toward Lord Archey, grabbing him by his jacket and hauling him up off the seat. He was vaguely aware of Grace's uncle protesting the rough treatment, but Fox didn't care.

"Where is she?" Fox yelled, when he'd yanked Lord Archey's face to within an inch of his own. "Tell me, or I'll kill you with my bare hands, so help me I will."

"Fox!"

"Mr. Morgan!"

Hands were pulling at his arms.

"Help us over here! Someone."

There were two men tugging at him, and though Fox could have fought them both off, some of their words started to penetrate his frightened mind.

"Lord Archey can't tell you anything like that, Fox. Let him go."

Slowly Fox lowered the earl till his feet scraped the brick walk. But he didn't let go of his coat, and he didn't step away. "What did you do with her?"

"Who, Fox? Who is it that's missing?" his grandfather asked.

"He knows who." Fox tightened his fingers in the fine silk of his jacket. "Grace. Where is she? And damn you, she'd better be alive."

"I haven't," Lord Archey began, his voice pitched high. He stopped and began again in a more natural tone. "I haven't seen my dear Grace since last night. She was leaving the ballroom . . . with ye."

"Liar!" Fox lifted him off the path again. "You're a liar and murderer."

From his ungainly position Lord Archey looked to the other two men for help. "He's mad. What is wrong with him?"

"Fox, put him down, this instant." There was something about that voice, remembered from his childhood, that made Fox obey. "Now we shall have an explanation of your actions."

Bristling, Fox decided it might be better if he related what he knew. "Grace is gone. She left this note." He let go of Lord Archey with one hand and opened his fingers, displaying a wrinkled piece of parchment. "She was meeting him." Fox gave Lord Archey a shake as a hound might shake a badger. "Here. This morning."

Lord Morgan took the paper and, to Fox's way of thinking, took an inordinately long time smoothing it out. He glanced over the few scrawled words, then glanced up. "She does say that."

"Well, she hadn't informed me of a meeting, and I didn't see her. You two have been with me. Tell him."

"It's true. We've been conversing for nearly a half hour."

"There, ye see. More's likely Grace just decided to take leave of ye for a while. They *are* lovers," Lord Archey added with a smirk.

Fox could feel two sets of eyes turned on him. He let loose his hold on the earl and stepped back. "He's been trying to kill her. I caught his servant William in Grace's room with a knife to her throat."

"Ridiculous. William is a trusted man." Lord Archey brushed at his jacket. "Look at him," he said, pointing a finger toward Fox. "He's obviously mad, running about, his hair wild, barely clothed, frightening decent people. Making up lies when this is obviously nothing more than a lover's spat gone array."

"Her note does mention meeting you, Hugh. And she does ask Fox to come to her when he awakens."

"Well, she must have gotten waylaid somewhere. Perhaps found a more presentable fellow to take up with."

The last word was barely out of Lord Archey's mouth before Fox's fist was in it. Lord Morgan and Grace's uncle dived forward to grab Fox's arms, but there was no need. He'd finished with the bastard.

Unfortunately Lord Archey hadn't finished with him. Eyes wide, he dabbed at his bleeding lip. "Ye are no longer welcome here, Mr. Morgan. Get out."

The first thing she noticed was the damp. Beneath her cheek. Then the pain. Her head hurt. A spot behind her left ear ached the worst, but her entire head felt as if someone had taken a board to it.

Grace moaned, and opened her eyes when she heard a scurrying sound. Inside the windowless building it was dark. Gingerly she lifted a hand to her hair, and grimaced when her fingers felt moist.

She remembered following Lord Archey inside. *Stupid,* Grace thought, and shook her head, only to feel a wave of nausea flood over her. Had she fallen? Or had he hit her with something? She couldn't remember.

But she did recall all he'd told her.

Grace pushed to her feet, ignoring the dizziness and the squeaking sounds of scattering mice. She steadied herself against the stone wall and waited for her eyes to adjust to the darkness. She could make out what appeared to be a table of sorts. Along the walls hung tools. And on the floor were rounded mounds of what she thought were burlap bags.

Carefully Grace made her way across the dirt floor. The only light was what seeped through the crack around the door. Pressing her hand along the wooden panel, Grace found the latch. When it refused to budge, she sank back against the wall. But only for a moment. She stood again and called for help. Over and over, till her voice grew hoarse, then faint. Either no one could hear her, or no one cared. Finally she stopped. Then, using touch more than sight, Grace moved back along the wall, looking for something to pry at the door, or—if that failed—to use on Lord Archey. She would be ready for him if he returned.

"Well?"

"For God's sake, Fox." Alex jerked around, his cloak swirling in the light from the lantern. "Have a care for my nerves."

"Has there been any sign of her?" Fox had a care for nothing but Grace.

"No. I did as ye asked before being so forcefully evicted from Maymont, and spoke with Lord Morgan and the MacLinn. Surprisingly enough, both men believe yer story. Though I don't know why I should find that amazing." He shook his head. "I do. Anyway, Lord Morgan has stuck to the earl like a bad stench. They are both in the ballroom, and yer grandfather swears Lord Archey has not left the main castle. The MacLinn has his clan searching the gardens and grounds." Alex's voice softened. "So far no one has seen her."

"I've followed all the roads and paths leading from here for miles. She didn't leave. She must be in the castle somewhere."

"But how could he have smuggled her in without someone seeing her?"

"I don't know." Neither man wanted to broach the possibility that she was dead. "I'm coming back with you to Maymont."

"Lord Archey has said he plans to arm many of his servants. They may have orders to shoot ye if ye return. He's trying to convince everyone ye're a disruptive presence and a threat to these talks."

Fox was pretty sure Alex didn't think his news would sway him, and it didn't. "How are things going? Any progress?"

"Nay. The Hanoverians still are in control, and they know it. The Jacobites still threaten revolution at every turn, and I'm feeling the only thing we can all agree upon is the need to find Grace."

Both men walked in silence toward the castle, their only light the lantern Alex brought. When they neared the rose garden, Alex stopped. "I don't think ye should go any farther, Fox," he called after him, for Fox had not even paused, "where are ye going? I wasn't lying about the armed servants. Fox, they'll see ye."

"You said he was in the ballroom."

"Yes, but damn it, Fox. Let me go. I'll bring him out here." But it was too late. Fox had already pushed through a kitchen door and entered the castle. Alex hurried after him, pulling his pistol from his coat. He took it upon himself to cover Fox's back as he strode down the hallway.

When Fox burst through the double doors to the ballroom, Alex was right behind him. Fox had his own pistol leveled, and after the first scuffle of excitement, Lord Morgan came forward.

"He's not here. I turned my back for a moment to discuss a point with Andrew Fletcher, and when I looked back Archey was gone."

"When?"

"A quarter of an hour, no longer. The MacLinn sent his clansmen to find him, and I've just been relating your theory to Grace's uncle."

Fox didn't remain to discover how the earl of Denbigh viewed his ideas. Turning on his heel, he stormed out of the room, then stopped. Where in the hell was he to look? The castle was huge, the grounds covered acres. Lord Archey could have taken her anywhere.

"Fox, have a care for yerself. Ye can't just stand here in the hall."

Fox turned to respond to Alex, and saw her. Wrapped in her plaid, Maude stood in the shadows of an alcove. Their eyes met, Fox was sure of it, even though he could not see hers for the woolen shroud she wore over her head. He strode toward her, almost afraid she might disappear.

"Fox, for God's sake, it's only Maude. She doesn't know anything. I already questioned her."

"You know more than you tell, don't you, Maude?" Fox said. "You always do."

"I don't know where yer lover is, Traveler. I have not seen her."

"But she's alive?"

"For the moment, aye."

There was no way Maude could know that with any more certainty than he did, but relief rushed through Fox at her words. "Tell me what to do, Maude. Where would you look?"

She shrugged, a frail figure beneath her wraps. "I would look for her where she said she'd be."

"But we looked in the rose garden. Fox, this old woman doesn't know anything."

Fox ignored Alex. Turning, he started down the hall at a run, heading for the door, only stopping when she called out.

"Traveler! She does not need ye."

"Well, she has me," Fox called back. "And she always will."

* * *

The night air and damp soaked through her silk morning gown. Grace didn't know how long she'd been locked in the building. She was hungry, but considered it a minor annoyance compared with the others. The chill. Her head. Her hands.

She'd worked for what seemed hours, until her arms were sore and her hands bloody, trying to hack through the door. She'd made little progress. With the night settled firmly about her, the notion that Lord Archey would return for her seemed far-fetched.

He probably felt it safe enough to keep her here. Obviously no one could hear her pleas for help. And no one knew where she was. He'd probably made up some excuse for her absence which everyone but Fox would believe.

Fox.

Grace wished she knew where he was, and if he were safe. Lord Archey was capable of anything. She knew that now. If he hurt Fox, she would never forgive herself for pulling him into this.

Her head fell back against the wall, and she must have dozed. She was dreaming of Fox, of being warm and safe in his embrace when she heard the sound at the door. Her first instinct was to yell. Her second was to flex her stiff muscles and crouch behind the table.

He carried a lantern. It threw off enough light for Grace to see who it was.

And to see the gun.

She held her breath and waited for him to come farther into the building.

"Grace dear, are ye hiding from me? It will do ye no good."

He lifted the lantern, and she could imagine him peering into the building. "Or did ye crawl off someplace to die? That blow ye took to the head was hard. I should know. I gave it. Come on, Grace. Show yerself. Save both of us some trouble."

She'd come up with a plan, and now had one chance to make it work. Carefully, quietly, Grace closed her hand over the stone she'd found earlier. When she'd been able to see, she'd placed a large crock directly across from her. She tried to picture it now in her mind's eye, the way she pictured her needlework before beginning. When she threw the stone her eyes were shut.

The stone hit the crock and Grace saw Lord Archey jerk, aiming his gun in the direction of the noise. Her hands were already encircling the heavy staff of the pitchfork. Trying not to think of Fox, of how much she loved him, Grace lurched forward, the pitchfork's prongs aimed at the earl's back.

Brandishing a lighted torch, Fox was tearing through the rose garden when he heard the shot. He was sure his heart stopped beating, but somehow his feet kept moving toward the sound. He ran and ran, surprised to see the small outbuilding nestled behind a hedge.

Fox burst through the door, stealing himself for what he might find. His pistol was cocked, ready to do what needed done.

He saw the body first. Lying on his stomach, a pitchfork balancing precariously on its embedded tines, was Lord Archey.

"Grace?" He was almost afraid to say her name.

He could swear his heart started beating only when he heard her hoarse reply. Dropping the torch, he ran toward where she crouched against the wall. Pulling her up, Fox wrapped his arms around her.

"I think I killed him," she whispered.

"He deserved to die."

"Ye were right about him. All the things ye said. And he killed Dugald, too. He told me."

"Hush, Grace. There's no need to talk now." Fox buried his face in her hair. "You're safe. And he can't hurt you anymore."

Grace pressed her cheek to Fox's chest. "But he'll be back. We all come back."

Chapter Twenty

They were going home.

It amazed Fox that he no longer thought of England as home. Nor did the time seem to matter. He was here, in the summer of 1705, and he was home because Grace was here as well.

For nearly a fortnight they'd traveled north, toward Glenraven. This was not the mad-dash trip they'd taken to Edinburgh. Nay, this time he and Grace traveled at a more leisurely pace, enjoying the mild summer weather, the aching beauty of the lochs and glens.

Maude accompanied them, along with near a dozen horses and pack animals. For his part in the ruin of the Darien Project, Lord Archey's lands were confiscated. Grace had asked that the money be used to reimburse those impoverished by the colony's failure. Fox doubted the coin would find its way into too many deserving pockets, but then he wasn't certain it wouldn't.

Grace had taught him not to be too cynical. Whatever,

Lord McKinzie had insisted a portion of the estate, a reward, of sorts, should go to Grace. She'd demurred, but finally agreed to use some funds to refurbish Glenraven.

The notion intrigued Fox. And at the same time frightened him. Buried deep in his memory was the niggling thought that he'd never seen the castle at Glenraven when he'd been at Culloden and Drummoissie Moor in his other life. If it had been repaired and updated, wouldn't he have noticed it? His mind wouldn't let go of the idea that the castle had crumbled to decay by mid-century. But that would be impossible if Grace and he did as they planned.

Fox shook his head, trying to dislodge the plaguing thought. He would concentrate upon what made him happy.

Grace.

She rode beside him, her fiery hair unbound, her lovely face alight with anticipation. They'd come ahead, Grace and he, leaving Maude and the slow-moving caravan behind. As soon as they'd reached the moor, Grace had been unable to contain her enthusiasm.

"It won't be long now," Fox said, gaining her attention.

She smiled at him, warming his heart. "I know. I can hardly believe we are almost there." Despite her words, she slowed her horse, then reined him to a stop. Fox did the same.

"What is it? Is something wrong? Your head?"

"Nay," Grace laughed. "I've told ye my wound is healed. Ye've seen for yerself."

"But the headaches . . ."

"Are almost gone." She noted his expression of disbelief and took a deep breath. "They will disappear soon." Grace looked out over the landscape. Vast. Barren. Breathtaking. "I have missed my moor."

"We never have to leave it again." Fox did his best to restrain his mount.

"I know," she responded, her tone pensive.

"Are you saddened by the state of the union talks, Grace, for if that is it, I will go back. I will do whatever it takes—"

She shook her head, slowly, gently, in that way she'd begun after Lord Archey hit her. The thought of it, of him hurting her, was enough to make Fox wish for the opportunity to kill him again. Yet, he hadn't even done it this time. Grace had, and Fox knew that bothered her.

He tried to force that from his mind and listen to her. She spoke softly, and he leaned forward, loving her nearness. "I know now that we cannot change what is to be. Even after ye told them . . . ye told them exactly what would happen, no one would change their stand. They all still insisted they knew what was best for Scotland."

"Grace, I doubt too many of the gentlemen believed what I had to say. Traveling through time is a concept hard to fathom."

"They knew. No one could have listened to you talk and not accepted your words." She looked at him with pride. "Ye were wonderful. Besides, ye know Alex trusts ye. He feels the pull between the two of ye, as does the MacLinn. I even think yer grandfather knows who ye are to him. They know they will see ye again in another life. And Alex and the laird know they will fight ye then."

The incessant wind caught a lock of her hair, blowing it across her face. Pulling his hand from the glove, Fox brushed the errant lock aside, letting his fingers linger to caress her cheek. "We did all we could."

"I know." Her hand covered his. "I have no regrets. None," she said with a smile. "Please remember that, my darling Fox."

Then, taking a breath and straightening in the saddle, she continued, "If nothing else, we helped Alex find his true love."

"Perhaps we should have waited in Edinburgh for his wedding with Elsbeth."

"And delay our own?" she said, looking up at him through her burnished lashes.

To Fox's chagrin Grace had kept firm on her desire to marry at Glenraven, so they were still not wed. But as she'd said many times, in their hearts they were one.

A rumble sounded in the distance, and they both looked off toward the north, toward the unseen bay. Grey clouds, dark and ominous, billowed on the horizon.

"A storm," Fox said, twisting in his saddle to look about. The caravan was not in sight, but he doubted they were too far behind. "We should ride back, set up camp. A tent will at least give you some cover from the rain."

"Oh, Fox, I will not melt. The storm is not that close. We have time to make Glenraven if we hurry."

Fox stared again at the boiling clouds. "Grace, I think—" But she was off, racing her mount across the moor. "Damn it, Grace, listen to me," Fox yelled as he spurred his own horse. He caught up with her, and reached, trying to catch her reins, but she swerved her horse and laughed.

"The tempest can't catch us, Fox. It can't."

But she was wrong.

The clouds, now overhead, let loose their fury with copious rain. Within seconds both Grace and Fox were soaked. The landscape, always austere, took on a menacing appearance. Even as he rode, keeping his horse abreast of Grace's, Fox's mind whirled in turmoil.

What should he do? This madcap gallop was not safe, not over such uneven terrain, not in this weather. But there seemed nothing he could do to stop it.

"Look," Grace called, lifting her hand and pointing toward the north. As she spoke a streak of lightning silvered the sky, illuminating a dark silhouette. Glenraven. "We are almost there,'' she said, her voice joyous. ''Oh, Fox, I love ye so.''

He couldn't help himself. Despite the danger he knew existed, Fox found himself hopeful. They were close. They would make it. Their life was just beginning. He opened his mouth to tell her how much he loved her. To scream it if he must, so loud was the thunder and the pelting rain. But the words never crossed his lips.

For in that instant, his world crumbled.

He didn't know what caused the fall. All he knew was that one moment Grace was riding at his side, laughing, loving. The next she lay still, crumpled on the soggy ground.

Fox didn't even wait for his horse to stop. He leapt from the saddle, his boots sinking into the boggy peat. He fought his way, slipping and sliding on the soaked bracken and heather, falling on his knees by her side.

His arms groped around her, and he drew her face to his chest to protect her from the onslaught of rain. ''Grace. Grace.'' He kept calling her name, though he knew, he knew.

Finally, when he could bear it no more, he lowered her, using his body as a shield, and looked into her face. Her eyes, those soft green eyes he'd lost himself in, were closed to him forever.

The storm raged about them as he knelt on the moor, cradling her body to his. The rain mingled with his tears as he whispered the words of love she'd never hear. And he cursed Fate.

''Why?'' The one word seemed to build in him. ''Why?''

Why had he been tossed about like a dead leaf in a tempest, thrown about through time? It hadn't been to save the world from its mistakes. Nothing could stop that. Mankind seemed destined forever to need reminders of its inability to learn.

The one thing he'd done was accomplished, the one thing that had made him a better person was finding love. Finding Grace. And she was gone from him.

"Why?"

"Why?"

"Why?"

Without even realizing he'd moved, Fox found himself standing, arms lifted toward the heavens. "Why?" he shouted. "Why?"

He knew it was coming before the light blinded him. He'd sensed it before. His last thought as the lightning flashed through his body was that he'd rather die than live without his love.

Summer, 1748

"How much longer till we're there?"

Malcomb MacClure peered at the landscape out the carriage window, then back at his daughter. "Not far."

Mary leaned back against the leather squab. "I thought we were close. Ye might think me daft for saying this, but I can almost feel its nearness."

"Ye've heard enough tales so I can believe ye'd think that."

Mary smiled gently at her father. This was difficult for him, she knew. Returning here. He'd almost changed their itinerary, and not because he faced certain death if caught here. She and her father had traveled throughout the Highlands with that threat hanging over their heads like a giant claymore.

Nay, it was this place, this moor, that he hesitated to revisit.

Culloden.

Despite the almost yearning Mary felt to see the area,

she leaned forward. "Papa, we don't have to go to Culloden House. We can simply go back to Inverness and wait for our ship."

"I need to tell them about our colony."

"Someone else can do it. I'll do it myself."

Malcomb tore his eyes from the passing countryside and looked with love at his daughter. "It's all right, Mary. Really. It's been years since the battle." He unconsciously rubbed his shoulder where he'd been stabbed by an English bayonet. "The place is not to blame. I can face what remains of the battlefield."

"I know ye can, Papa. Ye do so much good for those who survived."

"The colony in the Carolinas is hardly all my doing, Mary, though it does a father's heart good, to know ye think so," he said with a twinkle in his green eyes. "I'm glad ye talked me into letting ye come along with me to Scotland. Ye've been a joy."

"I want to help," she said simply.

"I know ye do. And ye've been nothing but a help to me since yer mother died."

Mary smiled her thanks. "And I must admit to wanting to see the Highlands once more. I was only eighteen when we left." When they'd been forced to leave or be hunted down like animals after the Jacobite defeat at Culloden. Mary could remember the fear and desperation as her father, wounded, and sick with fever, worked to get their family aboard a schooner bound for the New World.

They landed at Wilmington, in the Carolinas, had later moved up the Cape Fear River to Cross Creek. And they'd found many other Scots, drawn to the country in North Carolina. Her father bought land, and a mill, and had made a second fortune selling naval stores. Now he used that fortune to bring other Scots to America. He offered them a new life in the New World, a life free from persecution and fear.

Mary and her father had been in Scotland for two months now. They'd stayed with clan members and other Jacobites, eluding the English, and spreading word of Cross Creek. For each man, woman, and child who wished to migrate to Carolina, Malcomb offered passage and land.

This was the last leg of their journey. On the morrow they would head toward Inverness to meet with all those who chose to leave. Then the ocean voyage home.

But before they could do that, there was Culloden.

Mary knew the moment her father recognized the battleground. He tensed, and a faraway expression clouded his face. It was almost as if he were there again, hearing the pipes, the guns, the shrieks. She put her hand on his arm, and he glanced around, then used his walking stick to signal the coachman.

The wind seemed to sing a sadder song as it swept across the barren landscape. Mary didn't know what she expected, something sinister, she supposed. Bodies perhaps, or horned Englishmen leering at her. But there was none of that on the desolate plain. Just a melancholy wind, and the two of them.

They walked arm in arm, over the peaty ground, each keeping their own council. Her father paused, looking out over a rise, and Mary knew he was living the battle again. Seeing his brothers die. His sons.

She waited a moment with him, then started walking again. It was almost as if something pulled her, an invisible force that Mary seemed unable, or unwilling to fight.

The wind pulled at her bonnet, whipping tendrils of red hair about her face. Her step quickened, as did her breathing. She was almost running when she nearly tripped over the man lying in a tangle of bracken and heather.

"My God." Mary fell to her knees beside him, touching

his cheek. When she found his flesh warm she let out her breath. He was not dead, but he did appear hurt. Burned perhaps, though scorched might be a truer word.

She looked around for her father, but he seemed lost in his own world, so Mary turned her attention back to the man. She still knelt, staring at him, when his eyes opened. He looked at her a moment, bewildered, and she smiled.

The smile he gave her back warmed her heart.

"I had a terrible dream. I'd lost you," he said. "But now I know that could never happen."

Epilogue

Cross Creek, North Carolina
April, 1760

"Papa! It's them. I saw their coach turn in the drive."

Fox looked up from the ledger, giving his ten-year-old daughter a grin. "You're sure this time?" he said, pushing out from his desk and walking toward the window that faced out over the live-oak-lined drive. "No more false alarms?" he teased.

"Now, Papa, that other was hardly my fault. Camden started barking and I was sure she'd spotted them."

Fox laughed and pulled one of the auburn ringlets on his daughter's head. "Well, as it happens, you're right this time. That's your Uncle Keegan's coach, and I see he and Padraic riding along beside, along with Zoe's boys."

"And there's Lucy sticking her head out the window."

"So I see." Padraic's daughter Lucy was an impetuous girl a year older than his own daughter. They were best friends and any gathering the families had was made all the more exciting by the girls' enthusiasm. "Now run and spread the word to your brothers if you haven't already."

"Oh, Papa, you know I would come tell you or Mama first."

"Where is your mother?"

"I went for the baby," Mary said, as she entered her husband's library. "He doesn't want to miss all the fun."

"There's my big boy," Fox said as he lifted his youngest child, Thomas, from his wife's arms. As he did, Fox leaned down, pressing his lips to Mary's brow. She looked up at him, her green eyes filled with love.

"Did you finish yer accounts?"

"Just did. And I'm happy to tell you there is plenty of coin for ribbons and frills."

Mary laughed at her husband's joke. Their plantation, Glenraven, was one of the largest and most profitable in North Carolina. "Good. We'll need all our resources if we are to feed this bunch for very long," she said, looking out the open window. "It will be good to see Zoe again. And Lily. All of them," she finally said, giving her head a shake. "They're almost up to the porch."

"Did you hear that, Grace? Run off and tell Ben and Chris. No, wait. They're already out in the yard," Fox said, but his daughter had already raced from the room.

"Do ye think she's anxious?" Mary asked, linking her arm with Fox's, after giving the baby's round bottom a pat.

"I think we all are. Your idea to have a celebration was excellent, dear wife." They'd been married nearly twelve years, and Fox found his love for her growing with each day.

"I'm glad ye think so. Sometimes we just don't make the time to be with those we love."

"You're a wise angel," Fox said, leading her from the book-lined room. At the double door he paused. Turning, he glanced back at the framed needlework over the fire-place, and his mind seemed to drift.

"Are ye ever sorry, Fox?"

"Sorry?" He smiled down into her pretty face. "For what? Leaving Scotland, or England? Nay. Are you?"

"No, but then I was only visiting Scotland when we met."

"So was I."

"True, but sometimes I see ye looking at that needlework of a moor, and well, I wonder if ye miss it."

"I have everything I need. Everything I want right here." Fox bent to kiss his wife's lips, and was rewarded by a baby fist to the cheek. Laughing, he gave his son a noisy kiss. "I think I love that picture so much because it reminds me of when we met."

"I remember when you first saw the embroidery. We were staying at Culloden House with my father. Ye looked up over the fireplace and tears filled yer eyes. Ye wanted it so badly, Papa bought it for ye on the spot."

"It's beautiful. And haunting."

"Aye." She looked over her shoulder, then back at Fox. He was still as tall and handsome as the day she found him lying on the moor. He'd been struck by lightning, and the electric charge had done strange things to his memory. But he'd recuperated quickly. And they'd fallen in love almost as fast.

"Mary?" Fox draped an arm about his wife's shoulders. "What are you thinking that makes you look so sad?"

"Not sad, really." She smiled up at him. "I was just wondering about the woman who made that needlework. She must have loved very strongly to put so much feeling into her creation."

"Hmmm," Fox glanced over his shoulder. "She probably did. Perhaps even as much as I love you. Now come on, or we'll miss the greetings."

Together Fox and his Mary left the room. They stepped out onto the wide front porch just as the coach halted at the foot of the steps. The doors opened, and the sound of cheers and hellos, of friends and loved ones, filled the soft Carolina air.

To My Readers

I hope you enjoyed *The Rogue and the Heather*, and found it a fitting conclusion to my Renegade, Rebel, and Rogue Series. I love to write about things I believe in, so this book meant a lot to me. For those of you who might be interested in reading more about love that spans time, I recommend *Only Love Is Real*, by Brian L. Weiss.

As I researched *The Rogue and the Heather*, I discovered that the story of Scotland's dissolved Parliament did not die. Even today, centuries after Scotland's Parliament voted itself out of existence, many Scots worked to restore their governing body. During the time I was writing *The Rogue and the Heather*, the Labor Party won elections in Great Britain, and they offered Scotland the power to legislate themselves. A referendum was held on September 11, 1997, and the Scots voted yes to reestablishing their Parliament. I think Grace will be pleased.

Thank you all for your kind support over the years. You can write me care of:

Kensington Publishing Corp.
850 Third Avenue
New York, NY 10022-6222

Or e-mail me at CCDorsey@AOL.com.

To Happy Endings,

Christine Dorsey

BOOK YOUR PLACE ON OUR WEBSITE AND MAKE THE READING CONNECTION!

We've created a customized website just for our very special readers, where you can get the inside scoop on everything that's going on with Zebra, Pinnacle and Kensington books.

When you come online, you'll have the exciting opportunity to:

- View covers of upcoming books
- Read sample chapters
- Learn about our future publishing schedule (listed by publication month *and author*)
- Find out when your favorite authors will be visiting a city near you
- Search for and order backlist books from our online catalog
- Check out author bios and background information
- Send e-mail to your favorite authors
- Meet the Kensington staff online
- Join us in weekly chats with authors, readers and other guests
- Get writing guidelines
- AND MUCH MORE!

**Visit our website at
http://www.zebrabooks.com**

DANGEROUS GAMES   (0-7860-0270-0, $4.99)
by Amanda Scott

When Nicholas Barrington, eldest son of the Earl of Ulcombe, first met Melissa Seacort, the desperation he sensed beneath her well-bred beauty haunted him. He didn't realize how desperate Melissa really was . . . until he found her again at a Newmarket gambling club—being auctioned off by her father to the highest bidder. So, Nick bought himself a wife. With a villain hot on their heels, and a fortune and their lives at stake, they would gamble everything on the most dangerous game of all: love.

A TOUCH OF PARADISE   (0-7860-0271-9, $4.99)
by Alexa Smart

As a confidence man and scam runner in 1880s America, Malcolm Northrup has amassed a fortune. Now, posing as the eminent Sir John Abbot—scholar, and possible discoverer of the lost continent of Atlantis—he's taking his act on the road with a lecture tour, seeking funds for a scientific experiment he has no intention of making. But scholar Halia Davenport is determined to accompany Malcolm on his "expedition" . . . even if she must kidnap him!

ROMANCE FROM JO BEVERLY